A Harvest of Furies

Praise for *A Harvest of Furies*

The exquisite prose and innovative form of *A Harvest of Furies* draw the reader in, inviting us to share in a family's haunting by curses, blessings, dreams, and lore, their longing for loves both present and past. Hayden Casey is a storyteller of wild imagination and deep heart.

—Tara Ison, author of *At the Hour Between Dog and Wolf*

A Harvest of Furies starts with a curse, but it reads like a blessing. Musical, momentous, and utterly inventive, Hayden Casey's debut novel is a must-read update of a classic Greek tragedy. For while death stalks the pages of this book, every sentence brims with vitality, and every word feels sparkling and alive.

—Allegra Hyde, author of *The Last Catastrophe*

Hayden Casey takes a glinting paring knife to this retelling of Aeschylus's *Oresteia*—exposing how adults, held hostage to their own mythology, justify their violence, and how the children who survive must bury not just the dead but the contaminating generational trauma. Poetic, twisted, brilliant.

—Melanie Finn, author of *The Hare*

A Harvest of Furies is a remarkable and ambitious novel about love, tragedy, and fate, rendered in gorgeous language and possessing remarkable insight into the ways our families both make and unmake us. Hayden Casey is following in the footsteps of greats like Anne Carson, Clarice Lispector, and Rachel Cusk, but ultimately always finds a path all his own.

—Matt Bell, author of *Appleseed*

Hayden Casey's novel is a shock to the system in the best way possible. Things as quotidian as a morning cup of coffee and as extraordinary as earth-shattering rage are brought to life in visceral, poetic language.

Casey utilizes every word with needle-like precision and creates a haunting new take on a centuries-old story.

—Kayla Chenault, author of *These Bones*

Simmering, atmospheric, and full of twists, *A Harvest of Furies* exposes the secrets and tensions that erupt when an estranged man returns home. By turns a story of war, family, landscape, and the tenuous ties that hold us together.

—Barbara Barrow, author of *An Unclean Place*

Also by Hayden Casey

Show Me Where the Hurt Is

A Harvest of Furies

Hayden Casey

LANTERNFISH PRESS
PHILADELPHIA, PA

Lanternfish Press
PO Box 34569
Philadelphia, PA 19101
lanternfishpress.com

Cover Design by Kimberly Glyder
Cover Image: Elias van den Broeck, *Flowers, Lizards, and Insects* (1883)
(glimmer)
Interior Layout and Typesetting by Hadley Hendrix

Printed in the United States of America

Library of Congress Control Number: 2024953065
Print ISBN: 9781941360910
Digital ISBN: 9781941360927

“As soon as you discover the truth it’s already gone: the moment passed. I ask: what is? Reply: it’s not.”

—Clarice Lispector,
The Hour of the Star

Prologue

the house of atreus
a man and a woman two girls and a boy and all the countless before them
twenty-three stairsteps five chambers
it holds us all tight like ribs in a cage

The curse was only a story at first. That's all anything ever is to start: a story that can be woken from and rubbed out of the eyes. Something to spook us kids at bedtime. But stories are slippery things and at some point it latched itself into my life and became something I couldn't blink away. It latched itself into all our lives.

It started like this. Dad brought me and Emma into his bedroom when I was six years old and she was eight. Before he went off to war. I remember little from those years but this has burned itself deep. He sat us down just before bedtime, bleary-eyed on his bed, our presence here a rare privilege. He lowered the lights till the room was a vast shadow, looked back and forth between our bright eyes. Told us about a curse that had been cast on our family centuries ago. That it hovered over our heads like high-hung china and every now and then a dish crashed down and shattered and reminded us.

Its exact genesis differed depending on who you asked but he couldn't doubt its presence, its shadow that trailed him wherever he went. The way death had wandered in and out of our house like an alley cat.

I took his words in with a tremor in the chest. I was the kind of kid who could doze off against any car window or steal a last-minute nap on the bus ride to school but that night after the story I was sleepless. Rolled over again and again and when I looked down at my feet I swore I saw the shadows stretching to wrap themselves around my ankles. Couldn't kick them off couldn't get the feeling of filth off my skin.

In the morning Emma was unaffected. But I shook and spluttered as if an abyss had opened itself up inside me.

—I knew it was too early, Mom said to Dad. —Orrie you poor thing you're trembling.

Emma at eight had just learned to mistrust authority while I at six still clung to my parents as the sole source of truth. The boundaries of the curse my new scripture.

I hadn't even looked for its fingers digging into my own life. Hadn't needed proof. The mere suggestion of its outline thick and dark in the shadows was enough to do the trick.

Years later the shadow solidified. When Dad returned from war. In all the years before I was sitting and watching, waiting for something to happen. Watching the sunlight shift on the wall, watching it fill with dark. And then something happened and that happening spiraled into more happenings and I would give anything now to have my eventless life back. To have everyone back.

It's only a story, everyone said. But when story spreads a new kind of truth emerges. A truth that comes from several people holding something and regarding it in the same light. The story has swallowed us all.

< now now dear orrie settle in
time for the story to begin >

ORRIE IS CRUMBLING
TO DUST AND THE
DUST IS PILING UP INTO
SOMETHING NEW

&

EMMA WEAVES A
BASKET AND OVERFILLS
IT WITH FURIES

1

one time up and around the hairpin bend of morning

orrie's father we townspeople regale
as far-traveled war hero
as savior as benevolent

remember when tragic strangers
attempted to kill g's cattle
and aggie stepped in to deescalate ?

or when mama h (bake sale showrunner)
keeled over in the market parking lot in the biting rain
and he carried her beneath the awning and resuscitated her ?

world-saver always with a smile
and a firm-grip handshake it will be good
to have aggie back

while he was gone
rumor drifted around the town and settled in like ash –
dead ? dying out ? all we will receive

upon his return is a sack of his bones ?
but word has traveled all this way
and he is coming back

to my beginning now I have gone. The house knows us all in its bones, it remembers us and it is easy to slip inside and find myself back. There's fire on our TV: aerial shots of the war, the destruction in T_____, the explosions and smoke-pillars, screen-wide photos of the leaders we annihilated. Coupled with shots of celebration in the streets here, large crowds amassed in town squares. *Yippee*, they seem to be saying. *The war is over the war is over we did it and now we can get out of there.*

And now Dad can come back to us. He has been gone for six years, sent away when I was ten. Most of my memories of him have been superseded by stories, though there are a few old potent things that have stuck around in there. Lots of it is Mom, Emma, townsfolk telling me about my father, about times I was too young to remember. He has become more myth than man. Even Mom now tells tales of him with hollow light in her eyes as if she is beginning to forget him too.

She is in the kitchen cooking, preparing for his return. I sit in front of the TV and pretend-turn the pages of a book and roil inside. It's winter break and I have nothing to do. When the news goes to commercial I stare at the open page and read the same sentence again and again. It refracts each time, shifts its letters around, but I never grasp its meaning. The windchime on the porch chatters in the day's breeze. Every now and then I notice a (glimmer) in my periphery that makes me turn my head. Some twinkle in another world.

I feel as though I am on the precipice of some great change: my heart is beating in my hands.

My sister Emma descends the stairs and dips into the kitchen loudly as is her way and before I notice what she's doing she's set a mug of ginger tea on the coaster next to me.

—To settle your stomach, she says.

But it doesn't do much except get bile (glimmer) rising in my throat. Still that seasick kind of churn inside.

—Everything'll be fine, she says.

She is nineteen and says things definitively. Her eyes are stony, resolute.

We were allowed to take the day off, to skip our work in the fields, but I wish I had the tasks as distraction. My tummy does a tumbling-over thing again and again even with the tea. And the TV makes me think about him (where he has been, what he has been doing). But I think maybe Emma's right and his return will bring a change of pace, will level things out. We can reduce our workload on the farm. Mom can trade out some of the four or five hats she wears—she is so tired her touch has become loveless, her fingers have taken up an itching they cannot stop. All day long I see her scratch her arms her neck her shoulders. She cannot keep the worry out.

And I know she must have been someone else before. Flashbulb memories of her holding me so tightly I wondered if the love would squash right out of me. But I can hardly recall in a real ordered sense what things were like before Dad left. Six years is a long long time. And the life I have sunk into here is a life without him: doing my work and resting and thinking. Waiting. Wishing maybe.

Emma runs a thumb over my shoulder and slips down the hall. I click the TV off and decide to check on Ingrid (glimmer). My memories of Dad are all dulled from age but I sometimes remember my younger sister has none of him at all. He left when she was around five and now she barely recognizes him in photos. He will roam her house, this strange new man, like a boarder or a drifter. I poke upstairs and find her asleep in her bed (an accidental sleep, based on the book sprawled across her stomach, its bookmark jutting out awkward-angled).

The house splutters and shifts around us. Emma is downstairs tossing stuff in and out of the washer and dryer and Mom clanks and clatters the pans in the kitchen. And through it all Ingrid sleeps.

We live in an old family house, the kind with creaks and groans and gasps that have stuck around for centuries. The kind generations of us have lived and died through—it has nearly come to the ground and been brought back up. For a while I thought the curse was trapped in the house with us like a soul caught in its walls but it follows me like a cloud even when I leave. So it must be something that has followed me into the body. And Emma storms and splutters in combination with the noises of its ghosts so I reckon it has found life in all of us.

I let Ingrid sleep and shuffle down to the kitchen. The air down here smells of spices blooming in oil—Mom is making Dad's favorite stew. Before Dad left, he did most of the cooking, but we've had to fill in the gap in the time since. Uncle Enzo has left his day's farm duties untended, too—said it was a special occasion—left the property, went to the airport to pick Dad up and bring him home.

Mom wears a tight-knit brow. Scratches all along her arms, little red-stinging lines.

—I want this day to feel special, she says. —I want him to feel welcomed. She agitates the spices as they sizzle and pop. I say nothing and she turns toward me. —How are you feeling?

I don't really know what to say so I say —Weird (glimmer). I bring my hands to my temples where there's a strange pressure, a tightening. The churn in the stomach still and the vise at the forehead.

For so long this day has been legend, it has been lore. And now it is here and my body can't keep up, can't cope.

—Nothing to feel weird about it's just your dad. She pulls me in and sets her head against my hair. I tense at first, tighten like a guitar string, but settle into the gesture. How long since I have been this close to her. I wonder if she can hear what I'm thinking with her ear at my head. —It'll feel like no time's passed at all.

But the words don't assure, she doesn't sound convinced—something in the hunch of her shoulders. She releases me and returns to the skillet, tosses some salt in, cracks some pepper overtop (glimmer).

The glimmers stack together in my mind. I wish I knew what they were trying to tell me. Tempting to say they don't mean anything but so much of my life has been about looking for signs and following them to whatever ends. I'd just ignore them

but that cleo seems spooked she has
wandered round town with vacuous eyes
seems very much to "feel weird"

her husband soon back from t____
and it's almost like she'd rather sign
him up for another stint over there

, there, Cleo tells herself. Salt, pepper, stir. She cooks distractedly. She's been having strange dreams that linger with her in the mornings, stuck to her eyelids, and she can't rub them off. She stepped out of the house this morning, let the secret guest out the back door so he could venture on down to his place again, and then she stood there on the top slab of step, watched his broad shoulders round the bend to the road, tried to unstamp the dream from her eyes. When she'd woken from it in the night he'd held her, guided her down, but she'd not been able to let it go.

The way it goes is this. Dream-Cleo becomes pregnant—impossible in the real world, but how is the dream-woman to know this—gets sick, swells up, the whole thing. Goes to deliver, pushes and pushes, sweats and slides around, but instead of a baby, a snake slips out, and it leaps from the midwife's arms, sinks its fangs into Cleo's nipple, sucks out her blood. She can't stop thinking about it. The snake has beady eyes, and something about them, the shape or maybe the hue, is so familiar. It stares at her as it drains her of life.

She's never believed in dreams as things of meaning, found it a crackpot habit, but this one hit her in some strange place—she finds it portentous, strangely real. She remembers when her husband told her about the family's curse, the legend he'd been raised on, and she laughed and laughed. And he went dark-eyed, like she'd laughed his god out of the room.

In the scared half-awake space she turned to the non-husband man and said, —I don't know if we should keep doing this.

And he pulled her to him, tucked her under his arm, let his body say what his mouth couldn't: *I can be your shelter*. Looking at him, she saw the snake's eyes beading back at her in the early-morning dark. But she blinked them away, saw them again for what they were: just his eyes, soft and shiny in barely-light.

She doesn't think the man is the snake. She doesn't know who the snake is. But the dream strips her of sensibility. Her nose is filled with distrust, a scent like dried crusted blood.

In the scared half-awake space she looked out the blue-fogged windows and thought of her husband about to return from war and the pallid chiseled tattooless man in her bed and her children asleep in their bedrooms and she shook in her solitude.

What she didn't tell the man was that this is the fourth time she's had the dream this month, and that every time she has it, the fangs, their piercings, feel more real—she wakes with soreness in her breast, prods at the spot with sleep-slack fingers. And that every time he talks her down, sinks back into sleep himself, she sneaks to the bathroom, pulls a pregnancy test from beneath the sink, pees on it, taps her toes at the floor, waits, quavers.

Later in the morning from her spot on the step she watched the man disappear. As of today he has not been spotted by any of the children, she has not been caught with him. But she runs the risk every day and she knows it. She is waiting for the moment when she is too careless, the moment when passion overtakes rationality. She knows it is coming as it has always been her way.

Her children wouldn't wake for hours. On mornings when they don't have school, or farm work to do, they sleep till they are dragged out of bed, or till the smell of breakfast wakes them. She circled the house to its front, looked out at the oracle oak, whose last leaves littered the hill. The sunlight that caught in its branches.

The family has been invoking the oak tree's magic for centuries, operating on the lore that a god breathes through it. Make a request, ask a question, watch the branches twitch, wait for its answer. When Aggie told her about it, on her first visit up to his house, back when they were dating and dreamy-eyed, she'd laughed its powers away too, like it was a magic eight-ball he'd shaken behind his back. Now her resolve in the real world is crumbling and, more and more, the sublime is looking sweet. But she has not yet followed Zeus's breath, not asked the tree for a revelation of her own. She is too afraid of the truths it would grant.

Now, from her spot at the stove, she considers running out to it again, considers saying *Orrie would you watch the pan for a moment,* sprinting out the door, sinking to her knees beneath the tree, feeling the dew sink into the fabric of her pants. Asking, finally asking. But Orrie's eyes are on the far wall, his mind has shrunken into itself, and she looks down after a vicious sizzle and notices some of the garlic has gone dark, burned, taken on a rancid smell.

And

—OH GOD HELP ME, Emma shouts from upstairs.

A crash has sounded. Cleo turns to

look enzo's truck is making its way
up the hill round the bends our world-saver
is almost back !

our little town that has been
frozen beneath its longing for all this time
can finally thaw and resume ! we have been waiting we

have been holding in a giant scream for what feels like years. Someday I will let it out and it will feel phenomenal. But for now it's trapped in there like a burst of gas.

I have been lying in bed praying for the days to pass till Dad comes home and sets everything right, I have clung to his return, incanted it before sleep. I have read his letters again and again, gathered in the drawer in the front room. *Give the children my love,* they say, time and time again, and I hold them close as if the love will transfer. It feels like my life has been on a six-year pause, my limbs have been frozen in their reaches, it will feel so good to stretch them out at long last.

Yesterday Uncle Enzo asked me to sweep the kitchen floor, after Mom spilled flour across it, and I about snapped. He is my uncle, mind you—well, close enough. He's Dad's cousin but we have always called him *Uncle.* He lives in a large house a couple hills down and, widowed, he has thrown himself into our family, helped out on the farm, given Orrie a man to model himself after. He is not all rot. But at some point he became a man who delegated—*Emma, sweep the floor, will you?* framed as a question but delivered as a non-negotiable—while he sat at the head of the table and did nothing. And I did not approve of this becoming. I wanted to grab him by his ears, lift him above the table, tell him, *You are not the man of this house,* say it so close he could feel the rumble of my voice in his own throat. But I didn't, of course, I got the broom and I swept up the flour and deposited it into the trash can, and I even wet a paper towel and ran it in the grooves to pick up what I'd missed. And of course he didn't thank me when I was done, he merely turned the pages of his newspaper, started in on its next page. I wanted to pry his lips apart and feed him the paper towels, allow him to taste the command he'd given me, to tell him I am the only one who commands me.

All of which is to say there is a rage in me, and tempering it is the task of a lifetime.

I breathe deep, count up to twenty and back down again. Above all, I think, I feel stuck. By now most kids have left their flocks, gone off to college or found worthwhile jobs, unstuck the posters from their childhood bedrooms. By now most nineteen-year-olds are deep in love, learning languages, forming friendships, and I am here twiddling my thumbs. When it came time to entertain the possibility of leaving, I looked at Mom, traced the scratch marks up and down her arms and the frown lines that deepened by the day, and I decided to stay. It felt selfish to entertain my own desires. But now I'm looking up from the confines of my life and I wish I'd put myself first, because what of me remains? I fear it's only the rage left, I fear it's eaten up the rest of me, the dreams and desires and kindnesses.

I hold my breath, bite my barbs down, because I don't want to overstep, don't want to be kicked out, I have no money, where would I go. My best friends have left town, they barely remember to call. Something in the water in this place, something that makes me feel like I'm always an inch from violence.

Orrie has come to investigate the source of my *GOD HELP ME* anger-cry and I say to him:

—I wanted tea, too.

I have dropped the cup, the liquid is spreading. He is still as flush-faced as a child, cheeks dusted pink, but brutal cheekbones have emerged from his former softness and his jaw seems sharp to the touch. I remember when his face was buried in so much cheek his head seemed entirely made of the stuff. Remember Mom pinching them, running her thumb along them, turning him red. Back when the family was whole and hardy, before the wreck of war.

He sees me crouching.

—What happened? he says. Then he sees the pieces of porcelain on the floor, the sacred shards of a family heirloom mug, soaking in the pale, still-steaming liquid. —Oh, he says. —Well, I'll get some towels. He slips back into the hall and I hear the hinge-creaks of the hall closet door.

That cup's about as old as the house, I remember Dad saying when I was a kid. *Your great-grandmother painted its embellishments.* At the sound of his words in my head, a pain splits me down the middle. His voice still stuck in my cortex after six years. Why is the body primed to remember, to hurt?

Maybe in shattering the cup I have set some old thing free. Some old familial soul trapped in its porcelain, eager to escape. If I gave the idea to Orrie he'd eat it up, wide-eyed—so much fonder of the lore, the curses and blessings, than I am. But at the moment he returns with the towels, we hear Enzo's car in the driveway, the tires on the gravel, and I stop thinking about it. We look up at my half-open windows, then look at each other and stand, rush into the hall. Orrie goes to wake Ingrid.

—Come on, he says. —Dad's home.

From the top of the steps I see Mom at the door, watch her pull it open. Enzo stands at the other side, alone, and when he comes in, I see he has a look like a ghost has shuddered through him, his face bloodless. My stomach drops out.

He turns to Mom and tries to speak quietly, to evade our ears, but I hear him anyway:

—Something about him is changed.

2

two times hold it close draw the blinds in the windows of yourself

< so many . bloodbath >

Aggie hears while he stands out at the car, his boots in the cold dirt. He has pulled his bag from the car but does not think it looks like his bag. He knows he has gone someplace and now he is home but is this the bag he brought with him all that time ago? He looks up at the house and floats up the porch stairs, through the held-open screen door. The house smells like when he was thirteen and coming in from a hard day in the field, covered in dirt and sweat. He thinks, Maybe this is my life again, maybe I am back there.

Time has stretched and slid all about lately. But the woman at the door is not his mother and none of the children descending the staircase are his brother. And there's a new rug at the front door, a soft plushy brick-red thing he sinks his toes into when he pulls his boots off. For some reason this is the thing that yokes him back to the world. Oh, he thinks, the real life, I forgot. And then he hears

< this isn't going to be >

but he knows the war was not the real life either, that was a six-year ellipsis that continues to bleed out inside him. The woman at the door, he notices, wears an expression like he has slit a hole in her, deflated her. Why? What did he do, what did he not do? Cleo, he notes, her name dug out from deep within him.

—Hello, he says.

And she pulls him close, so close, but all he feels is a body. He wonders what happened to all the feeling. It seems to be trapped in the someplace before. He is tired, he is hardly thinking. Tomorrow, he hopes, after a long rest, he will come back to himself. But for now he is guided into the kitchen, yes, the kitchen, with its wide cloudlight-filled windows and its long slab of table, and he smells what simmers on the stove and feels again like he is a child. A purer place, a less complicated place. He keeps expecting to look up at the stove and find his mother there. She taught him this recipe, he remembers, and he in turn taught it to Cleo (and he can tell from the smell that if he were at the helm of the pot he would have added another clove or two of garlic, he prefers it zippy in his nose). She turns and he sees her face and he blinks his mother's face out of his eyes, sees Cleo for who she is. Cleo, his wife. The past keeps trickling in

< down !! gone >

Changed is the word Uncle Enzo uses to describe Dad. Emma whispers it to me as we slip down the stairs (glimmer), our palms on the banisters. I don't see what he means at first but it becomes more apparent as the evening unfolds. Dad holds my shoulders in his hands and sizes me up.

—Quite the man you're becoming, he says, though I'm unsure if he remembers who I was before he left. In height I stretch up to his chin and before he left I bet I barely breached his chest.

Mom dishes out stew and we eat it impatiently, we all burn our tongues.

—Not my best batch, she says, ladling the stew limply in her spoon and allowing it to fall back into the bowl.

—Delicious, Dad says after struggling with a hot bite. Sucking in breaths to cool his tongue.

The sky bleeds wound-red (glimmer) and his concentration slips and slips with the sunset colors. It is his same voice I remember from all those years ago coming from his mouth but it's as if someone else is commanding his head. No Dad in there.

After dinner while I am helping Mom wash up he calls out for me.

—Orr.

The sound rings some deep bell inside me. But by the time I reach him a fog has crossed over his eyes. Strips of lamplight spider over his arms and interlace with his exposed tattoos. Rigid-backed and tight-shouldered, he sits there like a marionette. I can nearly see the strings holding him upright.

—Do you need help getting up to bed? I offer. I can hardly look at him and figure sleep will help the both of us.

He beams bright like I clicked on a lamp within him. I could watch the brightness spread through him forever.

—Please, he says.

I meet him at the bottom of the stairs and lead him up. He's got an odd hunch in his back and strange tense knees. Seems ready to drop to the ground at any moment. He takes the steps with caution, his eyes leaping around the room at the sounds of dinner cleanup. We step into the bedroom and I watch him pull back the thick sheets and lower himself to the mattress still fully dressed.

He looks at me (glimmer) and says, —Is this where I sleep? His eyes are hazy. It's as if I dropped him in the middle of some new world.

This is where he told us about everything all those years ago. The curse and its complex knots up and down our lineage, where it could have come from, what it means for us.

Back then, Mom said, —Leave it alone, Aggie, you're gonna scare the daylight out of him.

Emma seemed bored and blinked it off like a bedtime story. But it latched itself a bit tighter into me. Right here in this blue-lit bed with the moon hovering high.

He gazes around at everything now like he's in a strange hotel room.

My eyes fill and I can't stop it but I blink the tears away. Hope he doesn't see them in the near-dark.

—Yeah, I say. —This is where you sleep. You and Mom.

—Orrie, he says, testing the sound.

—Yeah. Orrie.

—And Emma. And . . . Ingrid.

—Yeah, I say, though my voice splinters. Hope he doesn't hear. —That's all of us.

—Okay. His voice is sleep-soft. —It's all in here somewhere.

The clock ticks and it sounds louder in the dark.

I say, —Good night.

And he croaks, —Night, Orrie.

At the door I wipe the sad out of my eyes and walk back downstairs, reenter the kitchen. But my sisters have left and Mom is alone and her head is in her hands, elbows set on the counter as if she is holding up the heft of the house. It seems like her moment, the room filled with the weight of her feeling, so I leave her there and walk back up to my room.

When I climb into my own bed and click off my lamp (glimmer) my clock ticks louder. I pull a blanket over my ear to squash out the noise and wonder about Emma's earlier resoluteness: if she feels vindicated by Dad's return or if she feels like it is only another black hole in the house, swallowing everything up.

I have never had her stony dedication, never been able to hold onto a thing that long. Emotions and moods flow in and out of me. But love gets stuck in the gaps, accumulates. I have so much of it in me and I try my hardest to keep it contained, keep it from bursting out. When Dad left us, I was so jammed up with love and hollowed out with hurt staring down the barrel of a six-year loss that I vomited in my room night after night and kept it to myself. Washed the sick out of my trash bin in the bathroom tub. My soul was a megaphone and it was shouting DAD DAD DAD (glimmer) into the voids, into the empty fatherless fields.

In the first few years the hurt never really calcified, it just developed a thin membrane over it. A three-year-long wound. Any sighting or memory was enough to rip the thing open again. And now that he is back I have been black-holed again (glimmer), scraped out and replaced with questions like

when is aggie going to come into town
we have been waiting for him listening out our windows
for the sound of him whistling over his truck engine
how nice it will be to see him with his family
with his wife with emma with orrie with ingrid

is interested in the foggy man. She wants to reach into his eyes and rub the clouds out of them. She walks by him in the kitchen in the middle of the night, where he sits at the table with a glass of water, and he is so still she thinks he's dead. He has only taken a sip off the glass he filled, and the rest of it swims in the amber kitchen light. She looks at him and thinks the word *Dad*, holds these two things in her hands but can't bring them together. Emma said there would be some giant swell of feeling when he walked into the room for the first time, like he had never left, but all Ingrid really felt was curiosity. She tilts her head, watches the foggy man. *Is he always this foggy?* she wants to ask. It seems the whole house has grown foggy in his absence but the rest of them have woken from it while he is still stuck. In a strange way she is afraid of him—she sees in him something she could someday become, if she does not remove herself from the

fog in the town fog over all our eyes
you have to understand his departure
wasn't only a loss for his family the whole town
felt the gash of it

's simple, really: I sleep easier than ever, sink into a black resoluteness, at the realization that the thing I have been waiting years and years for, since a time when I still harbored dreams of escape, the thing I have held on my tongue every night before sleep, has brought no comfort, no resolution. Now that it has come, it's only opened another tar barrel of questions to get stuck in. Why did I think the sweetness of life was once again possible for us? The war has taken our name—Atreus—and drenched it in dark. The vitriolic hot-blooded resentment I have found myself in is not so easy to leave, it is my new everyday way.

It's like having a new child in the family, having Dad back. He looks at me with a purity in his eyes, a gilded gleam, and I think his soul has been swapped out with another, there is a new soul in him. He is still so fresh to this life, stumbling and unsure in his motions. At dinner I asked him how he was feeling—expecting him to say *tired* or *happy*—and he gave me a look, lost and searching, like I was a stranger in his life, that cleaved me open. It is simultaneous, the mourning of the old lost life and the celebration of the new. Mom seems unsure of how to conduct herself, as if she released him from her life in the six years he was away and now the old thing in her is being dug up. Several times during dinner, she left the room and came back with a wet face and washed arms. *You can't soap away your mistakes,* I wanted to tell her. But she didn't know that I knew.

The gears in my head have been spinning faster lately. Every room I'm in, I look around and feel like something is wrong, like some piece of the grand puzzle is in sight but I'm just not seeing it. Enzo was over earlier than usual today, in advance of Dad's arrival. I was making tea in the morning, waiting for it to boil. Mom often cuts the kettle before it boils all the way but I like the water hot enough to melt, and nothing wakes me in the morning faster than two bags of steeping steaming black. Enzo stood at the far side of the kitchen, hands clasped behind his head, hip against the counter, looking at something in the pantry—I couldn't tell what.

—I stayed over last night, he said. —Was working late on the docs.

But the guest bed was immaculate when I passed by, made up far nicer than any man could do, and Mom hadn't woken yet. No signs of life in the room, pillows fluffy, carpet vacuum-tracked and footstepless, air stale. A room held on pause since its last guest had left.

Some welcome-home-Dad it all is. What would he sniff out, I wonder, if he were able, which dynamics would feel disturbed? I have no proof yet, only suspicion, but some things you just know.

And what am I going to do if I find proof, anyway? Stomp, storm, raise a stink? Some good it has done up until now—whenever the sea-foam of my fury rises too high and I get a word in edgewise, I'm glared at as if petulant, sent to my room, commanded to think about my reactions. Like I'm fourteen, grounded after getting a bad grade on an exam. I still feel like a high-schooler, feel like I have not been allowed to age here—locked inside this house, I have been locked inside my habits, my patterns. In waiting for Dad to come home, we have all waited to grow.

Who am I going to tell if I uncover anything? Who is my complaint department? Dad can hardly tell one day from the next, one memory from another. His whole world is a blur before his eyes. Do I go to other relatives, to townspeople, to an old teacher? But what can they do? Nothing—we are all stuck-footed in this standstill. We wake and shuffle around till it is once again time for

sleep well aggie in your soft blue bed
after your long long homecoming
kiss your wife very hard for us

, Cleo thinks, but where is the *us*? There is Aggie, over there; here is her. She has cleaved him out of her body but there is grief at his loss. He's in what looks like a blackened sleep, trapped in the inky pool of his mind. She watches him in this deathlike state, wants to reach in and pull him out. This man, this father, stripped of capacity. She has been overworked, underpleasured, unhappy, and her children have turned from her as a result. None as outwardly as Emma, but she feels between her other children and herself a similar distance. For so long they hoped—she herself hoped—that Aggie's return would make everything normal again. They saw light in that promise and held it, held it.

In the silence she falls into her own sleep and has the snake dream again. This time in the dream Aggie is next to her instead of Enzo (did she mention that Enzo was next to her in all the prior iterations? How easily desire is able to overwrite the binds of fact) but the snake-baby still does its fang-latching thing and she watches herself drain out, go bloodless. And he does nothing, just watches and shakes his head. She wakes in a panic, hair glued to her temples, but Aggie is sleeping so deathlike that she doesn't want to rouse him, so instead she shuffles to the bathroom, fills a glass of water with a trembling hand, and again pulls a pregnancy test from beneath the sink—one of her last, but she is in no mind to ration them right now. As she relaxes and the stream comes, she remembers discovering her pregnancy with Ingrid, remembers the way the room seemed to fill with a brighter light. How she ran shouting out to Aggie, how her joy was the first thing he heard when he woke. She sets the stick down now, on the moonlit counter, breathes slow, afraid for any more emotion to

wake late aggie in your fresh fields
the ground does not need your tending quite yet you can sleep
off the journey till the sky is bright

and early Uncle Enzo comes and gets Emma and me up and out into the morning. He lets Ingrid sleep, says we only need two kids in the fields. The three of us pull our winter coats on. Here in A____ in winter, it doesn't normally freeze but the chill can sink into the bones. This year has brought a bizarre snow cover that's settled down over us, frozen us in a bit. At this point the work is minimal and more about getting the fields ready for soil-warm spring. Summer break is when the work peaks and the whole place smells beautiful, earthy and floral and vegetal like we're wandering a market.

I am still rubbing the sleep out of my eyes (glimmer) and almost fall down the porch steps onto the cold dirt. I catch onto the rail and guide myself down slowly. I was in the middle of a dream, I don't remember what about, but the feeling it left me with was like sunglow on the skin. I want to go back to that, to my warm room.

Uncle Enzo says, —Your dad'll wake up and he'll be back to normal. Just has to sleep some things off is all.

Emma's frown does not fall away at this.

The coldest time has left us just slightly, so we clean the fields while Uncle Enzo and Mom sit on the porch and work on financials. The fallen foliage has gone mushy and its mush has frozen to clumps that crunch beneath my rake. The scrape of the rake's metal teeth in the earth sends shivers through me. My teeth chatter in the cold.

The farm in winter is a lonely enterprise. In the summer, when everything rushes up, we hire helping hands, but for now the work is ours to bear alone. The quiet swallows me up sometimes.

Today from the fields we can hear Mom and Uncle Enzo going back and forth about things—crouched over the documents, faces flushed with cold. We look at each other (glimmer). Tidy the tree lines and puncture the ground and reinvigorate the earth. All the while the two of them discuss matters in their chairs and Dad slumbers away inside. I pray that when he wakes he will remember everything, he will be back.

He drags himself out the front door at 10:37, at which point the sun is higher in the sky and the sun has begun to loosen the earth further. He stares at the horizon with sleep-narrowed eyes. I run up to his side and he pulls me close. Being tucked into him like an envelope feels familiar.

—Morning, kid, he says.

It's a big burst of joy pure and lifting. He's slept off the trip and his mind is back, he is here. But when he looks at me I notice that distance still (glimmer), approaching recognition but not quite reaching it. A sinking now. I focus on his palm on my head, the warmth of it. His body still bed-warm. If I lean into him I can stop thinking and focus on that feeling.

It doesn't work. I want to ask him things like Do you remember when I was seven and you took me ice skating for the first time and I circled the edge of the rink with my arm hooked over the wall and a fear like death in my eyes and Emma did laps around me laughing and hooting but you stayed with me the whole time held onto my other hand or Is your favorite color still green like mine or has it changed to something else because I worry mine is becoming red or How often did you think of me when you were in T____ how often did you wish you could tell me a story before sleep how often did you think of coming home were you a years-long wound too but he removes his hand from my head and shuffles over to the table the adults are clustered around and the moment falls away, there's a bird squawking in a spindly tree, and I make my way out into the fields again and listen to the quiet sounds of the

town feels different with aggie back there is
a pulse back in the earth like it knows
he is going to tend to it once again, aggie with his
delicate assured farm-destined hands

Enzo a glass of water and he drinks desperately from it. His brain cannot focus on the numbers; they keep seeping out of his ears. He is a melted ball of emotions, like a bag of candy left in a hot car. On one level he feels like he is finally at home in his bones—next to Cleo, at work on the farm, managing its affairs. He feels like he has finally stepped into his real life, the real life he always pictured, after his cousin stepped out of it. But also his cousin is back and something is clearly not right with him. Something has been switched off in his head to preserve the rest of him. What kind of preservation is that, really, if it shuts off the soul?

Enzo cleared his traces from Cleo's bedroom in the days before Aggie came home, prayed his cousin didn't find him smell him see him in there. He had to give his cousin this one thing, had to give him his life back. Even if his body is now more of a trap than a thing to live inside, a thing to move through. He wishes he could pry the trap open, release the soul inside,

but the man of the house won't be at work
for some time he must recover he must rest
regain his strength he has served us so honorably
look at the weight in his walk

back from the fields, breath fogging in front of me. Orrie stands next to Dad, his head cupped beneath his hand. My fingertips are numb and I try, to no avail, to rub warmth back into them. On the porch, the air is static with argument; Dad's face is dark, shadowed.

—I appreciate what you've done, he says to Enzo, —but you aren't needed in the same capacity anymore, I'm perfectly able to manage.

His speech so slow, so different from before, when sentences sprinted out of him.

—Ag, Enzo says. —Come on. You're not ready to take on all this responsibility again. Just let me stay on a bit longer, till you're back to yourself.

Orrie watches them both with fear pooled in his eyes. Dad has peeled away from him and stands with his hands in tight coils.

—I think he's right, Aggie, Mom says. —You need some time to get readjusted. And while Enzo is here and willing to help, I don't see a reason for you to rush back into things.

The sight of Mom and Enzo, the closeness of their bodies, his hands nearly at her wrists on the iron table, sets my blood alight. Dad doesn't see it but I do, now that I am looking for it, now that I've rubbed the cloud out of my eyes. I want to tell Dad that it has nothing to do with the farm, nothing to do with his conditions, nothing to do with anything beyond their bodies calling for each other. Want to tell him to look, just look.

But he seems to buy that their urging is a kindness, accepts it. He says, —All right. Well, I think I might head into town today. Pick up some stuff. Feels like a good day to grill.

Something about this, remembering the smells Dad can coax out of sizzling meat, the herbs and spices and oils he drenches them in, and I can't help buying into the vision. I go all warm-chested for a moment. Orrie smiles too—it seems to reignite some hope within him. Maybe a glimmer of how things used to be passes before his eyes. Some distant memory floating across his vacant sky.

Dad turns to him. —You want to be my helper? he asks. —Like the old days. He speaks hesitantly, turns the sentence upward at its end like a sort-of question.

Orrie nods. —Or, he says, eyes lighting up, —you could bring Ingrid, she's been excited to . . . catch up with you.

He almost said *meet*, I could see the word there hovering in his mouth.

—That's a great idea, Dad says. —When does . . . the little girl get up these days?

I try as hard as I can not to let it ruin the moment, not to take it as a sign that he has forgotten her name, or that he can't access it, it's somewhere out of his reach. My heart splits watching him stand there, supplanted from his former life. The unfairness rattles around in my head like a marble knocking around. How can I find out about the term he served without asking him, without making him revisit it, bringing it all rushing back up to his surface? Because I need to know—I need to know what changed him.

Orrie says, —She's probably up, just still in her room.

No one ever knows because Ingrid moves through the house silent as air. Sometimes I see her in her room and then moments later I see her in the kitchen. She drifts through the shadows of this place. She rarely speaks, never throws fits, only stands there and slow-blinks her big eyes. She has a wonderful, pure singing voice, and sometimes when Mom cooks, she requests that Ingrid sing to keep her company. Orrie and I hover in the living room, listen to her voice, feel it melt us. I want to grab her by the shoulders and shake her up a bit and say, Don't you have a scream deep down in you too? Don't you have a roar to let loose?

But she never screams, never howls. I don't understand it: my own body is built so differently; everything I feel fights its way out of me. She keeps it all inside her, delicate as a latched box. She appears at the door as if summoned, and when Dad asks her if she wants to go with him into town, she slow-blinks those big eyes, smiles, nods. Sleep has barely left her but her eyes are pooled wide. She goes back inside to grab a coat, to slip on her shoes.

When they leave, Ingrid buckled up in the far-side bench seat, Dad with his left hand on the wheel, something in his eyes makes me pause. Nobody else notices, they just watch him put the truck in reverse and back away, and Mom sets a hand on my shoulder, cocks her head as if to ask why a shadow has passed over my face.

But it's not worth raising a fuss over. So I follow Orrie back out into the fields and join him in his silent work, amazed, now as ever, by the quiet out

here comes the man
here the man comes
the man comes here
into town across our roads

pass beneath the hood of Aggie's truck. So long since he's gotten behind the wheel of his truck but the act of driving it, he finds, is like slipping into an old coat. He notices the way the town, its streets twisting and crossing, unfolds its map in his mind as he goes. He has missed the wheel's judder in his hands. His daughter is beside him on the bench seat and she clasps her hands together to keep them warm. Oh, the heater, he remembers. He looks down at the panel of buttons, waits for the symbols to cross the bridge toward meaning, and finds the one that makes air whoosh from the bottom of the windshield, blast his face with warm air. It recalls a simpler time for him, when he was on the bus ride to school, those whooshes of air that nearly put him back to sleep till the bus crossed a speed bump and jolted him awake. The heat keeps the

< DOWN !! >

s out of his ears. He's still not here but he's closer to here than whatever his six-year thing was. Sometimes he feels as if he is back there, as if he never left. The excerpts feel so real, is the thing; they envelop him. Their sounds stamp out the ones of now and the memories of before.

He sits with the now-sounds for a while.

He looks over at his daughter and feels a pang. He thinks maybe he should ask her a question but he's not sure what it should be or how he should get it out. In his absence, she has solidified into a person, with interests and dislikes and desires, and he has no idea where to begin. But the urge to ask a question claws at his throat. When he left she was pure child, napping in the afternoons, living on a diet of baby carrots and orange juice. How many phases has she crossed through from then till now, how many identities has she held? He prods at those blanks in his memory, feels his fingers sink into their nothing-spaces.

But she seems content to sit in the quiet, holding her hands in front of the heater vents, warming herself. At the first stoplight, when he finally makes it out of the hills and into town, he is listening to an old bit. Somewhere in there, somewhere back again. He tries to remember whether to turn left or right

but we don't want to see
this next part
everybody look away

< you can't though orrie hard as you may try > <those final moments will always lie under your skin >

is pallid, freckled, dark-blued with tattoos. He has a brow curled over like a cat's tail, eyes fixed on the road. He is going fast, Ingrid notices—why is he going so fast? This man, she has been told, shared a life with her for years. She has seen the pictures of him atop the tractor, holding the little bundle of her, his youngest girl, her face squashed up like a raisin. She looks at his face, its shape, and something washes over her: it is hers too. Some bond in the body there. In the truck he is shaking his head in quick jolting movements, like he is batting away insects that approach him. He is going so fast. Speech rises in her throat but when it comes out it's nonsensical, a burnished sound, and he doesn't notice. She sets her eyes forward, keeps her limbs tense. *Ice everywhere,* Enzo always warns, *the snow's just a fluffy blanket covering it up, like how your blanket covers you up at night.* Then he grabs her sides and tickles her and she squeals, jolts herself away. Maybe the foggy man forgot about ice in his time away from home—got used to the desert. He sucks in a breath and cranks the wheel. His foot slips from the brake, a panicked look overtakes him, and

< here we go one two three : >

The news spreads quick as smoke. You know how small towns are. And that is how A____ is. From the highway where it happens, it slips up the streets one by one. And it reaches us at the top of our hill.

I am back inside the house when a car tears up the snow-slick driveway (glimmer) and a man from town leaps out. A man I don't know, but something in his urgency makes him trustworthy. Mom, who has been watching her breath fog the window, runs down the front porch steps. He shows her a picture on his phone and I watch her sink to her knees (glimmer) (glimmer). Uncle Enzo goes to the screen door and pokes a quiet foot out. Goes to meet Mom on the ground and sets a gentle hand on her shoulder and listens to what the man has to say.

This moment, right here, this moment: this is the last moment Emma and I look at each other and can pretend the world is still whole (glimmer). Everything happening with Dad has put fractures in the ground but this moment here is the one that ruptures it open and gulps us up. We hear everything through the open front door and feel the cold air rushing in, though it does nothing to us who are already chilled all the way through.

The man says, —Ingrid's dead, the little girl is dead (glimmer) (glimmer).

Emma leans over and vomits on the kitchen floor (glimmer). I find myself outside. Look at the photos of our truck (glimmer)

its engine wrapped around a sturdy pine (glimmer). The metal at its front splinters like paper on fire. My throat is raw as I say, —Where's Dad.

—Huh? the man says.

—Where's Dad. Aggie.

—An ambulance loaded him up. He's still alive.

(glimmer) I can't conceive of a life without my sister. It cannot occur without her.

I stop living (glimmer).

Take up a post in some false life.

Emma is screaming, running, hurtling (glimmer) through the door. I walk back into the house but all I can see is my soul (glimmer) as it rises out of my body and leaves me behind to live out (glimmer) the rest of whatever this is.

Doesn't feel like there is anything in this house, not an I, not a she, not a

we the chorus have
nothing to say
at this time

A silence falls over the property. Then a noise sounds upstairs, loud and sharp, as if the house is sending out a grief-noise too.

nothing at all

3

three times the charm or maybe four who is to say whos keeping score

The curse wrangling us in its hands again (glimmer) and it's all my fault. Parents of our friends used to disallow friendships with us once they learned who we were. Didn't let us in their houses, relegated us to playing in their yards. Thought the curse could float off us (glimmer) and settle onto their skins like ash. Didn't want our smudges and I can't say I blame them. At times I have wished I didn't have to be part of whatever this thing Atreus is. Sat beneath the oracle tree, looked at its twisting trunk and thin branches, and cast wish after wish all for the same thing. Watched it refute me again and again. Not a leaf shook loose. Why, I wanted to know, was I being punished so? Why had I been born into a tangled net? Born helpless? It seemed like

only death sounds from us

mewls of agony
our dear ingrid

is floating somewhere in the world. There is a place where souls go but hers is not there yet. It is thinking of her brother Orrie and remembering when they used to play outside together. Emma was too old to find amusement in such games but Ingrid and Orrie still had fun. They used to stand at the base of the tallest oak tree in the yard clutching handfuls of stones and try to launch the stones as high as they could. She liked making the branches shake their leaves loose. Sometimes Orrie called out RUN because a stone was coming down too close and he didn't want either of them to be pelted by it. He could always win because he had four years on her but sometimes he let her win. And she ran inside, flush-faced and buoyant, and said, *Mom, Em, I got highest, I got highest!*

She will never throw stones again because she can never hold them, they slip through her soul-hands. It was a silly childhood game anyway, but something about it got stuck in her throat and she is keening about it

now listen you can hear us
from the hills
howling like hyenas
unable to rest unable to sit

at the base of the oracle tree, before everything falls apart entirely, before the planet splits open and swallows us up, before we gather in the car to visit Dad, before we find Ingrid, whatever bits of her remain. THE CURSE, everyone shouted at me from all sides, THE CURSE, Dad and Orrie and Enzo and the town and the house itself in its floor-creaks, the last of the true believers. I have never asked the tree a question in earnest, only in mockery. Laughed it off, thought trusting the wind through it was like trusting a horoscope to steer my fate. Now I am tearing my nails into the frigid dirt, seeking the tree's roots, trying to get to its basest parts, trying to atone. FOOL, YOU FOOL, I want to shout at myself. I want to dig the veins out of my arms and give them to Ingrid, the organs, the meat, all of it. She has her bones but I can give her every other part of me that is still living, she can thread them through herself. She can have my body, I have done nothing with it all these years, it has not loved, it has not cherished, it has only soaked in the sludge of its own hatred. I have done nothing but keep it alive, as if I knew she would need it someday. She can use it for good, she can use it to dream. She can clear out the cobwebs, the gunk I have filled it with.

There was a day a couple years ago when I walked by the kitchen and saw her seated at the table with sharp fear in her eyes, her lip trembling, but I was in a mood of my own. I didn't stop to ask or to assure—I stormed upstairs and raged at whatever I was raging at, I don't remember, it doesn't matter, it wasn't the important part. What was important was that I walked past her and then later when she shut herself in her room I didn't check on her, I didn't do anything, I let her suffer alone and I hid in my selfish pit. And I'm clawing open the earth looking for why she was hurting, why she was afraid. I had theories at the time, but they have all fallen from me now. I keep my ears open for the peals of shuffling leaves, ask again and again, Am I next, Am I next, Please am I next, Am I

next hoarse-throated we fall silent
sit in our misery

is a beast Cleo cannot fight off. She is thinking about the morning last week when she let Enzo out the back door, kissed his fuzzy cheek. The secrecy has given every moment with him a grave importance and as a result she has felt like the star of her life. She shut the door after he walked away and turned to find Ingrid sitting on the steps, looking out the front windows of the house. The light had taken on a blueness in the early sun.

Cleo said (tone brush-light to mask her fear), —Jesus, you're so quiet, do you even walk or do you just float? Why are you up so early?

Ingrid just looked at her with those big hazel eyes that always shone like she had just been crying. They say eyes are windows but Cleo didn't believe it till her second daughter. Emma's were always dark with vitriol, and Orrie's shone with some other kind of dreaming, but Ingrid's were pure as spring mornings. Cleo can't stop thinking about them. Maybe at the hospital she will pry them open for one more rich look. She will take them in and hold them forever. Though she is sure they look dead now, potpourri-dry and lightless.

She says, —Enzo, get the truck started.

He doesn't hear, some other world's pulled down over his ears, so she says it again, shouts this time. He leaps a bit in his skin, darts from the room like a scared cat, grabs the keys which jingle on the way out. She has misspoken—the truck is gone, the truck has been destroyed, wrapped around a tree. She hears Enzo fire up the SUV instead. The jingling of the keys still hovers bright in her ears—she feels that nothing can be that bright again, not now, not

here they come tearing
down the road toward the hospital

and there she goes little girl blue
toward the underworld black

-ened by the time we get to the hospital. I have gone flat like an autumn leaf beneath a boot, and Dad has been wheeled into a room of his own, unhurt, surprisingly lucid. They want to keep an eye on him for a bit, make sure there's no damage on the inside. He looks silly, a giant man in that sea-green gown. He sips from a cup of water. It feels like nobody is in the room but me: Mom and Enzo are out in the hall and Orrie's eyes are fixed in the branches outside, looking for birds, squirrels, martens. Things that patter in and out of the remaining slush.

Where is your grief? I want to ask Dad. It has somehow brought him into focus, cleared a bit of haze from him. My grief hangs before my eyes and shrouds everything in itself. I feel as though I have hit an emotional peak and gone cascading down the other side—my body, having raged and wailed and torn the ground apart, is pulling me down into exhaustion. But I know in a matter of time my heart will seize and my blood will run hot, will rage, once again. Like all else in me, my grief is a thing that rages and calms. While the adults deliberate outside, and Dad stares at the bathroom door's wood frame, and Orrie tracks a finch twitching in the branches, I leave the room, wander the hall, look for water. I look in the other rooms, at the doctors, nurses, patients, anything not to think of Ingrid. I imagine their stories, imagine them far worse than my own. But it doesn't help, it only adds to the

wreck everywhere in the bodies
in the souls in the air of the town
they will wreck the frozen earth
for her they must it is their way
they will lay her next to the other
fruit fallen from the family tree

shudders and the bird I am watching flies away (glimmer). I have given it a name—Harold—and assigned it a home seven miles north of here. Babies to feed, a nest to preserve. He is flying home now, I reason, with a fresh worm in his mouth. I lower my eyes from the window when Dad says something and note that the room is now empty save for the pair of us. I hadn't noticed its loneliness but it comes crashing down on me now (glimmer). The plastic seats at my sides are empty and the hall seems clear from the sliver of it I can see through the door.

—Huh? I ask.

—I have to say something. Now that Em is gone. I feel like you're the only one I can say it to. And I have to get it out of me.

—Okay.

—About today.

—Okay.

Why does my heart rate ratchet upward like a bird's (glimmer)? He looks like a giant fairytale bear tucked into a tiny bed, his heels nearly hanging off the bottom edge. And his eyes are filled with a vacuous hurt, his hands folded together politely in his lap like he is attending a talk. He tries to speak then swallows. He is choking on the words.

—The wreck was an accident, he says. —Slid across some ice. But at the last second I had the choice to turn the wheel and save her, or save myself. That's how it seems to me, looking back. I had the choice. And I was going to save her. (glimmer)

Glimmers assemble in the margins of the room and dance like flashing bugs in the air.

—But at the last moment, he continues, —I saw her in my periphery and I had the sense that—

Some demon seems to overcome him now.

—that she was evil and I had to rid the world of her. Like it was in T____ in the time I was gone. I was back there. In T____. The orders to just do it without thinking.

His eyes are empty now (glimmer), everything in them has died.

—I did it, he says. —I turned the wheel. It was me.

Still with those prim hands folded (glimmer).

I watch him breathe. He barely moves. Like the air is moving in and out of a plastic-shelled dummy. I have nothing to say, so I stand and walk into the hallway.

—ORR, he calls after me. —ORRIE, KEEP THAT SAFE.

Mom and Uncle Enzo are down the hall seated in the waiting room (glimmer) but I turn in the opposite direction. I don't see Em. I realize I am also looking for Ingrid (glimmer) (glimmer) and want to rip my eyes out because she will never fall in their light again. I walk out the front doors of the hospital (glimmer) which part at the sight of me and I lie on the grass (glimmer) for a while (glimmer). It is wet against my legs (glimmer) and back. I look up at the sky (glimmer). Clouds all over up there (glimmer) big puffy things (glimmer).

And the glimmers that are piling up (glimmer) turn to fragments of sound and the fragments combine to say

< hello >

I look around to locate the sound but no one is near me. Only a man being wheeled into the building in the distance. I wait for another sound but none comes, only branches rustling and the wavelike rush of passing cars coming to and from the hospital.

4

four times find an eye inside yourself and look out through it what do you see

a hospital is such a sad place
congregations of mourners hopers worriers
sicken themselves with feeling

aggie will be there for a day or two and then they will
release him when they deem him safe, it is the way
but he will never be normal

-cy will never find them again. Her daughter's bedroom is full of toys that will never be played with again. What is she going to do with all the toys? Mostly books, now, she is—*was* (little soul-death)—turning into a brainy girl. The clothes could be passed on but no one is going to want clothes that belonged to a dead girl. The increasing probability: everything will remain where it is and the room will become a shrine to her, to the little dead girl. It could become another guest bedroom, it could become an office, but who is going to want to work in a space that will forever smell like the memory of the little dead girl, no matter how many chemical solvents and sprays and vacuums and sponge-scrubs they take to it.

And there's the bit of her that wants to murder Aggie for what he has done, though it was an accident, the bit that wants to tear out his eyes and rip out his tongue and unsocket his limbs and toss them all in a pyre, burn it big, bright. She has a fury in her that often goes untapped—it's where Emma got hers—and today it's ravaging, she feels it on the reverse side of her skin, burning away at her muscle, her blood. It burns its way up her skull, behind her eyes, she can hardly see around that ruddied rage. She shouldn't have let him drive, shouldn't have had such trust in his abilities, she should have gone with him instead, driven him there, escorted him up and down the grocery aisles. Should should should. All she can do with all the *shoulds* is count them up on her fingers and shove them you know where.

The fact too that when she dozes off in the hospital chair, pulled down into its spiral by lack of energy, her head closer to Enzo's shoulder than it should be—easy enough, she reasons, to blame on sleep and gravity—she dreams again of the snake. But this time Enzo and Aggie are both there, and Aggie's holding his family heirloom scepter, which has been in their closet for years and is only invoked in doom-times. She doesn't know why he has it but the dream, she notes, is morphing. She could fill Medusa's head with the snakes she has birthed in dreams, could feed a lakeful of leeches with the blood they have drained from her.

When she wakes she is so close to Enzo that she can smell his hours-old deodorant, the way it mingles with his shock-sweat, and her eyes flit around the room to see if anyone has noticed. She pulls herself upright, shifts away, but her nose is still dizzy with his scent. She doesn't like thinking about it but it is easier than thinking about other things. At least she holds some capacity for love, even if the gods have misdirected it. She worries she is drying up into a loveless thing, a sour mother, a bitter wife, an elusive sister, but Enzo makes her feel like she is blooming with life, like she is growing.

And the fact she wants to confront least of all is the fact that the man down the hall—her husband, the father of her children—makes her feel nothing more than a deep guilt. When she looks at him, no love wells in her eyes. When she entertains the prospect of his death, the fact that he could have died alongside or instead of their daughter, she feels—she can't say it. Can't think the name of it. But there is a freedom, a lightness, in the thought. Her vessels relax. And, again, a blip of guilt that she could feel that way. But it is the feeling she has and it is a feeling she can't change.

She hasn't been to visit him in his hospital room yet. She watches Orrie round the corner of the hall and step outside, figures now may be the time to steel herself and do it. So she stands, brushes her hands along her legs, brushes off the guilt that seeps from her pores, and heads toward Aggie's cracked door. It's true, she thinks to herself, call me what you want, a liar, a deceiver, a

hypocrite lecteur the family has never hurt worse
but they have never felt more alive and they have never wished
more strongly otherwise they are wet with ill feeling

but nobody is thinking now. The four of them go home, without Aggie, and pick at a bar of chocolate. They split it between them but none has more than a pinch before their stomachs go to tumult and they give up. It sits on the counter, split into untouched squares, set between the

prickly basket of grief holds them
all together the house is cold (aggie turned

off the heater in the middle
of the night and nobody noticed)

that I fell asleep. I wanted to knock myself out with valerian tea, thought a drug-addled sleep was the only sleep I would get, and I was right, and it worked. I wake in Ingrid's bed and hear her singing voice jolting around in my head. For a moment I think she is here but it is only my brain. For a few moments I roll around in sick-seeming agony, hear her everywhere, see the crash play out in my mind though I wasn't there to witness it and have no idea how it went. But a specific metal sound is in my head. There's rage in here too, there's always a rage in here, but it has no target so I can't let it out and it just sits and boils, burns its way up my throat. The only gladness I have, the only one I can find amid the dark shards of anger and sorrow and regret, is that I never left home, that I lived with Ingrid for her entire life. I had never thought of my home-stuckness as anything but a burden and suddenly it's a gleaming gift. The agonies in me outweigh the gladnesses but there is the one at least. The one smooth warm stone in my pocket full of glass.

I nearly vomit on her pillow but catch myself in time, stumble through the dark and hurl into the sink instead. The sick sticks to the sides of my lips and I wipe it away with a wet cloth. I think of when she was seven and had her first bout with the flu, fear shining so brightly in her eyes but she never complained, never let her tremulous heart out. She was our Pandora's box, that girl, she gathered our darknesses and kept them shut tight inside. All she gave us in return was her pure voice. And now that she is gone I fear our darknesses have all slipped out into the world, I fear they will strike again. If only we

townspeople toss and turn
in our sleep tonight

our world is emptier
and it cannot be refilled
nothing left of her we can keep

my ears open wide as I can to hear the voice again but it never comes back. By one in the morning I'm convinced I made it up. Or maybe it was a piece of some memory that came back to me and felt as real as life-breath in my ears. In the dark of my room I wait for my eyes to fill in the blanks. Wait to see the crevices in the walls and the crackles in the ceiling, spaces where a voice might hide. But I don't hear it again and all I see is glimmerless dark.

The hope I cling to is that the voice belonged to Ingrid. Come on, Ingrid, I want to tell it. Say something again, make yourself known to me. Sing for us one last time. Tell me you forgive me. Because in the end it's all my fault. She climbed into the truck with Dad at my suggestion and in any other world the body splayed across the dash is mine. The death is mine and she gets to go on living, she gets to see twelve and thirteen and each year beyond. I catch a wisp of sleep when the sun starts to rise and then consciousness finds me again nearly as soon as it left me.

At the kitchen table in midmorning I rub sleep from my eyes. Mom slides a cup of coffee in front of me. She describes coffee as an adult ritual and prohibits me from drinking it but maybe yesterday's events have turned me more adult than before. It's dark and bitter and scalds my throat but I drink the whole cup and ask for another.

She shakes her head, says, —You'll get the jitters or just throw it all back up.

The coffee sends a jolt through me but overall today things feel uneven. I have never gone a night with this little sleep and I feel as though the world is lopsided and everything is sliding slowly across its floor. I hear Emma or Dad shuffling around upstairs and wonder when Ingrid's braided head is going to drift around the kitchen column and slip a wedge of muffin from the counter tray. And then I think, No, it's too early for her to be up. Give it a few hours, she'll come down like always. And the world shifts further off its alignment. In the house all of us together

we see it too
we see the world shifting

overnight. Before bed I was thick with relief, glad I stayed, glad to have lived out Ingrid's eleven years with her. But when I wake, back in my cold bed, I am staring at the shackles of more time here and a pit has opened up in my stomach. I realize I could have left and taken both her and Orrie with me. Gone where, I don't know, but I would have found something. So much world out there and our sorry little slice of it fills me with a longing I can't suppress, a longing that replicates inside me, spirals outward into something severe. I feel as though I've robbed myself of life here, watched my friends pack their lives into boxes and leave, watched them head to glittering cities and gleaming coasts while I gripped at their fading coattails and moaned TAKE ME WITH YOU. But here I am still and going rotten on the inside. A mind without stimulation is a mind that steeps in its own stale juices. And I feel as though my mind and my body have gone to rot. I am the stench that fills my own life. I wish I had gotten out. But in my head, I hear what the townspeople would have said as my car made its way past the town limits:

silly girl trying to outrun fate
the curse is in you no matter where you're headed
the curse IS you

won't believe this, I tell Ingrid in my head, but the voice came back. In my delirious state, eyes woozy and head topsy-turvy and stomach sick-feeling with lack of sleep, I have taken to talking to her in my head. She is a better listener than anyone living. And she never pips back she just listens and looks (glimmer). I'd like to believe it's her actual soul in there listening to me but also I want her soul to be light years away by now. Wherever the good souls go, whatever fields they dance across.

The voice came back, I explain to Ingrid, and it said

< hello again >

and I wanted to ask it, When are you going to say something more adventurous? I'm ready for the voice to pull me out of my body and spill me onto the ground. I'm ready for an unfurling like that.

I remember, Ingrid, when you pulled me into your bed one night and said, *You're not like a usual boy.* And I went a bit red and said, *What do you mean?* And you said, *All the boys at my school are so mean, they say bad words and do farts and throw rocks at each other, but I don't think you ever did any of those things.* And I said, *Well, I threw a rock at my friend Patrick once and it split his head open, but that was it, never again.* And you said, *I hope you never become like the other boys.* It was the most talking I'd heard you do in quite some time, though at most points I could look at you and tell what you were feeling. Whether your eyes were shining with love or disappointment or fear—you were legible in that way. And I always wanted to be held in your love-light. I wanted to earn that from you.

I catch myself speaking aloud and clamp my hand over my mouth. Don't want to let these things go to anyone but Ingrid; they are for her. I hope that, floating across her Elysian field, she catches my words as they drift by. The night is dark and I hear something (!!) that says:

< third time's the charm >

and I grab a book and start mashing my head with it (glimmer). Again and again the maroon hardcover between my eyes. There is a thing in my head and I've got to get it out so I can speak to it. Then I try each of my temples, think maybe I can fling it out one of my ears. I feel my head rocket to the side each time.

But Emma is here pulling the book out of my hands, shouting, —What the fuck are you doing, Orrie? and sitting me down.

There are tears in my eyes (glimmer) that I only notice as she wipes them away. —Trying to get something out, I say.

But she doesn't understand, she just slants her brow and shakes her head and takes the book. As if I can't find another and resume thwapping. But for now I leave it be. I lay back and think of Ingrid. Sorry you had to see that, I think to her. I think of Emma now retreated to her room. Think of Ingrid's empty (don't think about this) room (don't think about this) and the kitchen (stop) free of her song (stop !!). Think of the voice I kept waiting to hear. Think of it giving me what I need most, telling me it forgives me. Think of Mom's half-empty bed, think of

aggie is mucking up the hospital we hear
he is making a commotion calling out to his
daughter

but doesn't he know she is
too far away to hear him now
?

a simple question is all, but I shudder when I recall the intensity with which I delivered it. The firestorm in me sometimes forces its way out, hard as I try to tamp it down. My system was flooded with shock and some preservation instinct kicked in, some bone-deep need to make Orrie safe. I tell Mom about it when I see her in the hall. She pulls me into her room, sits me down on the bed.

I run through the whole thing. Her brow goes sour, prickles with sweat, and she sets a hand to it.

She says, —Let's keep an eye on him these next few days.

I think, *Or longer*, and I think she does too, based on the further slant of her brow. The wind has picked up and an olive branch thwacks the outside of the window, that rustly sound of leaves stirring like rain hitting the roof. She walks me back out into the hall, shuts me outside her room. I stand there in the quiet for a moment, watch the branches slice through the moonlight on the hall floor.

I hear a sound from the other side of her door, set my ear to it. Breathing fast, struggling to hold something in that is trying to get out. How many years has it been since I would have gone in to comfort her? Since the sound of her upset has triggered something in me beyond a general, cool sort of sympathy? I have no problem leaving her there, letting her settle down by herself. Sad, isn't it, that sort of realization. So I head across the hall, open my

door again have you ever had one of those dreams
where a door opens to another
door

and you rip them open with abandon thinking surely
you will reach a room or a hall sooner or later
but you only come face to face with another door

is cracked open and the slice of lucid hospital-hall light falls in on him, and he tosses and turns in his bed. It is funny, he thinks, how the noise of a place like this, loud and bustling at all hours of day, can fall away when the door is shut to just a sliver, and the rest of the room can go dark as pitch, the blinds shut to keep out the moon. He tosses and turns some more, reaches out in half-sleep to cradle his daughter's head. For so long he has not had this luxury, the ability to cradle a head in his hand, but some sense comes to him and he feels his daughter's head is as cold as faraway earth frozen over in winter, and he remembers, yes, it is my fault, I killed her, it is my fault she is this cold, and his hand continues its reach toward someone else, another head, another child, but he pulls it back, doesn't trust himself not to kill the others too, doesn't trust his hands to love and not to hurt. Killing has become an eye-blink, life before and death after, giant vast indefinable space between, and now some emotion is coming over him, consuming him in his entirety the way a large wave strikes a beach, and he is juddering and mucus-covered and though he tries to wipe it away it doesn't stop, everything inside him is attempting to rush forth at once, the love the sorrow the earth-fissuring remorse, it all floods out, and in the light somebody appears, some scrubs-wearer opening the

door opens to let ingrid in though she tries
to turn around tries to fight
her way back to the body

but the body can
no longer hold
her

heart is racing. She has found Enzo perched in the fields like a bird and pulled him into the shed on the other side of the property. She is feeling risky these days, or rather she is no longer judging the merit of risk itself. A horrid feeling is bubbling up in her and she would rather shove Enzo down and take him into her mouth to trade the feeling out for something better. She knows that's not quite how it goes but she isn't thinking about that, she isn't thinking about anything but the sensory. Enzo is beet-red and pulsing in her hand and she slithers up to meet his face and there is nothing between their mouths anymore just one two-tongued organism trading breath and slick spit in and out of itself.

He tries to raise objections. —What if one of the kids stumbles in, or, for God's sake, your—

But she silences him with her tongue. —Just fucking let me have this, she breathes into his throat.

She remembers when she first met him. At her wedding rehearsal dinner, sitting next to Aggie. Enzo walked around the corner and his face, his broad slopes of shoulder, hit her like a fist to the throat: she couldn't breathe, needed to excuse herself for a moment. Dressed so stunningly, too, in a crisp blue suit with a pale pocket square. When she passed by him on her way out of the room she smelled him, the sharp burst of his cologne but also the hot-blood body scent beneath, and something in her body started to burn up. She wanted to slip the square from his pocket and run it beneath her nose, see if it smelled of him. She felt alive, finally. It had been so long.

This was, as she soon learned, the famed cousin.

After the dinner she slipped into one of Aggie and Enzo's conversations. Things seemed tense: they rarely looked at one another, spoke to opposite ends of the lawn instead of to each other. They were, she thought, opposite sides of the same coin: each seemed to hold himself in higher regard than the other but they were one and the same. She hoped her face didn't wear her feelings, kept her gaze leveled at the ground when she could manage. She thought of the inevitable moment, leaving the wedding reception at the end of the night with Aggie, watching Enzo's blue suit recede in the sunless lot, taking Aggie's clammy hand. Her heart writhed.

Aggie growled about his cousin, but when she pressed him on it, he couldn't explain why: he fumbled around for something, settled on, *Just the way it's always been. Theo and his kids are good-for-nothings. Surprised Enzo even showed up.*

Thus it became Cleo's mission to reconcile the cousins, ostensibly in the name of posterity. *I don't want our children,* Cleo said, *to have mindless prejudices.*

And so when the house down the road went up for sale, and Enzo and Melanie were looking to move to town, Cleo leapt at the prospect. She pulled Aggie close, straddled him on the dining bench, said again and again how great an opportunity this was for the family. Used the memory of Enzo, the possibility of his proximity, to heat herself from the inside.

Her marriage had been built on a lie, on a shoving-down. She'd met Aggie when he'd come to town with his brother, two years before. The two of them had stayed in a beaten-up place down the road from her; she'd seen them move in, and when she passed by on nightly walks she always saw his window light on, wondered who he was, where he'd come from. Then one night he was out on the porch steps, extinguishing a cigarette and looking up at a half-obscured moon. He waved her over, smiled plainly, and after some pleasantries told her about his life, the parents he and his brother had run from, the farm work the two of them had taken here. All across town, all sorts of plants to take care of, all sorts of earth to tend. And he asked about her life, the bustling family, the desires, the regrets. She couldn't remember the last time someone had been so curious about her, so willing to listen. She remembers little from that first conversation, nothing more than the dizzying amount of ground they covered: they seemed to have gotten it all out of the way, seemed to walk away from the conversation with solid outlines of each other. She felt nothing for him beyond a gentle kick in the chest, but she and Aggie got along. Something in their souls was compatible.

She doesn't want to think about what she is doing to him now. So she shoves it down, listens to Enzo breathing heavy at her neck. Feels the heat of his breath there. Her foot hits a rake and it clatters to the ground, clangs against the floor. As they fuck, its metal teeth bite into her calf and she thinks of the snake's fangs. All the snakes, all their fangs. Shoves that down too. When they are finished and the room has filled with the scent of them, Enzo pokes out to make sure the coast is clear. He can blame his redness on the cold. Cleo waits a while, tells a story to herself. Then she leaves, shuts the door behind

her heart has gone solid it's clear when she
ambles around town with a sulk in her step
aggie's long absence has broken her down

is there any salvaging what she has lost
or is the family hopeless in its aims
have they all fallen to rot to ruin

my night and my morning too. I don't know what I was thinking but I wake with a pounding sensation (glimmer) like hammers at my head. I go to the bathroom mirror to check for bruising but there is none. It was only the brain that thrashed around in there, screaming out for me to stop. Now I know the voice cannot be bludgeoned out, and so I will not try to do so again. I will listen to what it has to say and keep it within me. There is room in me for multiple voices, multiple ghosts. I can hold them all.

Emma assembles an ice pack for me in a plastic bag wrapped inside a paper towel and shows me where to hold it. I stand at the window and watch the late morning. Feel the ice's chill spread through my skin. Birds—jays, maybe—skitter along distant branches. A squirrel hops through the weeds and bristles its tail. Overhead the sun shifts through gaps in cloud, here one moment and gone the next. Upstairs, I hear Emma running a shower, I hear the handle-squeaks. Then another shrill sound joins the squeaks and it takes me a moment to place it. The phone is ringing, I realize.

I shuffle to the table and pick it up. —Hello? I say in my newly changed voice. For years, telemarketers and receptionists thought I was a woman. Then my voice plummeted to something strange and I was never mistaken again. Sometimes I speak and forget my new confines; I rumble and am frightened of myself.

—Hello, the other end says. —Is Cleo available?

I look around. —She's not here at the moment, can I take a message? I see motion in the front window—heads bobbing, figures moving (glimmer).

—Sure. Tell her Aggie is cleared for discharge whenever he can be picked up. Have her give us a call?

I agree and we exchange kindnesses and sign off. When I set the phone down I see Mom and Uncle Enzo wandering in from the field. He is smiling, ruddied from the cold. He skims her shoulder with his thumb and something about the gesture rings out in me, stops me cold. I can't pull my eyes from them now. Some invisible thread has traced itself across the distance between them and it shines in this sun (glimmer). They separate. He walks up toward the side of the house and she toward the front, but I watch her watch him. Her body leaves his side but her eyes stay with him for a long time.

—Phone call, I say when she comes inside and hangs her coat on the front rack. —From the hospital.

—What'd they say?

—Dad's ready.

She steps into the kitchen, pulls a bottle of water from the fridge. Twists its cap off and takes a long drink from it.

—I can pick him up, she says. —I'm sure he's ready to get home.

Something else awakens in me, some noticing. I think: have you always regarded him this lovelessly? Or are you holding him in some new light? I think back to my childhood before he was summoned away. Think of how the two of them used to look at each other, love flickering in their eyes like fire licking at a skillet. Or was that something I made up? Maybe I am just getting older and clearing the cloud-light of childhood (glimmer) from my eyes. Starting to see things for what they really are. Or maybe it's the scrim of grief snuffing out joy. But I don't want to see them this way. I want to go back to being a child, regain trust in the foundation our family was built on. I tried to take matters into my own hands, sending Ingrid to the store with Dad in my place, and then, well.

I feel frozen, I feel like the house is freezing me. Suddenly I am seeing the cracks, feeling the splinters as they form. I am tired of being

worried about the family so much is happening
in their world these days

hope they can hold themselves
together

in the kitchen till Mom peels away to head to the truck. Coming down the stairs, I watch Orrie's face go hollow, his eyes following her as she leaves the room, some glow in him seeming to have died. Once the garage door shuts, he hovers there, blankened, for moments, his eyes on the knob. I enter the room and he attempts to slacken his face, to lessen the grief, but it's too late; I have seen.

—What's going on? I ask.

His hands are nervously circling his wrists, then set before his stomach like he is trying to calm its quease.

—What's happening to us? he says.

His voice is a bassy splinter of a thing that, even when nothing more than a croak, splits the room in two. I see Enzo outside, heading down the drive in those big gunked-up boots of his, and I don't even have to ask, I know what Orrie has deduced.

And then I remember another moment. It was staring me in the face then, the truth, but I wasn't looking, was I? A few months ago, I was folding laundry in the living room, the basket of clothes set on the far side of the couch. Mom had her needles out and she had been knitting a scarf—she had a phase for a while. She set the whole thing down and came to help me put clothes away, now that it was only down to unmatched socks. I'd made piles for Orrie and

Ingrid and Mom and me, but a pair of socks didn't look like anything Orrie had ever worn. I figured Mom had gotten a thick large pair for fieldwork, to keep her toes warm in the unconventional cold.

—These yours or Orrie's? I held them out to her.

—Oh, no, you can just leave them. A shadow went over her face, or so it seemed then, but she turned away so I didn't get a very good look at it, and I thought I'd invented it.

—Whose are they?

She gnawed on her lip, weighed her words. —I think, I think they're Enzo's, maybe.

I grunted some version of *Hmm*, left them on the couch. I supposed everyone needed their socks washed at some point. But I wasn't onto the two of them yet, wasn't shining lights on their shadows, looking to reveal. I had the strangest sense then, but I couldn't place it for what it was. Enzo never had his socks off—he never had his boots off; he hovered outside the house like an uninvited vampire so he wouldn't have to take them off. *These fuckers,* he always said when Ingrid was out of hearing range, *take years to lace up*. So how had his socks cropped up in our house?

And besides, I'd only pulled clothes from Orrie's, Ingrid's, Mom's, and my hampers—how had the socks gotten in one of them?

Mom took her clothes pile in one hand and Ingrid's in the other, carried them upstairs. I took Orrie's and mine up, set his on his bed. He was at school, wouldn't be at home to put his clothes away for another few hours. Downstairs, Mom had left the innocuous socks on the end table. It was so obvious I want to whack myself over the head with it now, but then I was distracted, thinking about having to pick up Orrie and Ingrid from school later, bring them home; thinking about the grocery list Mom had left, things I could pick up on my way to the schools, but also about Nic and Claire, who had left together for university months ago and were planning to call me that night and fill me in, have a good catch-up. Nothing much here, I was planning to say, just the same day on repeat—tell me about you! The three of us were once the tightest knit among the larger friend group, and then the two of them woke up one morning and realized they were in love with each other. And they left for school. Left me pacing around my house wondering what else I had to do that day and was forgetting about.

All of which is to say, I wasn't much thinking about my mother. But now, standing in the kitchen with Orrie who has gone pallid with truth, I am looking at our family, at the integrity of its structure, and watching it start to give. At least he is not thinking of Ingrid at this moment, at least he has a slight reprieve from that. But I know it won't last—it may survive till Dad comes home, till Orrie looks for the little girl he left with and remembers she won't be coming home. I can hold myself together and also keep him upright. It has always been my way.

I don't know what to give him, don't know what to say to him. I flounder through a dozen sentences in my head and all of them ring false. So I stand here, hold him in my arms, as we wait for the headlights to return, to wash over the front windows

are shiny with light
aggie and cleo are coming home
seated together in the car

how they can face each other after
what happened
we do not know and cannot guess

< who >

the dull spot on the surface of Aggie's brain says. The spot that made impact with the front of his skull when the truck split itself open around the tree. He can feel a tickling almost on his cortex, the place where the brain split. But again the spot says,

< guess guess who >

and Aggie doesn't know who the spot is referring to till he looks over to the driver's seat and sees the woman there. The woman—come on, Aggie, she has a name—Cleo. His wife. Things shuffle before his eyes but he cannot tell which are memories and which are inventions that fit the shape of his tongue. They have known each other for twenty-three years? Leaving a lock of her light-spun hair at her father's grave, pouring out a drink onto the soil? Or was it his hair—his father's funeral—his own glass—

—Bump coming up, she says, and he holds the door handle as they are jostled around.

The old crumbling roads that he loves so much and has loved for eternity. She says it without feeling—there is something there but he can't access it, there's a thick layer of shroud in the neurons. She looks at him, smiles; it is a hollow smile, more gesture than feeling. He considers taking her hand, but something would feel wrong about it. What is this place they have found themselves in?

In the late winter afternoon the sky is pale violet, baby-soft. He thinks of holding his own babies. Here, there, gone now. The snow at the sides of the roads is melting further. As they head up the hill, the tires skid through the mucky slush.

They approach the house, watch it become visible as they crest the hillside. The warm orange inside light filters out to them. —It's like a new start, he says.

—What do you mean?

—This, here. Coming home today. New start.

He loves the thought so much, its effervescence, he can hardly keep it down. And

they cannot pretend like everything is normal
because nothing is really it gets you wondering if
they ever had normalcy or if it was only something
they reached for grasped at

night, Cleo slides into bed and sees Aggie give her a slithery look that only means one thing. There's an innocence to his lust, a big-eyed kind of fright to it. She feels an absence where any desire for him used to reside, a pit of no-feeling. But she sees him glowering bright.

She wonders how much he remembers from before he left. Apparently not much—he is needing, persistent, in his press-against. He looks at her.

He starts, —Do you think . . .

She keeps her body away from his. Feels him worming his way toward her beneath the sheets but she maintains distance. Hours earlier she was in the shed with Enzo, she felt his hot skin beneath her hands, felt herself coming awake. Nothing like this shriveling, this turning-away.

She feels a speech brewing, something about not being ready to resume their old life, about time and distance and shock and readjustment and how the hell is he in the mood given the past forty-eight hours, but something in her resistance, her emotional steeling, awakens something in him. She watches it overtake him, first in his hands as they freeze halfway toward her, then working its way up his arms, to his chest, his shoulders, his tensile neck. His head, his eyes, the way they go cold.

—Yes, he realizes. —It was like this. He swallows. —It wasn't . . . we weren't . . .

He pulls away limply, lies back against the pillow. His eyes are cast at the ceiling and she can see all the uncovered emotions swimming in them like wisps of cloud across the moon.

—I don't remember what was between us, he says, —but there was always something there. Between us.

Something that halted his hands in motion, that melted him where he'd been firm. She nodded, then, turned over onto her side.

—Yeah, she says, —there was.

5

five times floating down like snow a sidewind lace of memory

was aggie holding his breath the whole time
he was in the doom-place
counting the steps the hours back to home

or did it become a pretend-home for him
the way anything you come back to again and again
takes on significance familiarity

lessens, actually, the more time I spend with him. I am not becoming more familiar with the new, shallowed version of him, only less familiar with the old. There's a rift that's opening in my head between who he is and who he was, and nothing I do, no attempt at bridging, at reconciliation, makes it easier to swallow.

He is vague, dateless, placeless, he floats on a cloud of pleasant non-knowledge.

—How was yesterday? I ask, as a test.

—Lovely, he says, eyes clouded, —it was a good day.

I watch him grope for specifics, combing through his memory hoping to catch on something, but nothing shows. Just a blissful warm driftlessness. Even his grasp on our past is slipping; he is sitting in a room with someone he cannot hold on to in any capacity—every new fact falls through his fingers.

Orrie can barely sit in the room with us, so visible is the pain in his eyes, in his frazzled brow. He excuses himself several times but always returns, always keeps trying. Looks at Dad like a burning house, thinks watching the shutters go up in smoke will help him, will make him stronger. There's no shame in softness, I want to tell him. But he sits here straight-backed and stalwart.

When Dad leaves the room for a moment, stumbles down the hall to the bathroom, I reach toward Orrie. I worry the slightest contact will shatter the dam he's built inside, but I set a hand on his forearm and his eyes flicker over to me.

—It's okay, I say. —You don't have to be here.

But he shudders in a rigid way and I see the dam in him is still built and he will still try. Dad wanders back in, sits back down, looks around like he thinks he's left his wallet somewhere. Eventually settles into the discomfort of now.

Once, at dinner at Claire's house a few years ago, I watched her and her father tease each other about broccoli, something about the way she couldn't get the piece off the fork onto her plate once she'd speared it. She struggled and struggled. And to demonstrate the stuckness of the vegetable, she flung her fork toward him. To her surprise the floret arced across the room and smacked his lower beard. It fell to the floor, splattered its butter sauce on the hardwood. Sniveling with laughter he leapt to the kitchen for a paper towel. And she looked over at me and saw a look on my face like my soul had split into shards. *Oh god,* she said, *you must miss your dad so much.*

So much it could kill me, I wanted to say. But I choked down the swell of feeling and laughed alongside them.

And now he is back, and I think of how sad sixteen-year-old Emma would be, sitting here with drunk-seeming Dad, memoryless and sweltering in the heat of his own confusion. How sad and vengeful, though she'd have no one deserving to take the feelings out on. She could only shout at her family, only shout at herself. Wake the walls up with her shouts, make the house feel the vibrations of her

pain in everyone's hearts these days
pain like a river splitting through us
mama hamford thought about organizing another sale
to raise funds for ingrid's funeral but when she ran it by cleo
at the hardware store at the edge of town cleo laughed

said ingrid didn't even like markets she laughed
and laughed like it was pure comedy
and then she had fallen to her knees and was sobbing
sludging up her knees in the mud they were all still
thinking about it nobody could stop thinking

of Aggie's face as they fell asleep, the door they closed together. It is for the best, she knows, but it is not what she aspired to in youth: a loveless marriage, a gestural marriage. Not what she aspired to demonstrate for her children. She wanted to build something sharper than her parents' lovelessness, wanted to build something lasting. Something immovable, something that trembled in no wind.

But she has heard him whispering in his sleep, a word, over and over, that she can't make sense of. His lips too close together to let the sound loose—just a sibilance, a plosive. In a certain light it's a puzzle, a thing to take her mind off Ingrid, at least for a moment.

But last night he finally gave the word some oomph and she heard it: *Cassie*. The moon tried to creep in through the curtains and the sound came quick and sharp in the room like a burst of rain slapping down on the roof. *Cassie*, again and again, though she couldn't tell if the far-off word was a longing or an apology.

She doesn't know a Cassie herself, figures the name must belong somewhere in the six-year memory chamber. But she has an inkling of sense that she isn't the only guilty party, that they are on more even ground.

She wants to confront him, raise the question of the name, but she doesn't want it to devolve into argument. Doesn't want to scare the children with the heat rising in their voices, knows she won't be able to keep it out of hers. And Ingrid, oh, Ingrid, always catching up to her in the end, no matter how she tries to distract—Cleo is split open, she is losing bits of her strength every day, her daughter has soaked into her, softening her bones.

As she transfers the wash to the dryer with trembling hands, she can hear Aggie upstairs drawing his bath. He asked Enzo to help guide him in, which hit her in the gut, but she supposes she shouldn't be surprised. Maybe he is still stinging, maybe it feels new to him still. And the children, she knows, are out in the field. When she hears Enzo coming downstairs she waves him in, pulls him toward her, shuts the laundry room door with her foot. Her lips are at his neck and she can feel him leaping against her leg already. She unbuttons her pants and pulls them down, glides up onto the washing machine. She feels twenty again, wild, wind-swayed, unburdened.

—Cleo, you're losing it, you're losing it.

She feels heat licking at the skin of her neck. He hovers above her like he has a chance of lifting himself away, but she knows he's ensnared, he's netted here forever.

—I didn't ask for your opinion.

And she pulls his face down, sighs, sways her hips into him. Chases the feeling, just once more. And at the moment she reaches the precipitous edge, veers through it like a stone shattering glass, she hears her child call out from the front of the house:

!!!

Emma is standing above me. She has removed a trowel from my hand. My head is against the cold ground. My back and legs don't feel it through my jacket and pants but my head is only covered with hair, no hat, and the snow-sludge melts against my scalp.

—ORRIE, I DON'T TRUST YOU, she shouts. —I DON'T TRUST YOU WITH THIS THING.

She throws the trowel into the field. I don't know what she means till I look down at myself and see hack-marks all along the tops of my arms. My sleeves are rolled up, which it seems I did myself. Emma's face is red as a held breath and her cheeks tear-streaked as she guides me up into the house. Mom and Uncle Enzo are there, flush-faced, like they've been in an argument.

—I don't know what's happening with him but it's scaring me, Emma says.

—I'm right here, I say.

Mom takes my arms into her hands, skims the stab-spots with her thumbs. Consternation flashes across her. My wound-welts look a bit like her scratch-marks but deeper and wider.

—I don't even remember doing it, I say. —I looked up and Emma was shouting.

—Well, you were trying to kill yourself, you should've seen how it looked!

—I don't *mind* that you were shouting. But you were. I was just very confused.

Mom looks around the house—at the roof, the walls, the arches, the floors—as if the curse is leaking out of it like a gas, seeping into all of us, causing this mayhem.

—Okay, she says, —here's what we're going to do. Orrie, you're going to sleep in my bed. I think you need somebody to watch over you at night. Aggie can sleep in your bed.

—Of course, Emma says.

—Of course what?

But Emma bites her tongue and shakes her head. Her arms are crossed over her chest and her brows are sunk low. Mom huffs and turns back to me. Resigns herself to dealing with Emma later.

—We'll tell your dad when he gets out of the bath.

At that Uncle Enzo darts out of the room and up the stairs to check on him. I am staring at my arms still. There is a gap in my consciousness where the welts happened; I have no idea where I was. And then out of a patch of cloudless blue I hear:

< stop her >

and my blood goes chilly. The other things I have heard have been nothing, they have been silly half-sentence things. But this is a command.

Is it the house? I want to ask. I turn toward the wall, cast my best question at it. IS IT YOU? my brain-space says. But the wall doesn't answer, the floor doesn't rattle, the ceiling doesn't shake. I have no answers.

When night slides over us, Mom brings me into her bedroom and lies me down on Dad's side. She leaves to get him settled into my bed. I hear the soles of her slippers shuffle across the wooden floors, the little *hush-hush-hush* that gets quieter as she disappears. I wonder if, when he lived here with his parents, he slept in my bedroom. If some memory will reignite him there. The pillows and blankets and mattress in here all seem heavy with the weight of his struggling, as if some part of his soul has seeped out of him and into the bedding.

Mom comes back and turns out the lights and whispers me off to sleep, and at some point I pull a pillow over my face, because I am worried about what I will say in the night, worried about what I will give away. I don't always remember my dreams, but when I do, they are heavy things I carry with me for the duration of the next day. And I don't want to let any of it out, don't want her to worry. I am normal, or rather, I want her to think this. I want her to feel free to let me go back to my room, back to my dreaming.

While falling asleep I imagine future situations. Like: she hears me whispering to Ingrid in the middle of the night and pulls the pillow off my face to catch my words. Or she wakes when suddenly I start screaming, she wakes and tries to calm me. Or she has to pull a trowel or sharp tool out of my hands (though how would I get a trowel in her bedroom? maybe something more appropriate for a bedroom like a fork or a pair of tweezers), because again I am trying to dig it deep into myself. Or she has to bind my hands to the bedrails because I can't be trusted not to tear at myself.

Where did this come from, everybody wants to know, myself included? Who is to say. It feels like another person has taken up residence inside me and every now and then he rises to the surface and makes me do things. He has blocked me out, taken me over. I need to learn how to wrest the control back, to return it to

myself i think there's no way
this is just a gleam in the family's mind
i think this will stick to them forever

everyone's always said they were cursed
and now we're seeing how it leaps out
from nothing and strikes them down

-stairs I see Ingrid's thick old coat hung over one of the pegs of the coatrack, and I want to pull it down and huff it, see if she still lives inside. She wore that coat once, I remember, when we went to the store to get ingredients for a birthday cake for Mom. She said, *Let's go to the store, just us sisters,* and something seized up in me, at being held in that perfect light. I didn't deserve it, I knew, but she said the word *sister* like it was a fractureless thing, magical and clean and crystal-clear. And she sang the radio songs the whole way. She had a lovely, quiet voice, the notes I knew were somehow right but they were so quiet. Till one random song's chorus when she started screaming along and I nearly swerved into the median. We laughed and laughed, how hilarious it was, this near-death experience, till we got to the store, slid in our boots across the wet early-February parking lot, and picked up some boxed mixes and canned frosting, the kind whose sugar melted on your tongue. Ingrid wouldn't remember this, but before Dad left, he used to make all our birthday cakes himself. He didn't much enjoy baking but he refused to buy store-made ones. He used to let Orrie and me (if we were home, and it wasn't too late in the day) lick the batter out of the bowl, taste-test the frosting till it was right. Orrie used to pretend he needed a second and third lick to form an opinion, used to re-dip his finger again and again, clutch his chin, make a deep pondering face. But that day, Ingrid and I brought home the store-bought cake mix and whipped everything together in the kitchen, splatted frosting between the layers, set the candles on top. When Mom came home from work—she had a different job then, a standard office thing, before she left it to work on the farm exclusively—she flushed at our handiwork. Some ghost passed over her at, I think, the memory of Dad's labors, but she shoved it down, we all shoved it down, and sliced up the cake and forked away at it. And now I am heaving, clutching my hands to my stomach as I sit on the bottom stairstep, as if the memory is something that needs to be retched out. Everyone else is asleep. I didn't even know I remembered any of that.

Oh, and on the way home from the store—it's all coming back to me now—Ingrid pointed at the park, the one right next to her elementary school, and I pulled into the lot. We went and sat on the swings, kicked our feet out and in, watched a few kids shift a ball around in the grass. *When I went here,* I said, *none of this was here. The equipment is all new, these swings weren't even here.* Ingrid asked, *What was here?* I said, *Just dirt, imagine how bored we were.* She laughed and laughed. And I'll never hear that sound

again and again and again
we imagine it must hit them
the force of it

enzo driving through town
with wool-ghosts over his eyes
how long can he hide from this

is the worst part: at night, when I wake and it's dead silent. I don't want to shift, don't want Mom to hear me shuffling and think something is the matter. But really, isn't everything the matter? Glimmers wink in my periphery though it's pitch-black in here (Mom has great blackout curtains that keep any hint of moon away and she draws them shut for special sleepless occasions like tonight). I try to blink them away, like debris that sometimes gets in there, specks of pollen or dirt or dander. But the glimmers don't go anywhere; they just hover. I am waiting for enough of them to accumulate to where a message forms like last time. I am not science-minded but this evidence I can follow to its end.

Maybe if I nudge it, a voice will come. If I tap-tap-tap at the borders of the glimmer-image. In my head I tap against it, waken it within me. I scoop the glimmers together, mash them into a ball. Bounce it around a bit, try to knock the voice out of it. Toss it back and forth between my brain-palms. Eventually it says

< stop her stop them both >

and I say to it, Stop who, stop what? The glimmers are apparently susceptible to expenditure, as they have disappeared from my vision and nothing further comes from their glimmer-mouths. I will wait for them to accumulate and try again. Slowly they pop up (glimmer) around me. Just a couple. There's a cough at my side, a figure turning, settling into her pillow again. For a half-second my brain tries to correct the figure to Ingrid (glimmer), remembering the night a few years ago when she pulled me into her room and I fell asleep there. Feels like yesterday, doesn't it. Feels like one of those moments you'll carry around for the rest of your life, doesn't it, Ingrid. Hovering over your shoulder or twitching in your ear. It's that way for me too. It always will.

6

six times slipping down the slope of oneself what can be excused and what cannot be forgotten

be with us atreus clan let the town
warm you in its earthly embrace let its people
restore you restore some warmth you have been missing

from herself and she doesn't know where she has gone. But she has had an idea and she hasn't been able to let it go. Outside the house Cleo sits at the little table in her jacket and pants (she likes to sit out there and be briefly cold) and sips from her steaming mug. She's planning out the details of Ingrid's funeral, shivering through phone calls, drafting an obituary, figuring out how to distribute. At some point Enzo comes to join her, pulls the other chair out, regards her with his warm browns.

—What are you thinking about? he asks.

Her brain is all aswirl, it's no wonder he can see it. But over the years he has learned her quirks, her thinking face, the hitch in her voice when she's lying, the flat affect she takes when sinking into a mood—of course he knows. Sometimes her head tilts off its axis, twirls around and around, and she can't hold it up.

—I'm thinking about Aggie, she says. —I feel so bad about everything.

She stirs her tea with a slow hand. Earlier she walked by Orrie's room, where she'd put Aggie to bed, and the most tranquil look had overtaken him. She hadn't seen him at peace like that since they were just married and she'd woken up in their marriage bed for the first time. Looked over at him and he looked like that, blank-slated in sleep, all the day's worries washed away. When the honeymoon swell of feeling was so strong she wanted to lean over and kiss that blankness off him, rouse him, let him loose.

When he finally woke that long-ago morning—she'd been lying there for a while, staring at him, his wrinkleless forehead, the curves of his shoulders and chest, thinking about the thickening outline of their future—he pulled her hand to his mouth and kissed it again and again. *This is it,* he said, *this is it.*

Enzo takes her hand for a moment, jolts her back to the present. —Nothing you can control, he says.

—I know, she says, —but . . . it's almost like he's not even living. Like he'd be better off . . .

She doesn't finish the sentence but the sentence finishes itself inside her head. And she looks at him pointedly—she's unfed, she's been rocketing in and out of half-sleep for so many nights, she's fucked her way into any traces of happiness she's come by, she's not in her right mind, but this thought possesses her with a vigor that pulls her from her seat. She looks at Enzo and a fire overtakes her. Even when things with Aggie were sublime, when not a stone was misplaced in their world, the kids glowing with love and the crops prospering and the sun a beacon above them, she never burned like this.

—What are you thinking, Cleo? What are you going to get us into?

No time to explain, only time to act. She stands and takes his hand, pulls him down the driveway into the garden shed, where the mowers and trowels and fertilizers and weed-eaters and seed are stored, rips the door open, shoves him in

and

she says, —Just think about it, in his ear, with her hand around his cock, her breath jerking, —just think about it, we could do it.

His head spins with the smell of her, the sensation of her, the dizzying thrill of her lust, its midday menace. He seems to blink himself in and out of these situations, he has gone delirious in these sudden moments of intense feeling, in and out of time.

—It would be so easy, she says, —so easy. But I'd need your help, two masterminds are better than one. We could do it.

The first time they hooked up was like this. He doesn't like to think about it because Aggie hadn't even left for war yet, which meant that Enzo wasn't even filling a gap in Cleo's life. Or maybe it was a different gap, the gap had been there from the beginning, the gap of feigned love. But one day Cleo just walked down to his house, which he had kept up by himself since his wife's death years back.

He was sipping a gin and tonic on the porch, looking out at his vast property. The alcohol swam up to his head; he hadn't eaten much that day. He imagined a field populated with children and a wife beside him. Sometimes he still felt her there, hands on her swelling belly. They were going to name their girl Eileen, which was a family name he hadn't loved, but sitting on the porch, drink in hand, glass sweating onto his thigh, he would have allowed her any name to have had the opportunity to love her to pieces, any name in the world.

And then Cleo was wandering up his drive and she took a seat next to him, the seat his wife used to occupy, and something seemed different about her that day. Prevarication had gone out the window. They were inside before he knew what he was doing. *We can't be long*, she said, *Ag will be home soon, the kids'll wonder*. But they broke each other open that day, allowed some long-dammed emotions out. He'd been wild for her once, when the weddings happened, one after the other, hers and then his, and he thought he'd stanched the wound, thought his marriage had done the trick. To call it a hookup is wrong, he supposes—they lay there afterward staring down the corridors at all the reopened doors.

—We could, she says, here in the shed.

Ten years later and their bodies have been warped by time, but their beating hearts are the same.

—I'll think about it, he says. His breath razing his throat, he is breathing so hard. His cousin, his poor cousin. Cleo's got him inches from the finish but he's thinking about his cousin and it has a saddening effect on his body, on his spirit. The pleasure and the sourness feel wrong together.

—Say you'll help me, she says. —After what he did to Ingrid.

His softness angers her. She pulls his hand down between her legs, settles atop it.

—And it's so sad, she says, —don't you think. He barely knows where he is. Who we are. Who *he* is.

Inches narrowing to centimeters narrowing—

—He'd be so much better off, she says. —And we could finally have our life. Our house, our kids, our future. Together.

She makes little death-sounds in his ear that drive him wild (she knows they drive him wild they could drive him to ruin)

—Come on, she says, —come on,
but doesn't she know that she doesn't have to do this doesn't she know all she needs to give him is a look, a blink, that's all she's ever needed for him to go tender-centered and pliant

and

he stands at the kitchen window, looking out over the vast property, and he thinks he sees scurrying in the garden-shed window so he steps out to investigate. Time shifts and blurs but this moment he trusts as real. He remembers years and years ago he used to have to scare the raccoons out of this shed by clanging pots or baking sheets together. It used to be his morning job, delegated to him by his mother (he thinks he sees her face through the shed window, maybe). He made his own boy do it once, but the kid buckled in fear at the sight of the striped things, though Aggie himself had always thought the critters were kind of cute. Some traditions, he supposes, he'll have to maintain himself. So before he leaves the kitchen he grabs a couple of baking sheets (he remembers where they are). It's not morning but the raccoons must be active, clattering through his shed. Morning, afternoon, night, they work on their own schedule, he supposes. He treks down the porch steps over toward the structure.

He lifts the door, gets a sharp whiff of sex, sees the woman there—his wife—Cleo. And—his—oh. A flurry of buckling and zipping and breathing, sweaty palm-swipes on pants, quick-flung excuses.

He leaves his body for a second. Goes back to a moment in which he never knew of this. It is nice, he is waking in his childhood bedroom, pattering around the house, putting water on for coffee—thinking of his children, the hard work they put in to keep the place in order, the schoolwork they bring home and chip away at in the kitchen.

But sooner or later he has to face the facts, has to return to the real life. So he comes back.

—How long has this been going on? he says. He steps away from the shed, which has taken on a stench.

He doesn't actually want the answer to this question. He wants to click the button and switch the moment like a TV channel. Wants to leave all this behind. He turns and trudges back to the house, back up the steps. The cavern that opens beneath his clavicle is the strongest thing he's felt in weeks, months, even. This is the most grounded he has been. And for what. To open a sinkhole beneath him and kiss away the last twenty years of his life? He thought the last six of them were where the real rot lay but it turns out things fell from under him long before.

In the kitchen he decides on some chamomile tea, fills the kettle and sets it on to boil, ignites the burner with a trembling hand. He rummages through the cabinet, searches for a particular mug, bone-white with swirls of blue, but he cannot find it. Maybe it is in the dishwasher, or in one of the children's rooms.

He cannot get Cleo and his cousin out of his mind. The weak-willed, reddened man, panting like a sprinter, cock in hand, perched over Aggie's farm equipment. His wife pleading the man along, willing him forward. He can't unsee the need written into their flushed skin, their crawling hands.

His brain suddenly jolts him somewhere new. Or rather, he thinks it is new but it is actually deeply old, recessed in the trenches of his mind. It washes over him with the sharpness of the new: the last time he had a woman beneath him. To his utter shock, the woman was not his wife. Her name lay just outside the bounds of his tongue. His brother Mateo, who had slunk off to war with him (they are a ruined family now)—every night, Ag heard him wander in and out with different women. The memory has the immediate comfort and pleasure of the present. T___ is less a faraway place and more a segment of his brain he's folded away, and in this moment he wears it proudly. It didn't matter, Mateo said, that he didn't know a dozen languages; he knew the language of the body, and everyone understands that. *Bless the spoils of war*, he cooed once as he watched one of the women let herself out of the base.

This was Mateo's way, and had been since high school: how many times had Ag bumped into a girl his brother had snuck in at night, how many girls had he seen on his brother's arm at different events across the years? Mateo's tactic to forget their daytime atrocities in T____ was to make the base a paradise. He accomplished this through lust. Aggie's way was alcohol: he dragged himself out of bed in the mornings (he remembers it so easily now) with a throbbing head and a queasy stomach, a sunken feeling like nothing would ever right itself again. And then night came around and it was the same thing all over.

One night Mateo brought home two women he'd trawled up while wandering the streets. One of them peeled off with him and the other lay back and eyed Aggie, traced desire lines across her thighs. His head swam with gin, the leftovers of last night's find. He thought of his wife, not out of emotional fealty—the gods had bled them out, drained them loveless, long ago—but out of a half-held desire that they might be able to find their way back to emotional fealty someday. Things had been good at first, or so he thought. And then everything had fallen apart. But he cradled an agnostic wish for that future.

Funny how he is back in all of it now, clear as day—he is trapped in the synaptic past. He felt, at the time, blameless: his brother had brought her back, he was only trying to be welcoming, she wanted him, he was drunk out of his mind. But he'd done it all, hadn't he? He cursed his brother out in the morning, pinned his actions on Mateo, but he'd set it all into motion, allowed it all to happen. He slid toward her, and Cleo fell from his mind, easier than he'd like to admit. Her eyes were the color of sand. Cassie, her name was Cassie—she said it like a spell. She cast a lingering sort of magic, stayed with Aggie through it all. Normally when Aggie drinks his memories become slippery but this night stayed with him. He forgot so much else but he remembered her, kept her there.

Why are you here? he remembers asking slurrily.

To pass the time, she said.

She wandered in the next evening, too, found her way back. Again Aggie's tongue was a blur, and he thought the beautiful woman before him was vision, invention, but her hands found his skin and they were warm and real. Mateo gave him waggly eyebrows before he disappeared. When she worked her way down, undid his buttons and pulled his pants down, she said, *Your wife.*

Huh? he said.

Your wife, Cassie said. *I can taste her, I can taste the ruin.*

Her tongue sent a tingle like rain over him, raised goosebumps up.

I'm a seer, she said before she slipped out into the night for the second time. *I saw you coming.*

She wanted to study, wanted to travel, but the war had ruined both their economies, stolen her job, stolen her parents' jobs, stolen her brother from the house, so now she did what she could to stay happy, to stay grounded.

I like to live through the body, she said.

What happened to her he cannot say, but he brought a bit of her back with him, lodged in memory. The sweep of her curls over her shoulder, the dimple in her left cheek. He felt an ease when he was with her, felt himself unspooling, the way it's easy to speak freely to someone you feel you'll never see again. Were he less sauced, he would've given himself away, but he couldn't find a way to convert that openness to words.

She tasted ruin on him, she'd said, but never said if it was Cleo's or his. Or both, mutually assured. Who's to say and would he really have wanted to ask? (His desires are slipping from him now.) He does not doubt seers. She would have given him a piece of information that he would have held onto till it came true.

He remembers, as well, a seer he met as a child. Again with his brother, again goaded into action. *You've always liked the freaks,* seventeen-year-old Mateo said.

The seer—her name was Allie, he'd never forgotten their synchronicity—had said, *He's going to drive you crazy till you just can't take it anymore.*

And look where the two of them have found themselves now. Mateo in a giant house hours down the coast of A____, trapped in a tense marriage. Aggie back from war, here there and everywhere.

Which of them had cast the first stone, decided they couldn't take it anymore, he can no longer remember. But they never see each other, never call—no holiday cards, no birthday wishes.

The kettle boils, zips him back to the present. He doesn't remember what has happened today, his consciousness has been cleared by the past. It'll come back to him soon, he reckons, but for now there is a blissful emptiness. He is finally, he thinks, coming back to himself. He is remembering and grieving and knived up inside and he is convinced this is

living after that what kind of life can it be
how do the wounded patch up over themselves and carry on
can't be easy we should make a dish for them to bring up

to the next few hours—things must go smoothly. Her pulse keeps climbing; she takes deep breaths to lower it.

Near three, she wanders down the road. *Need some air,* she plans to say if anyone asks. She wears her thick coat with large pockets—plenty of room inside.

At the base of the hill, where the oleander grows, she plucks two, three leaves. Long, thin things she tucks into her pocket.

On the other side of the street, she clips a couple handfuls of chamomile flowers. Winter came very late and strong, and somehow the blooms still hold. She will play it off as impromptu. *I saw the flowers,* she'll say, *and they looked so beautiful—I simply had to pick some.*

She'll make the tea hours before his long, long soak. Before the war, his long baths used to happen on Sunday nights, but in his current state they've happened every night since he's come back. When the water gets too cold, he injects it with a burst of hot, leans back, settles in again.

She'll cook the leaves down, wilt them, extract their liquid. Boil water, steep the leaves and add the liquid, drop in the chamomile flowers. Down the disposal—evidence destroyed.

Breathe in, breathe out. Scratches on the forearms—settle the fingers, let the red lines recede.

Breathe.

7

seven times sliding steady toward an end hold the present while you can

Emma comes up the stairs to Mom's room to check on me. I can never hide anything from her, she always sees beneath whatever pleasant face I put on. She pushes and prods doesn't leave me alone. I admire that and also I am tired of lying or pretending nothing is weighing on me, because it is.

And today I don't have energy to go through all that, so I just spit out, —I heard something.

—What do you mean?

—Do you know of anyone making any plans?

She squints at me (glimmer). —I feel like you're in another universe, she says.

—But really, I say, rolling my eyes, —do you know of anyone making plans? Are you making plans? Is Mom, or something?

—Plans? What are you talking about?

—I heard a voice.

That seems to do it. Her eyes go all dark and concerned and yes, I feared this, but I knew it was coming. Guess it's better to get the reaction over with so she can start to cool.

—What kind of voice.

—I don't know. It wasn't in this world but it also wasn't in my head.

The concerned look worsens. Her brows crunch in further to where I worry the hair will start to bleed down onto her nose.

—What did it say?

—It told me to stop her, stop them both.

—Stop who?

—I don't know.

—From what?

—Exactly.

She sits with me in this for a while. The air around us has a new texture to it (glimmer).

—It feels like the curse is tying me up again, I say.

—There is no curse, she says. But I can tell she's not fully relieved. She gets all shifty there leaning against the door frame, like there's an itch in her she can't satisfy.

—I just get the feeling that something really bad's gonna happen and I don't know why. And the voice is making me feel like it's my fault.

—It's not. She delivers the words in that resolute voice of hers and for a second I am almost swayed.

But how do you know? I want to say. Because she doesn't know a thing. She can speak as sternly as she wants but she doesn't know what is happening to me or to anyone. The axis of our world has shifted and nothing is predictable anymore.

—Well, let me know if you hear it again, she says before ducking out of the room. She seems to move slower, like my news has weighted her

down at the bottom of the universe there tucked
into his own little corner is enzo he is trying
to figure out how to keep any graceless news from spreading

but it's here in our earth spreads in our roots and soil
he must know he can't keep it contained for long
can't keep his town from finding out his truth

be told, there is a strange atmosphere in the house, a strange charge in the air, we all seem to be dancing around each other. And of course, I want to pick everyone up by the shoulders and say WHAT IS GOING ON but I'm afraid to disturb the finely knit quiet, afraid it'll cause the whole structure of peace to come crumbling down. But I don't know how long I'll be able to keep up this balancing act. Mom puts the chicken in the oven to bake, listens to a song Ingrid used to sing for her, a version that feels inferior now, after hearing my sister sing it. Dad sits on the porch polishing his shoes. Enzo has gone back down to his lonely house and Orrie sits in the giant bed holding the giant gasp of his secret in his hands. And I bounce around between everyone, caught in the net of tension, breathing the air that's thick and humming with it.

Dad comes in, eyes heavy. —I'm going to draw a bath, he says.

—Okay, Mom says from the kitchen. Her tone is lighter than normal, like she is balancing on some high edge with him. She shakes spices across a tray full of asparagus, drizzles oil and lemon juice, and slides it into the oven—it all puckers up in my nose. I keep thinking of what Orrie said, feeling like something's going to happen. I don't normally believe him, his theories don't normally sway me, but tonight there's a shifting in my skin as the sun goes down. Mom is swirling a saucepan on the stove, but I can't tell what's inside, can't tell how to read her. Normally, she is more legible from the outside, painted with concern or delight or exhaustion, but today she is amorphous. I sit at the table, keep my hands folded together, wait, for something to emerge from

the world feels uneven tonight
the gods are breathing across it
setting it at a slant

so the liquid gathers to one side of the pan. Calm, calm. She has already fed him one mug of the stuff but she figures another to be safe.

For a brief moment, she seizes inside, wishes to undo the whole thing—but she's too far along now, there's nowhere to recede to. The leaves' toxins are crawling through him. Two to four hours, she's heard.

She hears him call out for her, ask her for more tea. Like the old days, bringing things to each other in the bath. Over ice this time, she knows—he loves a cold drink in a hot steamed room. And Enzo is back now, his twinkle of a knock at the porch door.

—Thought you'd gone home for the evening, Emma calls out from the living room.

—You can at least try to keep your tone kind, Cleo says as she passes. Tone light, voice normal. Trying.

She flips the lock on the screen door—an old habit, since Aggie left, not quite as necessary anymore, because who's going to come, who's going to bring evil, who should be kept out—and Enzo scrapes his boots on the rug outside, passes through the door.

In the kitchen he says, —Tea sounds nice. He grabs a mug of his own to fill, part of the deceit.

She is steeping chamomile flowers in hot water. She strains them, pours tea for Enzo and herself. She fills a third glass with ice, pours the tea over it, and adds the leafy syrup from the stovetop. Stir, stir. Calm face, calm face.

It will slow him down, make him weak, tired. More than he already is. Gravity will latch its hooks into him, pull him down. It will—hopefully—look like an accident. They will discover him sunk in the tub, breath stolen, and have to look the part.

She walks into the bathroom with the tea. The hair on his chest is glued down with wet. The parts of him that have been hidden from sun—the top strip of thigh, his feet and ankles—are so pale. For some reason, he has always loved a bath—when they got him home after six years, the first thing he wanted to do, the thing he had capacity to remember, was climb into the clawfoot and soak. She couldn't blame him. There was something childlike about it, being swallowed in all that porcelain—it was womblike, maybe.

But he is at home in there and she takes the tea in to him. He'd been so thirsty, he says, before the bath, but he'd gotten distracted. And now he's too tired to get out and make it himself. The bath is winding him down pleasantly. He hadn't needed help getting in the tub, he'd come in here resolute to do it on his own. He seems, in some way, able to remember.

She hands over the tea, watches him drink it down, leans back against the sink. He sets the glass on a nearby counter, lies against the tub's contour, looks at the ceiling.

—What are we doing, he says. —What is all this.

She feels her pulse rickety in her wrists. Looks out at the yard, the winter-bare trees rattling in the wind, against the glass panes. The clouds in the distance, gray faded puffy things. The bathroom is that cold blue of early evening.

How have they gotten here, how has it come to this? It's a good question. It was a series of lies, she thinks, hidden but simmering away. And every time something was added to the lie, some shift or twist, the pot would froth and nearly boil over. But it would settle, go back to its simmer, and maybe all the separate simmering lie-pots became too much.

Regardless, something strange starts to happen in his chest—she watches him clutch at it like he can level it out himself. His eyes melt into panic. His arm juts out and knocks the glass off the counter onto the floor. The shriek of the shatter jolts through both of them.

—What the fuck did you do to me?

She watches his limbs go slack and druggy, his blinks slow, his eyes sluggish from left to right. Steps closer—it is harder to watch than she imagined it'd be, but she has to see it through. She gets right up next to him, looks down at his pale limp body as he struggles at the surface. His eyes, their slow-motion panic. A gleam overcomes them, a murderous thing, and she imagines it, this frightening eye-light, as the last thing Ingrid saw before he swerved and killed her. She knows, of course she knows, because he talked about it in his sleep a few nights back when Cleo tossed and turned, sleepless. He confessed to his crime, though he didn't know he was confessing—sleep set his truth free. She lay glued to her side of the mattress and listened to him tell it, and her throat latched shut in their bed and hasn't come loose since.

Till now, when he reaches for her, slow-limbed but sure-sighted, and she releases a guttural scream. Even in his drugged state, the ruinous thing in him has come unstoppered, and she can't stop screaming. She reaches to the floor, grabs a shard of the glass, and rips it across like she's seem in films. The shard catches in his muscle-cords so she tries again, juts out with all her might, till his neck is red-rivered and the water is darkening and her hands and knees are soaked, and she slips on a splash of water, or maybe he pulls her down, he with his ironclad vengeful grip, and she falls in, soaks herself in his blood, soaks herself new.

ORRIE UNPEELS A LAYER FROM HIS SOUL AND IN THE SPIRIT OF GRIEVING DISAPPEARS FROM THE WORLD FOR A BIT

EMMA BURNING MAY JUST TURN TO SMOKE

1

—where do you want to go Orrie

I hear it from my left side I am tucked away in a pocket of myself

all the blood in my eyes

—do you need to go to the hospital

sheening down the front of them like a river-rush

—no he's fine just in shock

red bedspread fled dread sped said pled dead (glimmer) stead fed lead-head wed

red gives to black it's all I can see washing down over us all is it over or

—should I call

—who

the loud sound of a black look being exchanged across a short distance

the look ping-pinging around the black space

—orrie do you remember sil

—are you sure

—don't you think it's best

—you remember how they used to be

sil i think the syllable over and over again

at the name there's a black kicking-up that happens

—take me there

the voice comes from my own mouth blackened and new

—have to get out of here

desperate dark needing

—just till things wash over

—yes

instant and bell-clear.

2

we are driving that's all I can tell

we are in a truck. we being me and whichever body (glimmer) got me in here buckled me in secured my arms in my lap. maybe Uncle Enzo but could have been anybody.

my eyes have been too black-shrouded.

I have been drifting through clouds not-seeing. I hear the rumbling of one of the trucks beneath me feel it vibrating my feet in my shoes feel the seatbelt holding me within itself.

she came out of—it was the strangest thing.

a blinker begins to sound (glimmer) and the truck slows to a stop but still it rumbles beneath me.

it's the thick tick-tick of the gray truck's blinker not the brown.

because the brown truck is (glimmer).

she had eyes that I will never stop seeing.

I may as well tell it because it blocks everything else in my head anyway why not get it out. I was sitting in their bed with a notebook open in front of me but nothing recorded into it because I thought writing something out might help me but I couldn't find a way to get any of it into words.

and Mom went into the bathroom with a graceful swish in her step and I wasn't listening very carefully but a commotion seemed to occur and she screamed a horrid wrenching scream that melded itself to me (glimmer).

I can somehow see the glimmers still though I can see nothing else but black.

but anyway she ran out soaked in water and blood and trailed it all on the floor.

her hair was plastered down over her face red-dyed and

(it is a miracle I can think my way through this I have been choking on the memory for hours not able to get a word out)

(people of various voices have come into my blue bedroom and taken my hand in theirs and said ORRIE ARE YOU OK WOULD YOU LIKE SOME WATER WOULD THAT HELP but I knew it would take more than water to clear the memory-blockage, I couldn't say yes or no couldn't do anything but swallow around the lump of image that formed there)

sheenlike I couldn't see how any sound could get out but still those screams came.

then Uncle Enzo was there and his body shook at the sight of her blood-wetted and traumatized and she said HE WAS GOING TO KILL ME I HAD TO STOP HIM so Uncle Enzo pulled her in tight held her trembling body in his arms blood-soaked himself as well and I already knew what I was going to see when I rounded the corner into the bathroom but I had to see it for myself anyway.

dead man whose neck-skin folded open like a split in a curtain. the ground covered in splinters of glass.

dead man whose name was Dad (glimmer).

I am crying again and the person next to me in the truck sets a hand on my leg and hands me a tissue or paper towel or something to wipe my eyes.

we are going somewhere I don't remember.

it was discussed but all senses were shut down then everything but memory and hurt.

the sharp splint of the thing shoved up my middle.

but now at least I can hear.

my vision is still blacked out like another lid grew over my eyes but the rest of me is beating.

I keep waiting to calm down but when I feel a moment of calm there's a sudden wave of everything that rushes over me again and sends me into a state.

a sunny-sounding song comes on the radio and there's a bit of lift a shift under the skin but not long till it slips I know.

Ingrid would be humming it behind me in her right-side seat (glimmer).

when the car was Mom driving, me shotgun, Emma and Ingrid in the back. (Emma used to sit in the front till I shot up in height and she christened me the default front-seat passenger.)

Mom was wearing a red garment and it was rich-dyed red.

her hair that sheen of impenetrable dark.

—HE WAS GOING TO KILL ME.

didn't I hear it didn't I see it?

well I did and I didn't, I heard them conversing but it was like any other conversation at first and I was tuning it out.

you can't blame me for not being attentive because people talk about unimportant things all the time and how was I to know.

then a shatter and a brief pique of my ears but back to my tunings-out.

the house at this point was like an orchestra all the instruments going out of tune slowly one at a time all the instruments breaking.

the glass shattering like a too-taut violin string plonking out of place and curling up.

the shouting and splashes of water like cymbals dropped and mallets piercing the thick skins of drums.

Mom like the skid of a bow across a string that horrid shriek of sound.

I flounder with my hands and turn the radio dial all the way down.

—Okay, the person in the car says, and I think it is Uncle Enzo.

but who's to say if it is him or if any of this is even real.

I rely on sight to establish trust and I have none now.

nothing but this memory that won't clear.

Maybe-Enzo signals the blinker and I feel the vehicle turn to my left.

the texture beneath the tires changes crunching and jolting, potholes maybe or just uneven dirt road.

I rub at my eyes to see if the black-shroud will clear but still nothing.

—Almost there, he says.

when the car comes to a stop and Maybe-Enzo turns it off we fall into silence and my heart starts thwomping.

—It'll be fine, he says —C'mon, let's go inside.

—Where are we.

my left hand finds the edge of the cupholder and my right hand finds the armrest on the door and I hold myself there.

—You don't recognize this place?

—I can't really see.

—Well let's go in and maybe it'll feel more familiar.

he pulls my door open and guides me out of the car. I hold onto his arm as we make the ascent up what I presume is the driveway with gravel crunching beneath my feet.

then we're at a door and he knocks a couple times but it's only a few moments before I hear the hinge-creak of it being swung open.

there's a smell that hits me in some elemental place, a smell that takes the floor of what I thought I knew what I thought my life was and drops it out from beneath me.

there's another history in here a forgotten thing I'm feeling my way through (glimmer).

—Orrie, a voice says and I feel hands on my shoulders pulling me in. —God you've gotten tall.

I flounder in his arms a bit and Uncle Enzo explains my condition.

—Of course, the man says, —sorry to startle you. You remember me don't you? When you were a kid you used to call me Sah, it was all you could get out.

I don't recognize it the way you do a real memory but something about it is so familiar it cries out in me.

the smell of the house it's like maple syrup something sweet like that.

all the air in there is sweet it recalls birthday parties and elementary school breakfasts and staying here maybe.

it's a sense-memory deeper than general it's this place only.

Uncle Enzo says, —I'll come get you tomorrow and we'll get some of your stuff but for the night just hang tight, okay.

I say —Okay.

Sil grabs me by the elbow and leads me into the house.

there's a swoosh of fabric passing toward him and I think he's taken the overnight bag that was packed for me.

the house is quiet but I hear a washing machine whirring or maybe a dishwasher.

—I'll take you to your room, he says. —I'm so glad to see you. It's been so long since you've come over to play though I suppose you're too old for that now.

—Never too old, I say, —play is eternal.

—That's the spirit, he says.

—Where are your sons? Are they at their mother's?

I find a vague memory I don't know where it comes from of Sil being divorced and getting the kids on a rotating schedule and the question pops in me like a corn kernel.

there's a blink of too-quiet in the air.

—Yeah, he says. —Pio's at his mom's but he'll be back tomorrow. He's excited to see you. You remember Pio?

I hardly remember them it was all so long ago but some bit of my soul flashes out at the name (glimmer).

we approach the end of a hallway and he says, —Right turn coming up, and we swing our bodies over and continue down the hall.

he stops and twists a door open and guides me in.

—Bedroom, he says, with bunk beds and desk on the left, closet on the right, window in front of us.

—Wait till you see the colors this thing gets in the morning, it's a beautiful sight.

—Oh right, you can't see.

—Well, hopefully your vision will come back and you can see it 'cause it's just lovely.

—Oh and also I'll leave the door cracked for the night so if you need anything you can just holler, okay?

—Normally, Pio sleeps on the bottom, but I think for tonight it'd be best if you slept down there. I don't want you to have to worry about the ladder and all that.

—But for now I assume you just want to go to bed, yeah?

—Again, I'm just down the hall so call out if you need anything. The bathroom's right across the hall, just out the door. It's the door on the other side.

he swallows, takes a break from speaking (glimmer).

helps me lower myself onto the bed and I feel for the pillows and covers.

—It's really good to have you back here, Orrie, he says. —You're so much taller but I'll be damned if you don't look just the same.

he slips out of the room and I hear his footfalls recede on the wooden floor.

I turn over once and anticipate a long night of sleepless turnings-over but my body wrenches itself asleep and I have a few hours of black.

I wake in complete darkness and curse at my eyes for still being shrouded over but I look in the direction of the far wall and notice light slivered around the cracked door from a hallway nightlight or something.

my eyes are letting me see again.

I sit up and wipe at my drenched forehead and try to remember where I am, because this isn't my bedroom and this smell isn't the smell of my house (glimmer).

and after a long moment of floundering through my brain it all comes back to me.

the long drive over the song turned down on the radio the stumble through the house.

Sil.

a reacquaintance.

in the morning the house will be sunlit and I will see it I will see Sil again after years.

it is such a nice thought I almost forget about the bath.

the red all the red (glimmer).

it washes over my eyes even when I try to shove it away.

but that's the nature of things I try not to think about, always has been.

they persist.

hopefully in the morning he is willing to acquaint himself with the new Orrie.

there is an old Orrie in here too the one he knows but mostly I am a new Orrie.

here and

THERE IS AN AMBULANCE ROAMING ABOUT TOWN TONIGHT

crackle

WE HEAR ITS

SONG CALLING UP AND DOWN

crackle

WONDER WHAT TROUBLE IT SPELLS FOR US

3

we pack Orrie up and ship him off,

the protective wool of his soul pulled down over his eyes. Some things a child can't see, shouldn't see. I can barely look at Mom but I help her with this one thing, for Orrie—I stuff some of his things into a drawstring bag so he will make it till tomorrow, at which point he will come back and gather more. He lost his mind, there, in the bedroom—I heard shrieks from the bathroom and came around the corner, saw a trail of blood all over the hall floor, and stepped over it into the bedroom to see Orrie, thrown back onto the bed as if a demon had crawled its way out of his throat.

I gathered him in my arms, the splinters of his body, and he started sobbing, retching, clawing at me to pull him closer. He was trying to say something between his hiccups of sob-sound, and after a few splutters I understood he was saying, *Bathroom, bathroom*. So I stood and moved toward the bathroom door. I saw it, what he wanted me to see there, beneath the netlike hair floating. A little stone was put in me, then, a small thing that kicks around sometimes.

I ran down to the phone to call 911 but saw the one cordless phone had been knocked loose from its holster and the batteries had flung themselves out of it. I could only find one of the three on the floor; the other two had rolled off somewhere. *FUCK*, I shouted into the strangely quiet house—you'd have thought everyone in there was dead, it was so quiet. We were all dead in our own way, I suppose. We still are.

I found the batteries, I called, and things after that are blank for a while. I remember the gaps being filled in for me—the shattered glass, the attempted pulling-in, the bloodshed. And I had some sense beneath the skin that something wasn't right. I remember flashlights being shone in my eyes, one then the other. I remember the zipping and unzipping of bags, the gathering of my father's naked blood-dyed body, though I tried so hard to look away. I remember discussion about where Orrie would be carted. We couldn't keep all of us in one place, we needed a steady head somewhere, and Orrie had lost his entirely.

I remember feeling very little for a time, which is unusual for me. I sit empty, soak it in.

In my trance state, I do what I am asked, wander to Orrie's room and gather a change of clothes, his deodorant and toothbrush, stuff them in a bag.

When I meet them at the car and give the bag to him, his eyes are fixed in front of him at some indeterminate distance—it seems a strange kind of not-seeing.

—Here, I say to him, but he doesn't respond.

When he and Enzo have gone, Mom turns around and leans against the door, allows something to fall away, some guard, some pretense. I am about to head up the stairs but I catch sight of this slackening face and am intrigued. She has cleaned up since the killing, gotten most of the blood off, bunched up her hair in a pink towel. (I call it a killing because that's what it is.) She catches me looking at her and—I swear—she turns it all back on again, the heavy forehead, sunken eyes, slight quiver of her lip. I have witnessed a glitch in the system. It shivers in me.

For a moment I think I won't engage. I am beaten down, blurred at the edges. But the stone in my stomach has turned over, revealed its darker underside. The words won't let me swallow them.

—Look what you've done to Orrie, I say.

Her head whips up like I've walked up and struck her. —Excuse me?

I consider, again, backing down. But the gleam in her eyes suggests she wants a challenge and I'm more than happy to oblige.

—You heard me.

I never break eye contact, never allow my shoulders to sink, never turn away. I haven't showered since yesterday, my scalp is oily, I can smell a rankness wafting up from my armpits, bleeding through yesterday's deodorant, my eyes dark as oil pits, I am pure darkness. I face her and hold myself rigid as steel and my body says, Take what you want from me, there is very little I have left to give.

—You killed our father, I say. —Killed.

I keep my eyes up, push my luck.

—You were gonna do it anyway, I say. —You planned it.

Do I know that that's true? No. And I don't know what I'm looking to provoke—a confession, an outburst, a kind of pain she can inflict on the outside that matches the melting-beating I've suffered on the inside?

Whatever it is, she doesn't give it to me. She walks up from the other side of the room, stands in my face for a moment, writhes like she wants to reach out and strike me but is holding back, and then turns and storms toward the stairs.

—I am your mother, she says. —How could you say that to your own mother.

It's in her eyes for a moment: the fact that I'm making her acknowledge a thing she thought she'd justified away. Mercy killing, self-defense, vengeance for Ingrid, putting him out of his misery, however she pitched it to herself. A thing is only what you call it. And I want her to call it murder. I want to hear her say it, *murder*, the two rhotic syllables sweet as honey on her lips. She could say it and make it sound like bliss—she's always been a sweet talker. She could whisper it in Enzo's ear and he'd bend his neck for her, expose the taut-knit cords of his throat, present the blade. He, her sweet, stupid supplicant. Ripe for the slice, itching for the knife.

I think I've played the role for long enough. No more, I decide.

I wish I had seen it all, I just wish I'd seen. Wish I'd heard the first scream and leapt from my room, torn down the hall, watched her rip his skin open. Seen him pull her in, try to take her down with him. I know it all clear as day, know how she swelled the story up to cosmic size. Almost like the house lent me its senses, let me feel what it felt through the walls. I know it but I can't prove it.

I still haven't processed who is gone, only the fact of the killing, the outrage of it.

WE CANNOT REACH ORRIE HE HAS LEFT THE PROPERTY
WHY WOULD HE LEAVE US WHERE HAS HE GONE
WE MISS HIM LIKE A SOCKET MISSES ITS FORMER LIMB

4

there will be a trial—

of course there will be a trial. She will plead self-defense. She will tell the story of his slow dissolution since coming home from war, the way he sometimes looked out his own eyes like they were a stranger's. (This was all true.) She will enter into evidence the wrist bruises from his vise-grip. She will claim he tried to kill her just the way he killed their daughter: a basket case's last lapse of sanity. Something in her cries out at the injustice of the lie but it's too late to feel bad now. The deed has been done and she's washed clean and dried off, the last of her sins spiraling down the shower drain.

Enzo and Emma and maybe Orrie will be called on to testify. A trial is coming.

In the kitchen in the morning, Enzo kisses her forehead, holds her wrists gently in his hands, slow-steps left and right while they wait for water to boil. The boiling dance, he calls it. Orrie is out of the house, Emma is asleep, all the medics and officers have left the house—she and Enzo can finally live out some semblance of their truth. For the rest of the day, she plans to adjust funeral arrangements—Ingrid's funeral, planned for tomorrow, cannot run now. She thinks what's best is to push back a week and honor both of the fallen on the same day. But she's got a more immediate, more pressing concern.

—I need you to do something for me, she says.

He strokes her cheekbone, sets a kiss there. —Anything.

The love in his eyes is so weighty she thinks it's going to crush her. But she wouldn't mind, all her life she has wanted its smothering.

—After breakfast, she says. —Come upstairs and I'll show you.

They eat modestly. Eggs and toast and some sausage links. She saves nothing for Emma—after what was said last night, Emma can make food for herself later—and leads him upstairs. She clutched at her wrists in the presence of the officers last night, indicating that bruising might show up. Their bathroom is still cordoned off, so she guides him into the children's bathroom. Checks to make sure Emma is still asleep, sets an ear against her door. Nothing, no sound.

She gestures to the tub shower. Not the same as her clawfoot, but it'll do.

—I need you to get in, she says, —and grab my wrists. She gestures with her hands. —Like he would have.

His brow sinks. —You said he did.

—He did. But we need to make sure it bruises, that's all.

He turns to the wall, massages his forehead with his fingers. —Cleo, I don't think—

She grabs his shoulder. —Enzo, we have to make sure they think it was self-defense. That I had no other choice.

—Because it *was* self-defense. Because you *didn't* have any other choice.

—You know I didn't. You know he was going to drown me. But we have no clue what story Emma will spin. You know she's cooking something up.

His eyes are hollows. She pulls her sleeves up, exposes the soft freckles that dot her forearms. —But I've got thick skin. So we have to make sure the damage he did was deep enough to show.

After a stretched moment, during which she can see him see-sawing it over, he nods. With a deep breath, he steps into the tub, lowers himself down. She holds her hands out, waits, as if he is going to kiss them. He takes them into his own, gentle, at first.

WE CAN HARDLY

crackle

LIKE BAD RADIO

crackle

WHERE HAS OUR FAMILY

crackle

5

a shroud of dark when I wake

but a cascade of light waits behind the blinds. Sil has come in, in the middle of the night I presume, and pulled the curtains shut so the light would not wake me. It's the bright fire-hot yellow of midday. It reminds me of Ingrid's favorite sundress and a cavern opens in my eye (glimmer). The glimmers have mostly gone away I have watched them fade. But they still crop up every now and then. She always wanted to wear the sundress in the fields and grew sad when Mom made her change out of it at the door. *You're going to get mud stains all over it and be mad,* Mom said. *It's for your own good.*

I stand at long last. The desk has a shut laptop on it and a stack of textbooks. The closet drawers are shut and they are sliding mirrors so the room appears doubled, vast as a corridor. Mirror-Orrie has unkempt hair and heavy eyes pooled with bad memories which I suppose means Real-Orrie does too. Is that Mom behind me? No, it is a coat hung on the bunk bed railing the color of something Mom would wear. (Again her blood-bathed form and again I blink it away.)

The door is half-open so I pull it the rest of the way, let its door-stop tap the wall. To the left are a couple more doors. Sil's room and a laundry room and maybe a garage. I hear a washer whirring again—it must be laundry weekend. To the right is the hall that opens on the front room and kitchen. I haven't been here in years but my body is doing that thing where it slowly releases the memories it's been holding in its cells.

Family photos line the walls toward the living room. Pictures from Sil's wedding to his ex-wife, her cool brown skin glowing against the dress. Pictures of Pio and his brother—what's his name again—side by side at the walls of a crib or strapped into a stroller or sharing the glow of birthday candles. Their big grins beaming at me. Yes: these were children I used to play with, these are the halls we ran up and down. Why haven't I been here since? Sad, the kind of thing where you fall out of each other's lives. Unintentional but pulled in different directions.

I walk out into the living room. —Good morning, I say —God, I slept late.

—It's basically tomorrow, he jokes. —But good morning to you too.

He's in a chair on the other side of the room facing the front windows and I hear sheets of a newspaper or magazine rustling in front of him, see the back of his just-balding head. He stands and turns to look at me. Must notice something in my eyes, a landing-on-things that wasn't there before, because his face goes warm and glowing. —You can see again.

—Yeah. And it's good to see you again. Ha.

He smiles. He's quite a bit taller than I remember, lanky and long-boned. With an aquiline nose and a pair of kind, pale blue eyes that are familiar to my mind but placed elsewhere.

—Some leftover eggs in the kitchen if you want them. Probably cold but nothing the microwave won't fix. Pio'll be back in the afternoon and I figured we could do something.

—Lunch maybe? My stomach lets out a grumbling sound.

—Not a bad idea, he says. It's been a while since you've seen Pio.

—How long will I be here?

He blinks.

—Sorry that sounded bad. I didn't mean it to sound like that. I just. I swallow down the stones of sentences that keep plopping in my mouth. —I just don't know what's going on, you know. Wondered if you adults talked more about it.

He clears his throat—something must be lodged in his too. —I think, he says, —we just agreed that some time away from the house might be good for you. Don't think any sort of time frame was put on it, but obviously you don't have to stay anywhere you don't want to.

—No no, I'm grateful. To stay here.

I stretch out my back, let my hands fall to the floor. Fingers brushing against the floor-planks.

—And to be honest, I say, —it is kind of nice to get out of the house. I feel like there's some. I don't know. Lighter somehow.

There's a chasm in me at the splitting of the family but also some hard-to-describe new sense of possibility. Even the light feels different here, purer in its rays. At the house the light is often grayed out by fog or cloud cover and it brightens the place, as light does, but still it maintains its slight shroud.

—That's good, he says. —You hungry?

I reheat the eggs in the microwave and when I pull them out I hear them sizzling, see them buzzing around on the plate. Sil makes me a piece of toast and butters it and I eat it alongside the eggs and (sorry Emma) ketchup. Emma hates it when I put ketchup on my eggs but I can't help that it tastes so good. The sweet smack of it. Sometimes I lick it off the plate when all the eggs are gone and Emma is out of the room.

Sometimes I feel very kidlike in the bones, like I'm a seven-year-old that just got stretched out a bit with a rolling pin. This is one of those times: seated at the table, dwarfed by standing Sil, licking ketchup off my fork. I do a kid-grin.

I wonder what Emma is doing now. Whether she had breakfast of some sort, eggs or meat or yogurt or fruit. But the thought of her fills me with a pain and puts a crick in my neck so I rub at it and push that thinking away.

Sil washes up my plate when I'm done and I thank him. He says, —Do you want to walk around the property? Might jog your memory a bit.

I think about all the unvarnished light, feeling it on my skin. About hearing all the outside sounds on my way here yesterday, the gravel crunching and the leaves shifting and the birds flitting but not being able to see any of it. —Yeah. The word leaves my mouth soft as a cloud parting.

—Well, get some socks and shoes on and meet me outside. And probably a coat.

He is waiting on the porch for me. The outside of the house is a lovely pale blue color that reminds me of my bedroom walls. It's square and one-story with a small front porch, not very big, certainly no cross-generational creaky house full of chambers and ghosts but plenty of room for the three of them. They live across town from us and lower in the valley. Winter doesn't stick to this place like it does to our house. The ground, even in the cold, is sun-dry beneath my shoes. It's raining lightly out here and I am amazed by the way it falls and disappears. The strange snow at our house this year has made us remember. It has stayed in frigid plowed piles and turned to ice and then to slush and only when it's time for crops to poke out of the ground will it hopefully leave.

—Why haven't I been here in so long? I ask. —It's gorgeous.

—I don't know, he says, —just happens that way sometimes. Something in his tone's measured evenness suggests a greater cove of story. But I don't push.

Instead I turn back to the gardens, listen to Sil describe the herbs and trees and bushes. It's like our farm but smaller scale, more intimate. The kind of thing where you bend to the ground with somebody and nurture it. Not needing our amount of farmhands and planners: this is a place for only a few. Most things are dead now but I imagine the place brimming, imagine it green and growing. The gardens are right outside the doors, a slight walk down the drive. Everything gathered can be brought right inside, washed and eaten then and there.

—What do you remember from here? he asks, his eyes shimmering with hope. That some trace of him stuck around across all the years between. That he wasn't erasable. I could hear it in the lightness of his voice.

—Not much, I admit. —It all feels so familiar but I don't *remember* it, if that makes sense.

He drags his foot across an uneven segment of walkway and flattens out the rocks. —Yeah, that makes sense. Well, maybe more memories will come to you in time.

—Yeah. And it's been a long week.

We approach the back of the house and the property widens. I see a patch of bare dirt off to the side and something leaps out at me. Some tactile memory that springs up in my body turns over and over itself, goes queasy. I point to the patch.

—There was a trampoline there. I remember.

—Yeah, he says, and his skin goes red with memory.

—All of us out here. And we used to put a sprinkler under it, didn't we. I remember us all up there in our bathing suits in the summer sliding around and splashing.

Pio. I am remembering him now, the photos of him I saw in the hall all conjoining into motion. His light-brown skin and his big pale eyes and his smile gummy because he had just lost some teeth. *It feels so weird,* he said, *look, feel it.* Took my finger and ran it along the pink indents left behind. He left some slobber on my finger and I remember thinking what a strange thing, this kid who just put my finger in his mouth. Our lips blue-stained after downing sugary kid-drinks, our fingers orange-coated after the chips. Look how high we could jump look how far we could run. When everything was a quest, a challenge.

—When does Pio get back?

—His mom's bringing him at two.

I'm thinking of Pio's brother. He is in the photos too, another little squirt about a foot shorter than Pio. Pio is a magnet in every photo and his brother is looking up at him with the greatest kindness. But I don't want to bring it up in case it opens something else I can't close. Sil seems content, pleased, and I don't want to pull him out of that space.

When we've circled the house, admired the plants and flowers growing on the far side, walked past the water bowl he leaves out for the stray cats he sees wandering, we kick off our shoes and slip out of our coats and sit inside.

We decide we'll swing by my house before lunch to grab some more of my things. We sit in the living room and he asks me about school and friends and girls. There was conversation years and years ago between us and it feels like we are reopening it. Because some part of him too is the same as it has always been. Same eyes looking out at me from inside his body. Hair paled and thinned skin that's taken on new creases but the core of him is the same.

Does it help me to think that some things about us won't change? That at our cores we will carry on forever? It's pleasant in some ways—I'll always remain wide-eyed and curious, looking out at the world. But it also makes me think the curse is lodged too deeply inside me, inside us all, and there is no hope to excavate it. Which swirls around inside my stomach like a nasty rumor and doesn't quite settle, pounds around in my head like an ache. We wait for Pio to arrive, the gap between us like a held breath.

6

—and now a little history lesson

ABOUT OUR CURSE
WE MEANING THE ROYAL WE OF ATREUS
A FEW VARIATIONS OF TALE THAT HAVE THUNDERED THROUGH
OUR WALLS
(THERE ARE SO MANY A FACT WHICH SPELLS A BIT HOPELESS)
BUT IN ONE VERSION OF THINGS
A GREAT-GREAT-GREAT-GREAT-GREAT (PLUS MAYBE TWO OR
THREE DOZEN MORE) GRANDFATHER
LET'S CALL HIM T
WEASELED HIS WAY INTO FRIENDSHIP WITH THE GODS
STOLE THEIR FÊTE-FOOD AND SHARED IT WITH OTHER MORTALS
WHICH WAS SEEN AS TAKING ADVANTAGE
AND RATTLED OUT THEIR GOD-SECRETS
WHICH WAS SEEN AS TWO-FACED

THEN HE STOLE ZEUS'S FAVORITE HOUND DOG WHICH WAS
A LOVELY GOLDEN COLOR
AND LIED TO HIS FACE ABOUT IT
(OF ALL GODS TO LIE TO WHY NOT GO FOR THE PETTIEST AND WILDEST)
BUT T'S ULTIMATE SAVAGE TRICK (IF WE COULD CALL IT THAT)
WAS TO (GULP) GRILL UP HIS OWN SON AND SERVE HIM TO THE GODS
WHO RECOILED IN HORROR AT HIS SAVAGERY
AND KICKED HIM OUT FOR GOOD
OUR GREAT-GREAT-ETC. GRANDFATHER WAS A CHARMER
HE CHARMED HIS WAY
INTO BEDROOMS INTO BANQUETS INTO BANISHMENT
WHAT WAS HIS ROT WE WONDER AND HOW MANY OF US
HAS IT CARRIED DOWN TO
BUT REGARDLESS
THE GODS HAVE HAD THEIR NOSES TURNED UP AT US
EVER SINCE & SPRINKLED CHAOS DOWN ONTO US
LIKE A FINE SUGAR

7

energy drips from me like a leaky tap

so I climb into bed and don't get out for a day. The energy I used to hold within myself, the full-souled finger-warming flame, has been sapped to nothing and I find there is nothing I can do to function. I have a black sleep punctuated by dreams of Dad, supplementing the gaps in our life: he never left, he taught us how to exist in the world, taught me to cook and be gracious and temper the storm in me, drove me down-slash-over-slash-far-far-away to college, called me on the weekends. And when I wake there is some part of me, new and blooming, that accepts he is gone, whereas before I wouldn't even entertain the reality. I now hold that knowledge within me. I don't like it, I don't want it, but I take it, keep it here.

He didn't teach us to exist. Instead he forgot how to do it himself. He didn't teach me to temper my storm; he left and we watched it swell, metastasize. He didn't drive me to college, he drove himself into a tree, and I sat, I sat.

The house is so goddamn quiet—I'm close to inviting over some old friends who are still in town so they can stomp around upstairs, manufacture some illusion of life. Maybe one of them can ask me questions like Orrie did, one of them can hum songs in the kitchen at a high pitch, one of them can stir a wooden spoon lazily around the inside of a pan, one of them can go shuffle around on the porch, kick his boots against the steps to unclog them of dirt, and I can look out the window, sink back into the old world, where everything was the same. Who cares that it's all a lie, if it's easy enough to sink into.

—Orrie is coming by to pick up some more stuff, Mom says.

In the fantasy in my head she isn't here but rather locked away in some cell or room, where she has to sit with what she's done. Or, no—in the fantasy, she never had the chance to do what she's done. Instead she and Enzo ran off long ago and left us behind with Dad, who never hopped the sea and went to war but instead fathered us. He tried, of course, from abroad, but there's only so much a letter can do.

From her perch at the front table, she smiles, adjusts the flowers in the vase along the front wall. She didn't come to me in my day of sleep, didn't bring food, didn't leave tea or water. But still she smiles sweetly, she slides up and down the halls, in and out of rooms. It appears she has decided to continue on with me as if nothing happened, though I know my words hover right in front of her eyes every time she turns to me—I know that to look at me is to confront what she has done. I have given up the glower, gone for neutrality, but still I glow with pleasure at this fact.

—You want a sandwich? she asks. —I feel like a sandwich.

My nose twitches. So she wants to poison me too—great. After everything happened upstairs, Mom came down screaming and blood-soaked, and Dad was whirled out on a gurney, loaded into a low-set vehicle with less exigence since he was already bled out and helpless, and Orrie sank into his covelike thing he couldn't even see out of. I found the kitchen, the world, momentarily empty, and I peered closer at the stovetop stuff she had been swirling around. I was the only one who still had a head on her, everyone else had disappeared. I knew it would catch up to me, and in due time it did, but for the moment I was lucid and lifelike. I took a small amount of the steeped water into a Mason jar, swirled it around, hid it up in my room. Put my hand in a plastic bag, dumped out the saucepan, ran its contents down the drain, took it upstairs too, set it on a shelf in my closet, figuring someday, once a trial is opened, it may prove useful—I can guide them to the case I have assembled, say, Here it is, should have her fingerprints and everything. Demand toxicology for Dad, however that works. If I raise enough of a fuss, I'm sure someone will listen to me. They will investigate.

For now, I am out of care, so I say, —Sure, sounds good.

Poison me all you want, I think. I hear her shuffling around the kitchen, pulling meats and cheeses out of drawers, plucking vegetables off the counter. The *thwap-thwap-thwap* of a knife against a cutting board, the *shush* of the blade through an onion, the creak of the oven door as she sets the bread in to toast up—she'll assemble cold cuts that stack to the sun with those poisonous hands, and I won't taste her venom till it's already at work.

But what's it worth anymore! What's any of it worth. I want to know, I want to find an answer I can hold. Because lately everything has gone hollow. I'm no longer able to look at my actions and find purpose—my body is moving of its own accord, dragging me through faceless days. I look down at my body and wonder why it's doing what it's doing, what any of it is for. But still I move, still I'm moving.

Mom sets the two plates, stacked with sandwiches, on the dining table, waves me over to sit with her. The window light shines pale blue at midday, the kitchen is lit frigidly. I have brief dreams: of wandering a college square, visiting a campus bookstore, seeing a city in that pale blue light.

—Where's Enzo? I say.

—*Uncle* Enzo, she corrects. She fetches glasses of water.

—Where is he.

I lift the sandwich, open my mouth as wide as it will go—she likes to stack them tall.

—He's at home. Got some laundry and stuff to do. And he's got to work on his truck. But he'll be back when Orrie's here, to help out.

She lifts the sandwich to her mouth, crunches through its shell, its lettuce. A bit of tomato spurts out the side, slithers down the slope at the side of her plate.

—I don't know why he doesn't just do his laundry here, I say.

She cocks her head at me, though a slight blush washes over her cheeks. —Now why would he do that.

—Come on, now, Mom.

Our eyes are locked. I lift the sandwich and take another bite. A bit of crunchy sourdough shell goes through the roof of my mouth but I don't look away, don't back down. After I chew and swallow, I lift a finger to the injured spot and pull it away bloodied. I wipe it on my napkin and take another bite, though the sight of blood, the reminder that it rises, nauseates me.

Just then I hear the steady build of crunching gravel and turn toward the sound. A truck pulls up in front of the house and three people climb out, two people I don't recognize, and Orrie. My heart swells: he seems okay, and not only okay but happy, he is smiling, laughing at something one of the others has said, he's wearing a sweatshirt that isn't his, it pokes out beneath his jacket.

I stand but Mom says, —No, you stay here, eat your sandwich, I'll help. She steps into the living room, unlocks the front door, pulls it open. —Sil, she says to the man. —And Primo.

—Pio, Orrie says.

—Oh, yes, Pio, of course.

Sil steps to the side and the three of them wander into the house. —It's been a long time, she says. —Pio, do you remember this place?

Up close, the two strangers come into focus, and their features are familiar. The boy, Pio, is wandering the living room, looking up at it with big eyes. A wash of something goes over him, maybe recognition, maybe remembrance.

—Emma, Sil says as he comes closer, crossing the threshold into the kitchen. —Goodness, how you've grown. I thought it was just Orrie, but look at you.

I smile, prim as can be.

—Do you remember me and Pio? It's been a while. What, five years, six years?

—Something like that, Mom says.

She wanders into the kitchen and I can see a universe of feeling written on her face, in her body, and she scratches at her left forearm as she steps toward the kitchen. There's some history hovering in the space between her and these people, I can feel it. Nobody around here is very good at hiding their feelings, both of their skins are alight with it, they can hardly look at each other. Why, I want to poke at him and say, are you playing civil? What's the dark organ you want to let slide out of you?

—Water, anyone? Mom asks.

Sil and Pio look at each other. Orrie stands there smiley, vacant as a stranger in his own home. He takes the opportunity to escape upstairs while Sil and Pio come into the kitchen and gather around the island. I slip out of the kitchen, follow Orrie upstairs.

He is standing at the edge of his room, looking around. Sizing it up as if he's never seen it before: his bed dressed in blue, his dresser with clothes sticking out of the gaps (he's never been the tidiest), his wide, wide windows. Wide enough for the light to come in and swallow everything up. The first thing he does is pull the curtains shut and the room sinks into half-darkness. I'm not sure if he knows I'm standing here, so I clear my throat, step toward him.

—Are you feeling better?

—Yes, but don't look at me like that.

My face goes red. —Like what?

—Like I'm split down the middle. I'm fine.

He lifts his eyes to me and I see something swimming in them. I haven't seen it on him before, but it's a newness, a freshened-up sense. Maybe getting out of the house has cleared the cobwebs in him.

But I think of him leaving again, minutes from now, and my heart seizes—I want him to stay. How can I see the good that leaving has done to him yet still want otherwise?

—How long are you gonna stay there? I try to keep the desperation out of my voice but I'm afraid it has bled in. He looks at me tenderly.

—Don't know, he says. —It's only been a night but it's really nice. It feels really good to be there.

There's an implied AND NOT HERE that I can't bat away.

He digs through his closet and pulls out a suitcase, wrenches it open, pats at the fabric inside to flatten it out, make room. Last time he used it for a trip was when we flew to visit our grandfather under the guise of a fun vacation although really it was to see him one last time before he croaked. His room smelled of decay and raisins. Orrie regards the suitcase with a gloomy brow.

—Do you need help packing stuff up? I ask.

He shakes his head. —Thanks, though.

I hear a shuffle from behind me and see Pio has come up. He is quiet in his motion like Ingrid was; it makes me smile. His eyes are big gorgeous buttery blues that light some childhood history in me.

—Do you remember me? I ask.

He goes a bit red. Everyone is reddening around me today—the world is blushing.

—Yeah, he says. He's got an Adam's apple like a golf ball and it juts up as he swallows. —We all used to play here. And . . . He goes smiley, looks over at Orrie.

—And what?

—And I remember when Orrie and I were little, maybe seven or eight, and I came over, you always used to play it cool, like you were too good for us. You'd go off and do your own thing. But after an hour or two you'd finally cave and come play with us.

I choke out a laugh. —Sounds like me.

The three years between Orrie and me are nothing now; at this point, who he is—his dreaminess, his soul only half-tethered to this world—is what I notice rather than his age. But back then I'm sure I gave those three years a gravity, saw myself as older and smarter.

I look over at Orrie and notice how many shirts he is packing. My stomach sinks. Lots of clothes, and the comfort items he keeps in the place where he lives: an old glass figurine, an old copy of a favorite book. The items add up to time and time and time away.

I leave the two of them, as they get caught up in conversation about old games, and wander down the hall toward my room. There was a time, I feel its old glow, when I regarded this place as my emotional center. Dig deep, to the core of me, and you'd be in this room, with its olive walls, its curtains that shift when the heater kicks on. But something has happened in all these years, a souring, a scooping-out, and now I sit in here and it seems to have gathered all the negative energy I've cast off over the years till the floor is piled with coal-stones of hot hurt.

Mom calls for me from downstairs. —You didn't finish your sandwich, she says when I meet her at the threshold of the kitchen. The untouched half swims in tomato liquid.

—I know, I wanted to help Orrie.

—So, she says to Sil, turning a shoulder to me. —Bring him back on the day of the funeral? And he can decide what he wants to do from there?

He nods, curt. —Can do. We'll all come for the funeral.

—Of course, she says. —I can't thank you enough.

But there's that darkness hovering beneath the surface of her, I feel it like a glow of heat. If I get Sil alone, if I ever make it over to their house, I'll push further. For now, I pick up the sandwich and take another bite. The boys make their way back outside and Enzo arrives from down the hill, just in time to watch Sil load the last of Orrie's bags (my heart jolts at the sight of multiple) into the bed of the truck. Enzo reaches out for a handshake. I watch the interaction from the kitchen windows and dread runs up my back. Enzo approaches with a smile but Sil remains brusque, back ramrod-straight—he shakes Enzo's hand with civility, turns and climbs again into the truck.

Before the boys climb in, we meet them outside, and I hug Orrie for a long time, the kind of hug you still feel on your skin minutes after you pull away. I try as hard as I can to say it with my eyes, Take me with you, don't leave me here, I won't survive in this house, won't survive without you, I've lost Dad and I've lost Ingrid and I'm losing you and I feel hollow-boned walking around, like all the things that mattered in my life have melted into a puddle right in front of my eyes. A slight pleading sound leaves my lips but he smiles, takes it as a joke, climbs into the truck after Pio.

The truck kicks up dirt as it reverses and I breathe in some of it but it's better than going back inside. I stay out there as long as I can handle it, till I'm shivering and choking down sobs. When I get back inside, my jaw is chattering and I can't feel my ears.

In the kitchen, Enzo huffs. —Oh, yeah, also, my truck'll be out of commission for a month or so, probably.

Mom makes a cluck of disapproval. —What? Oh, that's horrible.

He goes on to describe a certain part nestled deep in the engine that'll take an eternity to get to, everything around it having to come out first, the cheapness of the part but the cost of the labor if he took it to a shop in town, or into a city further down the coast, so screw it, he'll just do it himself. I stand in the front room next to the coat rack. I wonder if they will mistake me for a coat rack if I stand here long enough, if I blink the leaving-pain out of my eyes.

—Emma, are you going to eat this sandwich? Can Enzo have half?

Of course, I think—what's ours is yours, isn't it. I nod, and he reaches over to take the half I haven't touched.

—You'll need something to get around, Cleo says. —You're more than welcome to use one of our cars.

—Thanks, he says.

—Emma, Mom says. —Make sure to ask if you need to use the car. We need to keep it available in case Enzo needs it, or Orrie needs us.

The walls feel tighter around me suddenly. Enzo looks up from his sandwich, innocuous. But there's a strange pressure on my ribs, like they're being pressed inward and they're going to snap off the cage one by one, poke at my organs. If Dad were still here, this would never have happened. Orrie would be here. We'd all still be split down the middle, without Ingrid to keep us whole, but we'd be together, at least.

They're careless now. When I walk up the stairs, I hover at the edge for a moment, and I hear the sloshy sounds of their mouths moving together, a low moan, a laugh. I walk into my room and shut the door, shut out the sounds of the happiness they've found. At what expense? I wish I could wrangle it back out of them, squeeze the glee from their guts. I'm not, I remember, supposed to drive. *Please don't do this,* is how she said it, but she really meant, *Don't you dare.*

The house is a vise I'm caught in and she just keeps tightening its jaws around me, so tight it's bone-crushing.

8

—if the last tale didn't convince you maybe this one will

VERSION NUMBER TWO RATTLING IN THE FLOORBOARDS
A COUPLE GENERATIONS DOWN FROM THE FIRST
TWO BROTHERS CAUGHT IN A POWER STRUGGLE
(AREN'T ALL BROTHERS ALWAYS?
NO WOMAN HAS BROUGHT A WORLD TO RUIN)
(THOUGH HELEN MIGHT HAVE SOMETHING TO SAY ABOUT THAT)
(BUT WE DIGRESS)
LET'S CALL THEM A AND T
(NOT THE SAME T AS EARLIER A DIFFERENT ONE)
THEY TEAMED UP AND KILLED THEIR UNCLE FOR HIS THRONE
BUT NO AMOUNT OF ROCHAMBEAU COULD SETTLE WHICH OF THEM WOULD CLAIM IT
ONE CAME UPON A GOLDEN FLEECE WHICH SHOULD'VE GUARANTEED IT TO HIM

BUT THE OTHER WON OVER HIS WIFE AND TOOK THE FLEECE
FOR HIMSELF
HE SAID TO THE FIRST
HA! YOU MIGHT GET THE THRONE IF YOU CAN MAKE THE SUN
MOVE BACKWARDS!
HOWLING AT THE IMPOSSIBILITY OF THAT
BUT THE GODS WERE MEDDLERS AND SOAKED UP MORTAL
AFFAIRS LIKE REALITY TV
SO THE BROTHER SIDLED UP TO ZEUS AND THE GOD SUNK THE
SUN BACKWARD
AND THE SCORNED BROTHER (OF COURSE
WHAT ELSE WOULD HE DO)
OFFED TWO OF HIS NEPHEWS AND BAKED THEM IN A PIE
FED SCRAPS OF THEM TO THEIR FATHER
SPLUTTERING AND RETCHING HE SPAT OUT A CURSE
ON HIS BROTHER AND ALL WHO FOLLOWED
ALL US LOVELIES BUNCHED TOGETHER IN THIS HOUSE
ROTTEN FRUIT SUNK TO THE BOTTOM OF THE BASKET

9

he appeared when I was not expecting him

I went to the bathroom and when I came back out into the living room there was a strange shape on the couch where I had been seated. At first, I thought my soul had drifted down the hall and left my body behind and I was just reencountering myself. But no, this body was different, with hair in tight coils and skin the color of wet sand and eyes so blue I felt a sinking when they landed on me. A body of water with tides that were pulling, pulling. That's why Sil's eyes were so familiar, I realized, because Pio got them from him.

He said *hey* or *hi* or something—the usual sort of introduction—and my eyes glazed over with history.

Sil drove us to a diner at the edge of town, its wall plastered with big yellow lettering. Now we are sitting across from each other in a booth and I am trying so hard not to stare. I don't want him to think anything of it but it is so strange to me how looking at him seems to launch me backward through some time-portal. His eyes, how they used to look up at the sky with me side by side on the trampoline, at clouds or stars or whatever was up there. They used to stare at screens lit with video games. And that whole cove of memory was locked up inside me till I saw him and he freed it.

—I love this place so much, Pio says. —I come here for every birthday.

Sil shuffles through the menu.

—Is today your birthday? I ask.

Pio grins all big, his nose and cheeks dusted with freckles I never noticed before.

—No, he says, —I'm a June baby. But we could pretend and get a free slice of pie.

Mischief darkens his eyes, like when he used to scheme a trip into the kitchen for something sugary. He loved sweets, soda, cookies, fruit. Why, my soul calls out, haven't we seen these people in so long? Why did I miss Pio's shot-up height, his crackling voice, his long-limbed stumbling? We could have had all those years. Instead, we skipped it all and I sit before a near-grown version of my childhood friend. Some parts of him are still child and those are the parts I recognize and reach out for.

—I don't know why you even look at the menu, he says to his dad. —You know exactly what you're getting.

Pio hasn't even opened his menu. Sil nudges his shoulder and smiles. They are nearly the same height but Sil is barrel-chested, bulkier around the middle. —Never know, Sil says, —something else could jump out at me.

I am staring down at the open-faced laminated sheets. Truthfully, I made up my mind minutes ago, but if the menu gives me something to look at other than the wide-open space of our memory, then I will do that.

—I get the bananas foster pancakes every time, Pio tells me. —Highly recommended.

I've already decided on something else but I look down at the pancakes and entertain the possibility. No, it doesn't feel quite right on the tongue. I order the French toast instead and stare at my hands. When it comes, it's smattered with berries and powdered sugar. Pio's eyes leap out of his skull and his tongue flails around in his mouth—he's sugar-crazy as ever.

His pancakes are set down next and the smell is tantalizing. The bananas drenched in some sort of caramel sauce that leaks through to the pancakes below. He catches me eyeing them and makes a gesture like, *You want some?* but I shake my head and lower my eyes to my own plate. The diner is hot; I am right next to a heating vent. I look up and Pio is holding his fork out to me, a triangle bite speared at its end. Banana and pancake and sauce.

—Here comes the airplane, Sil says, then makes an airplane sound.

—Hurry, before it drips, Pio says.

I reach out to take the fork but Pio says, —Open.

So I extend my head forward, neck craned like a bird. He places the bite on my tongue and I close my mouth around it as he takes the fork out. The sweetness is a bloom. I keep my eyes on my plate smeared in syrup, my napkin in my lap, my fork and knife intersected over the toast. The empty cup where my syrup was. The glass of ice water sweating down its sides. The dewdrop beads on the Formica.

—Good, huh, he says.

I choke out a *yeah*. Don't know what is happening, why my eyes are so skittish, leaping from one table-level thing to the next, but I focus on my toast one bite at a time.

Pio reaches over for a sample of his dad's biscuits and gravy. As he chews, he says, —Yours are better.

—I'll take that, Sil says. —I'll have to make it for you soon, Orrie. Maybe this weekend.

—You'll freak, Pio says.

I look up and Sil is smiling at me like I've made a joke.

—What? I say, going a bit red.

—I just never thought someone could make Pio look loud.

Pio laughs at this, a warm honey sound.

—I remember he used to be so crazy, I say, —just running around and bouncing off the walls.

—He's really mellowed out these last few years. Sil ruffles Pio's hair and Pio ducks away like he's embarrassed. —I know, Sil says, —we never thought it'd happen. But he's quite a mellow fellow.

—And so am I, apparently, I say. My fingers are knitted in my lap. I look like a schoolchild who has been chided: head down, blushing, curling in.

—Nothing wrong with it, Pio says.

I look up at him and there's a warmth on his face that brings me some relief. A slight wave of it up my arms cooling the fever-rush that's building in my skin.

I don't know how he would describe this moment but for me it's like there's a vestige in my soul that's rearing its way to the surface of me and demanding my attention, an area of me that has been long neglected and only now gathered the strength to kick up to my shore. To flail its arms in the air and say, PAY ATTENTION TO ME, NOURISH ME.

I imagine Emma and Ingrid and Mom and Dad in the restaurant. Though it's a faded imagining, now half-impossible and ever further from reach. Emma loud and causing a ruckus. Ingrid hardly there save for the sound of her chewing, taking sips, setting down her water glass. How would Dad act? Probably closer to Ingrid, though I would hope there was a part of him that could still reach for vivacity.

The car ride back to the house is blurry. Sil pays for our meal and I thank him, and at some point we make our way out to the car and climb inside, bump and jolt on the roads to the house, but my mind is too distracted for many earthly concerns. It's a whole new side of town I never experience these days, but it passes by in an instant.

We're standing in Pio's room now. He's looking at his bunk which is all disrupted from my sleep, its sheets pulled back and crumpled, its pillows uneven and partially exposed, one fallen to the floor.

—I love your bunk bed, I say. —Sorry I slept on the bottom bunk but I couldn't really see out of my eyes last night so I didn't wanna climb up.

He skates right past it like it's normal for people to temporarily lose their sight every so often. —That's okay, it was my brother's bunk.

His brother. I remember him from the hall photos. A figure who grew alongside Pio until he disappeared and only Pio stood there.

—Is he dead? The words fall out like marbles and my face goes hot. I am helpless to gather them up. They are rolling around all over the floor. —God, sorry, that was rude.

—It's okay, he says again. —Yeah, Angio's dead.

A pallor has fallen over the room in late afternoon, a sort of bloodless light. It's okay, I want to tell him, my room at home is a dead person's room too. Every day I get up and go through the motions of life but really, I have been dead for five days and it's hard to believe the world has been going on since. I died when Ingrid died. Now that Dad is dead too, I am dead again. Double-dead and drifting.

But I don't say anything. I shut my mouth. I am not helping.

—So I know what you're feeling, he says. —Or close enough to it.

I give him a look. Don't have any words but hope the leaky-feeling look is enough.

—Would you mind, though, sleeping on the top? he asks. —I normally sleep on the bottom.

—Oh, yeah, that's fine.

I pull my blanket from home out of my bag and throw it up on the top bunk. Nothing special in its patterning or color but I sleep with it often at home and it has taken on that homelike smell. I wonder how long it'll be till it smells like this place.

Pio goes to the bathroom and I go out to the living room and sit with Sil. The TV is on but the sound is muted so the room is just a blur of colors.

—It's really nice to have two voices in the house again, he says. —Feels more alive in here.

I smile and approach the couch. Not the spot Pio was in earlier—I leave that for him. Move slightly further down and sink into the leather. A well-worn couch with people-sized dips, it hugs me right up.

—So weird I haven't been here in so long. What's the story there.

For some reason I just come out with it; I surprise myself. Things falling from me left and right this evening. Every word feels petal-soft in my mouth and it's only when they leave that things sharpen and harden. Sil wears that look on his face like he's clamped his lips together in order not to let a sound out.

—It's not really my story to tell.

So strange, the fact that the best friendship of my childhood fell through my hands. But by the time I stopped seeing Pio I had moved up to middle school and met a whole crop of new people, made new friends, fell into new habits. I guess it makes sense that it happened without my noticing.

—Maybe later, he decides. Which has the tone of NOPE SORRY but still I allow a bit of hope to trickle into the conversation.

When bedtime comes around later I climb up onto the top bunk and lick at my minty-scrubbed teeth. My eyelids are heavy and I know it won't be long till I'm under. I feel a slight headache coming on. Pio clicks out the lamp and the room is washed in dark; just a bit of moonlight trickles in.

There's a slat of light on the wall right next to me and I watch it. Look at the texture of the paint on the wall, how it seems to be alive. I can hear Pio breathing below me and shifting from side to side.

He is a hard person for me to think about and describe. When I look at him, I remember when we were children. He was so wild and loud then. Now that he's sixteen, like me, he has mellowed out, though I can see there's something in him that is begging to be expressed. And then I consider for the first time that maybe grief is what buckled him over and locked him inside himself. Maybe it's something I can bring him out of. Or maybe I will become grief-trapped too and we will sit here side by side in our separate chambers of hurt.

Or maybe it's just the fact that he's not sugar-high all the time anymore: he eats more vegetables, therefore he has leveled out. There is a pensiveness to him, a sense when I look at him that if he opens his mouth, a cavern of himself could spill out.

And one fact of the day is that I have spent most of it thinking about him. Even when he hasn't been around. This is a strange fact I don't know what to do with.

—What was it like going back to my house today? I whisper into the quiet room. If he's asleep, I figure, it can roll off him. But he shifts below me and I know he's awake.

—Funny, he says. —I've thought about it a lot recently, and it was funny to be there. Feels kind of like I wished the whole thing into happening.

He rustles again, maybe itches himself on the neck or the arm.

—Well, not the. You know. What happened to. Agh.

Dad and sister (push it away) I move past it. —It's been so long, I say.

—Yeah. I just remember Dad making excuses when I mentioned you or the family. Saying you were going to be out of town or we had somewhere to be or shouldn't I be getting my homework done before trying to make plans. And then Angio. Which. You know. Kind of took over.

A pit of silence chokes him for a moment. I imagine him spitting it out into his palm, rigid and round like a peach stone.

—I can't believe Mom didn't tell me when it happened, I say. —I'm sorry it happened.

—It was years ago. Now I'm pretty much numb to it.

I turn onto my left side and look out into the dark of the room. On the desk there's a clock which shines out its red numbers. But the light doesn't make it very far; the room is still black. I massage my temples; there's a weird throb there.

—So this was his bunk? I say.

—Yeah. He snored so bad. I hope you're not a snorer.

—I'm not. I laugh as quietly as I can. —And his name was . . .

—Angio.

—Angio, I repeat.

—Angioletto. But we called him Angio or Ange. One of my first girlfriends used to call him Angie, which pissed him off.

I laugh again, less quiet this time. I cover my mouth with my hand afraid like we're kids at a sleepover and Sil is going to come chide us for not being asleep. How many sleepovers did we spend talking as the hours bled away. How many nights in my house doing the same thing with Ingrid and Emma.

—Why did he never come over when you came over?

—We had really different lives, actually. We weren't those kind of twins that were each other's shadows. Different friend groups and everything. But we were still close.

—What is Pio short for?

—You don't remember?

There's a bit of hurt in his voice and I want to pluck it out of the air and squash it between my fingers. —I wish I did, I say.

—It's short for Primo. Ange couldn't pronounce it as a kid, and his way stuck. When I asked Dad why they named me Primo, he said, *perché sei il primo.*

My eyes are heavy but the rumbles of his voice keep me awake and thinking.

—And I *have* always been first, kind of. Even over Ange. And then for a while I started calling him Sec, short for *secondo*, and that pissed him off too. So easy to rile him up. Kinda like Emma in that way.

I smile and we settle into a moment of quiet. I imagine him lost in memories of Angio, adrift on a cloud somewhere.

—Honestly, I used to have such a crush on Emma.

I laugh and laugh but there's some other thing in me I can't identify. Something darker. —Oh my god, really?

—Yeah, really. Drove me nuts that she never wanted to hang out with us.

I make some vague pleasant sound, some half-laugh. But he doesn't say anything else. I figure he's tired or doesn't want to talk anymore. I imagine him sitting there with me in my room, listening, waiting for Emma. Wondering about her. I keep thinking he's going to speak, keep blinking myself awake so I don't miss a thing.

A WISP OF

crackle

A SINGLE LITTLE WISP

10

Cleo wakes in a sweat and feels like life

, the whole thing, will ricket to an end. The dream, again, the same goddamn dream. She thought she'd rid herself of it, since the snake, the former husband, has been quashed. But the dream is back. Again the birthing, again the squelching pain, again the two men above her: Enzo on her left, golden-eyed subjugated spineless man; Aggie on her right, the family scepter in his hands, but this time he is different, his neck gashed open, blood flooding over his clothes and what shows of his neck. Yet he is alive. And on the scepter, the heavy wooden thing, a new branch is blooming.

She feels Aggie's spirit looming over her. Not in the dream but separate from it, in the body. What, she wants to shout at him, what do you want from me? I have put you to sleep and now you are supposed to stay that way. In the dream he moves, twitches, as the delirious pain of her birth washes over her. And that scepter is blooming, making more life, and the baby is free of her and looks at her with its snake eyes and says BRING ME HOME. And she realizes with a sick twist in her belly that the eyes she has recognized all along are not Enzo's or Aggie's but Orrie's. The fangs go in as she starts to understand.

She's sweating, shaking, in bed now. Enzo senses her discomfort, the looseness in her limbs, and, like a good watchdog, he rolls over and investigates. Plants a kiss on her bare shoulder, settles into her side, watches her tremble and think.

—In the morning, she says, —we have to finish planning the funeral.

It's been a few days and from the outside they've seemed too shaken to plan. But they must, if she wants to quell Aggie's restless spirit.

Another *but*, which is: Is she ready to have Orrie home? This is the bit of thread she spins around and around in her mind. Especially after seeing him in the snake, watching him drain her. She feels her trust in him shrink, though she is trying not to let the dreams work too much magic on her mind. At the beginning of everything she laughed at the curse, at the haunted dreams. Look at her now.

She climbs from bed when Enzo is asleep and sneaks into the bathroom. Pulls the second-to-last pregnancy test from beneath the counter. Breathes in and out through the longest three minutes of her life. Tries to remember her last period, though she knows they have come and gone through all sorts of stressors.

When the second line appears, pin-thin, she feels it like a stain on the soul. Rubs the dark out of her eyes, squints at it again in the mirror light. The faintest line, like the gods reached down with a dead pen. What are the odds, what are the odds.

She shoves it all back into the box, dumps it in the trash. Pulls out the last test, tries again. She barely has any fluid in her but the stress gets some out. She counts down from 180, and when it's over, she doesn't want to look. This is the last moment in which she doesn't have confirmation—only the black behind her eyes. She holds on to that not-knowing.

11

—stories are fun aren't they want another?

NEXT UP NUMBER THREE THIS ONE LIVES UP IN THE RAFTERS OF US
AND INVOLVES THAT DEAD-AND-GRILLED-UP SON FROM EARLIER
(THE FIRST ONE, NOT THE NEPHEWS—
WE KNOW, SO MUCH SON-GRILLING)
LET'S CALL THIS ONE P
THE GODS SENSED INJUSTICE AT HIS DEATH
AND PUT HIM BACK TOGETHER
BROUGHT HIM BACK TO LIFE
BUT AT THE GIANT OLYMPIAN GODS-TABLE
DEMETER WAS DISTRACTED BY GRIEF
(HER DAUGHTER HAD JUST BEEN SUCKED UP INTO THE UNDERWORLD)
AND SHE ACCIDENTALLY GNAWED INTO HIS SHOULDER
BEFORE REALIZING HER ERROR
(HAPPENS TO ALL OF US)

SO HEPHAESTUS CRAFTED AN IVORY REPLACEMENT
AND THE REVIVED IVORY-SHOULDERED MAN LIVED
HAPPILY EVER AFTER
UNTIL YEARS LATER IN COMPETITION TO WIN A BRIDE
(WHEN BRIDES WERE THINGS TO BE WON)
HE DECIDED NOT TO PLAY BY THE RULES
AND CONVINCED A SERVANT TO REPLACE THE LINCHPINS
IN HIS COMPETITOR'S CHARIOT
OFFERING THE SERVANT THE FIRST NIGHT WITH HIS WIFE AS A BRIBE
BUT WHEN HIS COMPETITOR'S CHARIOT CRUMBLED
AND IVORY-MAN WON HIS WIFE
THE SERVANT CAME TO CASH IN HIS PRIZE
AND IVORY-MAN BECAME ENRAGED
AND CAST THE SERVANT INTO THE SEA
WHERE HE SLOWLY MELTED TO BONES
BUT BEFORE HIS MELTING HE CALLED OUT A BITTER CURSE
THAT LEFT HIS MOUTH IN OCEAN-BUBBLES
FLOATED UP TO THE AIR
AND ONWARD UP TO THE GODS

12

coming back inside with a platter in my hands

that our neighbor John brought up the hill in his pickup. He said his wife Lorrie had made it for us in our time of troubles, said Lorrie was absolutely moonstruck at the loss. *You know Lorrie,* he said, *she taught Ingrid in school some years ago, always found her such a bright and calming child.* I thought I remembered my dead sister's teacher—grainy mental picture of a red bouffant and a warm smile. *Anyway, something to keep you nourished,* he said. *We still think about the time your dad came down to help us when Blitzen, that was one of the neighborhood deer, got his head stuck in a fence, and your dad bucked his legs up and got him out. He was a good man.* John got leaky-eyed then, his nose rose-tinted from cold. He said, *Sorry for all your troubles. Hope you enjoy the food.*

Enzo is in the kitchen, blocking my way to the sink. He's just come in from some earth-tending. I've had a quiver in my hands all day, a restlessness I can't quell—I worry I'll start scratching myself like Mom, leave long marks all up and down my forearms, little rivers of scratch. The fridge-fresh platter is frigid in my hands, sending chills up my limbs. I haven't really looked at Enzo in a while but I notice his eyes are narrower than usual, less alive in their opening. His wrists jut over the sink, bent strange, like they might snap. Like the world's weight is pressing on him. One of his feet is kicked over the other, toe pointed at the floor.

I slide the platter of hash-brown something into the fridge, knowing Mom will scoff at it, call it heart-clogging. I'll peck away at it over the next few days, and if Orrie were here he'd slather nasty ketchup on it for all three meals. Very little that boy loves more than breakfast food with ketchup. Competing desires duke it out in me: I want to leave, want to run and never look back, but I also want Orrie here, want my brother back.

Claire is going to call at eight—we set the time a few days ago. She'll tell me about college, about Nic, about new friends; I'll give her my updates afterwards. I walk by Enzo and grab the tea kettle. Stand, wait for him to notice me, to move. I'm sure the look on my face isn't the nicest but it seems a bit much when he turns and a shudder goes through him at the sight of me.

I fill the kettle with water and light the burner, head toward the stairs to grab the mug I used this morning. How we just keep living our lives, how time keeps on floating by.

—Emma. The word is a pained thing on Enzo's lips.

I halt, turn back. —Hmm?

The stovetop is doing the whisper it does when it's heating up. Enzo turns away from me, looks over at the far wall, at the paintings hung there. The light gilds his cowlick hairs.

—Never mind. Again that low voice, resigned, flat, lifeless. He uncrosses his feet.

—No, I say. —What?

He looks so frail. I'm used to seeing him stand tall, lug things around, operate machines, dig into earth. His hunched posture makes him small, sad.

—What were you going to say? I ask.

He swallows. The water begins to hiss a bit. The lights are dim; Enzo's laugh lines glow at the edges of his grimace.

—I don't feel like you've given me a fair chance, he says.

Mom's footsteps creak upstairs and the whole house shifts with her motion. Enzo's words boom through the space—she must be able to pick them up.

—I've always felt like . . . like maybe you hate me, I don't know.

He slices the room open right there—all the blood, the muscle, in the air comes spilling out. Ligaments of the space torn in two. When was the last time I regarded him with a smile or a laugh, I wonder.

—What have I done wrong? he asks.

I no longer want tea, I realize. I switch the burner off, hear the hissing of the water begin to recede.

—You haven't done anything, I say. It's a small kindness, a small lie. He's flashing his soft eyes at me so I keep my gaze focused on the slant of his brow.

—But you're not my dad. And you never will be.

He must know that's how I feel, but to hear it voiced must sting more. Doesn't matter. He slipped a knife into my side in asking the question; I can slip one into his in response. I turn away. Mom is making her way down the stairs with a box in her hands. She has just showered and has a towel wrapped around her hair. I slip by her, scoot up the stairs. In twenty words I have become the villain and I don't like the feeling on my skin like grime.

I sit at my desk, wait for my phone to ring. My room is cold and again I long for tea, for a blanket to wrap tight around myself. Claire and I used to huddle under one while we watched movies, with popcorn or ice cream. She often fell asleep there on the couch, but sometimes she'd come up to my room and we'd sleep back to back, talk about boys. Neither of us ever spoke of Nic. I told her everything.

At ten past eight, I dig through my email, find the last scant note she wrote me from school. Two months back: *You'd love it here.* Descriptions of weather, landmarks, architecture. *I'll send you pictures tomorrow.* Nothing since.

At twenty past eight, I call her myself. I would have called earlier, but I wanted her to have the experience of realizing she'd forgotten and to feel bad about it. I wanted her apologies, her pleas.

The phone tells me the number has been disconnected.

ALMOST THE END OF

crackle

WE MUST GET

crackle

GET HIM BACK

13

it seems like every day from now on will be a good day

because I am happy, I am with Pio, I am not thinking about school coming up in a couple weeks or tending the pit of loss in me. I am coasting on the energy of friendship. The rooms in the house are full of sun and the chill of outside only lasts seconds on the skin before the heater kicks on and the vents warm us up again.

But today I sit up in my bunk and something is off. The room is empty and a video game loading screen is on the computer. There's a heaviness pressing down on me, some sort of muck stuck to the exterior of my brain. Some other layer squeezed beneath my skull.

When Pio comes back from the bathroom, he sees I have sunk to the ground. He comes into the room and lowers himself to me. Looks into my eyes, which makes me want to fall through the floor.

—You okay? he says.

I don't know what to tell him, so I lie and give a gentle nod. He holds out a hand to help me up. I take it and he lifts me back to standing. In truth, I am a bit unsettled inside. I haven't seen glimmers anywhere in a long time but it feels like something else is building in me.

—I'm just playing video games, he says. —Wanna play?

I shake my head. Never played them at home, only a couple times at friends' houses, and the amount of buttons made me sick.

—I'll just watch, I say.

He smiles and sits back down in his computer chair. Lifts the remote and gets through all the settings screens to a game part.

—Gonna grab some food first, I say.

He puts his socked feet up, sets his heels against the desk edge, and kicks one foot to the rhythm of the game music. The sweatshirt he wears is a pale-blue, clouded thing that matches his eyes.

—I'll be here, he says.

I pad out to the kitchen. Sil is outside, but in the family room he has left something on TV and its sound drifts in to me while I pour myself a bowl of cereal. There's a strange trembling in my arms as I lift the box and the milk. An absolute absence of hunger. But I know it's important to start my day off with some food in me, and it might make whatever is in my head feel better.

Sil trudges in while I'm chomping. The light in the window is baby yellow and there are some vines creeping on the other side, their dark green leaves all acurl. He grabs his mug from the dish rack and pours some coffee into it.

—God, it's so funny to see you sitting there, he says. —You're hunched over in your seat just like Angio. He laughs and takes a sip. —Like he thought someone was gonna come up and steal whatever he was eating.

—You never know, I say.

He laughs again, then steps closer, puts a hand on my shoulder.

It's warm though he was just working outside—must have been wearing good gloves.

—You all right, kid? he asks. —Seem a bit ghosty today.

With a big bite of cereal in my mouth, all the little chocolate puffs crunching between my teeth, I try to give him my best I'M FINE look.

—I mean, I guess it only makes sense, given. Ahm. He flounders for something else to talk about.

—I guess I'm still pretty tired, I say after I swallow my bite.

—Well, lucky for you, you've got nothing to do and can sleep all day. He shuffles over to the fridge and pulls it open, inspects its contents like someone else stocked it. —You want something with more substance? Eggs, sausage, bacon? Something?

I pat my stomach, which makes a big groaning noise at being filled. —No thanks, I say. —I'm full.

—You know you don't have to worry here. You can eat anything. What's ours is yours, this is your home.

My heart lifts at that. There's something in the way he says it, like it's splitting him open to say it. —Thanks, I tell him. —No, I'm just not hungry is all.

—Okay, he says. —Well, I think I'm gonna make myself some breakfast. It'll be here if you change your mind. Did Pio eat?

I carry my bowl to the sink, rinse it out, and set it on the bottom rack of the dishwasher. Put the spoon down there too, a heavy, fancy-feeling silver thing. —No clue, I say. —I just woke up.

I go back to the room and Pio gestures toward his bunk. I pull a pillow down to the bottom end and lay there watching him play. He's between rounds right now, so he doesn't have to focus.

—Whatcha smiling about? he asks.

The game starts again and he propels his fingers around the remote. Some sort of shooter game; there's the pointy end of a gun on screen and not much else. We hear footsteps and radio communication reverberant through a dark tunnel. He presses a button to switch the view and the whole character comes on screen. When he shoots the gun he hits a complex series of buttons that make an array of pops in my ear. He is very good at the game, I come to realize. His eyes face the screen and have gone glazy, his tongue-tip stuck out the corner of his mouth. I feel light years away.

I drift away into an alternate version of my life. We never fell out of touch and I came here every week. Grieved Angio alongside him. Ate meals at his dining-room table, ate his dad's cooking. Watched him play video games even learned to play them myself. Got good at them, even. Beat him at one or two of them every now and then. Soaked him up into my life.

Somebody kicks in the door to get into the room and Pio spins his character around to take him out. One shot and the other guy is down. The screen flashes with bright congratulations.

That strange pressure still in my head. I start to poke at my temples, think it might make it ease or at least shift. But it doesn't. And I'm struck by the odor of myself—I should probably put on some deodorant.

—Do you play video games a lot? I ask.

—Well, you know, he says, —winter break. He catches another one of those dots and leaps over the railing to the bottom floor, takes out somebody else in the distance. A girl—he catches her right between the eyes. She goes down in a splay of limbs and again those celebrations flutter at the top of the screen. —But not usually. During the year I've got lots of homework and I spend a lot of time outside. And Mom doesn't let me play them at her house.

—How often are you over there?

—Few times a month. She's remarried and Darius, my stepdad, is pretty cool. But I like being here better.

I picture his life over there. The soft swells he feels when he comes back up this street. It almost warms me but the warmth doesn't get around that skull-layer.

I stand up, meaning to go to the bathroom and put deodorant

on, and my stomach suddenly seizes. I vomit into my hands and hear at the same time bell-clear

< come back >

and Pio turns around with a look of concern.

—Yuck, I say, embarrassed, holding the hot liquid in my hands, trying not to drip it onto the floor. I run across to the bathroom and dump it in the sink, slam the faucet on, run my hands under it. Pio comes across and turns on the light. The water is ice-cold and it takes a while for it to warm up. My fingertips go frigid and acid sits in the back of my throat and burns there. I rinse out my mouth while the water is still cold, swallow some down to flush everything out.

I stare at myself in the mirror and Pio stands there, his hand on my back. I'm leaning over the sink, my eyes six inches from their own reflection, and he is there behind me, his hand up and down, up and down—calming motions. I lean into it without realizing, press myself back against his hand. It feels good to be there.

—Back to bed you go, huh, he says.

—I don't even feel sick, I say. —I just feel—

—Hot. His hand is at my forehead and his brow sinks even further. Those big blues so heavy with concern. —Burning up.

He guides me back to his room, his hand still at the small of my back. Each of his fingers set gently there. Eventually I pull away from him and crawl back down into his bunk.

—Sure you don't want to sleep? he asks.

—More games, I say.

He smiles. —Oh, hold on. He leaps from the room and rounds the corner. I hear his footsteps fade. I assume he's telling Sil about my vomit moment. But he comes back with a big cup of water and sets it on the coaster near me. —For you, he says.

My ribcage is too small. I try to squash the beating thing down but it makes its own choices.

He switches to a driving game. The screen lights up with rainbow colors and a trailer of sorts plays. All the cars racing around the track, all the boosts and power-ups they can get. He sets the controller down on his right knee, balances it carefully there.

—Watch, he says, —I can drive with one hand.

He begins the game—blasts off into first place playing only with his left hand. His right hand he keeps at his side and then after a few moments he slides it over. Behind him and over to me. Finds my hand a finger at a time and holds it gently in his own. For a while it's just the two hands together, his fingers interlaced with mine, his fingertips on my palm. Oh god, I worry, I'm going to sweat the room into a pool. I lose sight of the game. Have no clue what power-ups he's getting or what turns he's making. It's only the feeling as he starts tracing his pointer finger over my knuckles and that giant, gold first-place symbol in the bottom corner of the screen.

—Is this okay? he says.

I nod, then realize he's looking at the screen, so I say, —Yeah.

—You feeling okay? Sil says from the doorway.

Pio whips his hand away laser-fast, pretends to reach to the floor to grab something. My soul slips on its feet.

—Yeah, I'm okay, I think I say. —Don't really know what happened there.

Sil comes over to inspect. He lowers himself to my level and sets the back of his hand to my forehead. —Good god, you're cold, he says. —You sleep without any blankets on?

Pio turns toward us, a ghost gone through him. —He's cold?

—Yeah, Sil says. —How about some soup to warm you up? Chicken vegetable or chili? I've got leftovers in the freezer. I can take some out and warm them up for you for lunch.

—Chicken sounds good, thanks.

Another dark wave of nausea goes through me but no vomit this time. And again that bird-quiet but frightening echo of

< come back >

which seems to dim all the lights in the room, suck the spirit out of me.

—Did anyone else hear that? I find myself saying.

—Hear what? Pio says.

—I'm hearing voices, I guess. I say it like it's a joke and Pio and Sil laugh like it's a joke.

Sil tells me to call for him if I need anything. Pio's hand returns to his remote and he switches over to the shooter game again. Both hands required for this one. I shift my hands around beneath the pillow, stick them out so they're visible, but his doesn't slip back over.

Till he gets obliterated (he isn't perfect at the game, just very very good) and lets go of the remote in frustration, and his smooth hand finds mine again. Dampened this time from the game, but still I hold on to it like it's keeping me whole.

—God, you really are cold, he says. —Don't know what's going on with you. You were hot as balls in the bathroom.

He leans in toward me, his face creeping closer inch by inch. My breath is gated in my throat I think he's going to it seems like maybe he might but he stops. Something moves through him and he pulls away. Has an idea—I see it in his eyes.

—Let's go for a walk later. You've seen a bit of the property but not all of it, not the coolest parts. And some time outside might clear your head.

The promise of it shines in his voice.

By the funeral, Mom wants me to decide what to do. To stay here or to go back there. I think of Emma, now the only child in that whole house. An adult now but still childlike in some ways. Nowhere to go, nothing to do, not even any schooling. This is the longest I've been away from her in a while and her absence is another pang in me.

I let my head fall onto the pillow and focus on the screen. More people to shoot and Pio does it without blinking. Running in and out of abandoned houses, up and down corridors. I find I am watching the shooting game but thinking of my dad. Still feeling that strange skull-pressure.

14

—version four now (though our bones are aching

WE ARE TIRED OF TELLING STORIES)
A MAN SOME GENERATIONS LATER LET'S CALL THIS ONE A
BUT AGAIN NOT THE SAME A AS EARLIER
(MAYBE WE SHOULD HAVE CHOSEN DIFFERENT LETTERS)
AWAY AT SEA WINE-DRUNK AND WILD IS TAUNTING ARTEMIS
HAVING KILLED A SACRED DEER IN A SACRED GROVE
AND BOASTING AT HIS HUNTING PROWESS OVER HER
WELL ARTEMIS TESTY GODDESS SHIFTED WINDS
STRANDED THE MAN AND HIS CREW AT SEA
UPON THE CONDITION THAT TO BE LET GO HE WOULD HAVE TO KILL
THE THING MOST PRECIOUS TO HIM
THAT HAD COME INTO HIS POSSESSION
DURING THE YEAR HE KILLED THE DEER
WHICH HAPPENS TO BE THE YEAR

(GUT-SWAY)
HIS YOUNGEST DAUGHTER WAS BORN
HER MOTHER SAYS NO OF COURSE A YOU CANNOT DO THIS
BUT FOR ONCE THE GIRL IN THE CONTEXT OF WAR AND FAMILY
FEELS IMPORTANT
AND SHE LEADS HERSELF TO SLAUGHTER
AND THIS TIME THE CURSE ISN'T BROUGHT ON
BY SOME EXTERNAL FORCE
BUT BY THE MOTHER HERSELF
MOTHER RID OF CHILD THANKS TO HER HUSBAND'S
PRIDE AND HUBRIS
WATCH HER TURN THE HOUSE INSIDE OUT ALL ON HER OWN
(HOW'S THAT FOR A WOMAN'S POWER)

15

from the top of the stairs

I notice the light on in my room, when I thought I'd shut it off. But the door is nearly shut, this unexpected light shining through a narrow gap, when I know I left it open. When I go back in, the closet door, normally closed, is ajar, and a pair of shoes has fallen from the top shelf to the floor. My skin prickles. Is this one of the house's tricks (which I have no evidence of but have long suspected), or has somebody been in to pay a visit? Mom hasn't so much as looked at me in passing today. She's kept her eyes forward, kept her face neutral—she doesn't seem to be hiding any new secrets, but maybe I'm wrong.

I remember, then, what I have in the closet: the evidence. I sprint over, tip-toe stretch up to the top shelf, find the saucepan gone. The jar, which I'd kept in my middle dresser drawer, is also gone, the drawer contents askew, a few pairs of leggings hanging over the side.

Out in the hall there's a shuffling noise, and I stick my head out to see Enzo headed into Mom's room. With the comfort of it being his own space—my heart rages. I storm downstairs and into the kitchen, see Mom at the sink, hear water rushing. I already know what's happening but I look anyway.

The saucepan is there beside the sink, washed spotless, dried. And she's got the Mason jar unscrewed and she's dumped its contents down the drain. She's scrubbing the metal ring and each of its grooves with the sponge, letting the glass fill with hot water. She dumps and fills it again, dumps and fills. Calm, measured, like she cleans these things in this order every evening.

I envision the water hot enough to shatter the glass, imagine it falling to pieces in her hands, shrieking through her skin, pinking up the sink.

—Your words to Enzo earlier weren't very kind, she says.

—He's a grown man, I say, —he can handle it. And stay out of my room.

—I'm pretty sure while you're living under my roof there is no *your*. She sets the lid down, shuts the water off. —You're not paying rent, are you. Would you like to start?

I swallow, don't say anything but don't look away. My face answers, *No*. She is speaking to me with her face at a quarter angle—her lashes flutter down as she blinks. One has fallen onto her cheek. I near her, extend a finger to brush it away.

—Lash, I whisper.

She presents her face, eyes gently shut, as if I am going to dab blush on her cheeks. My hand tightens, constricts into a fist, but I loosen it and scoop the lash up and let it flutter into the sink. She runs the faucet, washes it down.

—Or maybe you've got somewhere else you'd like to live, she says. —Maybe with Claire.

Inside, I recoil. I think of the phone message, the disconnection, the email unanswered. How dare she poke so hard where she knows it hurts.

—Didn't think so, she says. —It's my room, it's all mine.

She takes the saucepan and hangs it back on its hook, sets its lid up on the rack. Picks up the Mason jar, dries it out with a rag, screws its lid back on.

—And be nice to Enzo, she says. —He deserves so much better than your attitude.

Then the worst part of all, worse than any word she could have flung: she smiles at me, steps around me and out of the room.

Alone later, I think back to her standing there at the sink, and I see it there, that contained rage. What are your secrets, I want to ask, what are your ways—how do you keep it from spilling over? I am at a rolling boil at all times—I was tempted to rip the rest of her eyelashes right out and scatter them along the sink while I was that close to her. Evil mother. She has given me this rage but not shown me how to temper it. She has cleared my evidence against her, washed it away—a guilty hound, sniffing out the stuff that would lock her up, doing away with it. The guilt gleams on her skin, shines in her eyes.

A crushing weight overtakes me: I have driven Orrie away with my furies and cries, just like I drove Claire away, just like I drove Ingrid away. But then I remember a day when Ingrid was ten, I think, and I was in a rage about a CD that had started skipping, and I threw the old player across the room, watched it strike the wall and shatter into plastic pieces. What was I doing listening to CDs still, anyway? But Ingrid came into the room and sat next to me and laid herself back across my legs, let her hair hang onto the floor, and something about the weight of her there was so quieting. No, she wasn't afraid of my fury. She had held it, guided it down.

16

—which of the tales do you believe?

WE HAVE HAD TIME TO SIT AND LISTEN TO THEM
WHENEVER THEY'RE TOLD
AND HAVE COME TO ADMIRE EACH IN DIFFERENT WAYS
BUT THE THING WE CAN ALL AGREE ON IS
THAT WE SHALL ALL FALL TO RUIN

17

—are you gonna take orrie to the

—SHHH, said Pio, DON'T GIVE IT AWAY, so Sil never finished his question.

But now I'm looking for a thing to be led to. The strangeness in my head is still here and maybe even worse than it was earlier. But I am trying to ignore it. I am looking up and down the trees and out through the branches for some sort of clearing, some sort of something.

Pio says, —Just look around, that's all.

His head of tight curls bounces as we walk and I want to reach out and touch it. I don't know how I could stand to leave. I imagine heading back home after the funeral and feel cleaved open.

He looks over at me and laughs.

—What? I say.

—You're really not good at hiding your feelings, are you.

My face goes red. I think. I can't see it, so I don't know for sure, but it's a feeling of blood-rush.

—What do you mean? I ask, like I don't know exactly what.

—The first time I saw you when I got back from my mom's it was like I'd hit you with a shovel.

I laugh, a loud burst of a thing, and lower my head. —Was not.

—No, it was. He kicks a pine cone. —But it was cute. At least I knew then. He grabs my hand for a moment and my organs clash together. My palm is slick from nerves but he doesn't drop it, just holds it tight.

—Knew what?

—I don't know, Orrie—what do you think?

He turns me bashful. I sink down into a shell of blush.

—It was funny, I say, —when you pulled your hand away so quick. Earlier, when your dad came in.

He goes clam-tight, his lips sealed like they're locked, and his hand slips from mine and falls to his side. Why'd I have to say it. My hand follows his for a moment before my mind catches up.

—You know, I say, —he's really cool. I don't think he'd mind if he knew.

—Knew what.

—That you're.

A little bit of cloud over him, maybe. —I'm not, though.

A pine cone falls out of a nearby tree and slaps into a leaf-bed.

—I don't know what I am, he says, —but I'm not that.

—Oh.

He swipes something out of the corner of his eye.

—Are you? he asks.

—No, I don't think so. I mean. Kind of.

—Clearly, he says, skimming my wrist with a finger.

The squawk of a bird up high in the branches. Some kind of small-bodied thing, I don't know, I have never been good at identifying them. Ingrid could have picked it right out of the sky. From a hundred feet up.

—We're almost there, he says. —Just a little further out.

His cheeks have gone raspberry in the cold.

We burst through a couple trees and come to a giant rock where you can get to the top if you climb either side. Not too high—twenty or thirty feet—but high enough that you feel momentous standing up there. He leads me up the right side and when we get to the top we stand there and look through the trees at the terrain we just crossed. He points way out in the distance toward where their house is. We can't see it through the treetops, but I feel its presence out there like a guiding star. Already this place has that warm-weepy feeling of home.

He sinks down onto the rock and finds a smooth part. Sits there and looks at the loose tufts of cloud. I sink down next to him and play with some pebbles that are near my feet. Like little bits of ice in these temperatures. I shuffle them around in my hands and try to warm them up.

—Actually, I say, —the way I feel when I'm around you reminds me of how I felt around one of my best friends who moved away. Her name was Liv. It was like a . . . lifting. And like when I'm there it's the exact right place. I don't know. I know it was something else but I never got the chance to find out. 'Cause she moved away last year.

He touches my chest and says, —Orrie, keep a little bit of yourself in there. It's all spilling out.

He's so close all of a sudden. I didn't realize it till I felt his hand on my skin through the puff of my jacket and somehow it was such a warmth. Or maybe the rest of me was already warm and what I felt on my chest was just a pressure. So natural, the way he just glided over here. Like our bodies were built for nothing else but to drift toward one another. Close enough to his nose to count the freckles that dotted across them and for a moment I think I feel his lips through my coldness but again oh worst possible time there is

< COME BACK ORRIE >

booming through me, dark as sin. It wrenches through my gut, presses my skull tighter, and I pull away, let out a cry. If there was anything in my stomach left to spill, it would have come up, but this morning emptied me and I haven't eaten my lunch soup yet, so all I do is turn away from Pio and dry-heave over the side of the rock.

His hand is on my shoulder. —God, you all right? he says.

I lie there and shiver; I can't speak. He takes a tissue and holds it to my nose, which I realize has started to bleed. There's a spray of blood across the rock that I didn't notice before, maybe released at the moment I thought my skull was going to squeeze itself tight enough to explode. I would speak, if I could—I would placate him, tell him everything is fine. But it's like a metal ring has fastened itself around my throat and I can't get anything through it. I lie there and suck air in little shallow gasps of sound. He is so scared his eyes are buglike. I take his hand in mine and trace little circles on the skin between his finger and thumb. I hope the gesture says JUST STAY WITH ME, IT'LL BE FINE. Hope and hope.

I dream up the next moments. We go back and eat soup, warm ourselves from the inside out. He plays more video games, holds my hand the whole time, strokes little circles on my skin. Maybe he tries to go in again, tries to get close to me, and this time my strange sick body lets him. I hold on to this dream.

—

AND NOW

(JUMPING UP A BIT
MAYBE A WEEK)

A PROCESSION

—

18

he is coming back he is coming back we are beaming bright with this fact the full-house chorus is back and ready hush hush time for preparations get out of the way sink back into your walls a gathering of the tribe today

is the day—the moon is still high and dancing in and out of a few scatters of cloud when I'm dragged from bed and given tasks. My brain barely ticks, but there's a leaping in my chest. I just want to get through it, then let it settle into memory. Thinking too long about Ingrid or about Dad gets me keening like a dog. It's Mom asking for help—she has put on a gorgeous black gown and daubed her face with faint blush, the innocent stricken grieving maiden. Pah. She is slipping into character early, before any guests arrive, and asking me with piteous, doll-wide eyes:

—Emma, please fluff up the flowers on the entry table, they're looking a bit wan.

and

—Emma, please pull out the veggie platters. While you're at it, if you want, you could cut up some of those cucumbers in there.

(which, of course, means DO IT OR I WILL END YOU)

and

—Emma, would you please vacuum the upstairs rugs? They're looking a bit worse for wear.

Even though no one will be allowed past the base of the stairs. She is looking for ways to run me ragged. I am up and down the stairs, in and out of rooms, tip-toeing up to dust the high shelves and crouching to wipe the baseboards, running on three hours of fitful sleep. I am servant. She is wearing me down to waste. I am shoving it all down, looking for new ways to smile, to say, Sure, Mother, Of course, Mother, Yes, Mother, Anything for you, Mother.

Enzo has dug a nice suit out of his closet—he's gone all the way down to his house for it. He and Mom, for the day, are out in the open, now that they don't have to hide themselves from me. They touch hands and brush kisses on each other in passing and wipe tears from under eyes and whisper things back and forth. This morning, I went into Mom's room while the two of them were outside, and I found one of Enzo's shirts, a tan, collared number, draped over one of Dad's hangers. My heart lurched hard enough to launch itself out of the ribcage, but I slid it back in, swallowed it all down. For Ingrid, for Dad. (Really, I went back to my room and shouted a bit into my pillow, till the tension in my throat was relieved, but I said nothing to Mom or Enzo about it. A small victory, if you ask me, because everyone knows I could have ripped them both a new one.)

Enzo climbs into his truck to make his way toward the ocean: something about saltwater. I don't remember the family's long-held funeral rituals—it's been so long since our last grandparent died—but apparently this is one of them.

Mom notices the confused look I wear and says, —You don't remember scrubbing down the house?

I shake my head and turn back toward Enzo's departing truck, which is loaded with buckets and a cloth bag full of herbs. The red lights fade out at the hill's edge.

For hours, we tidy, we ready the house. Near sunup, light floods our front windows.

The day is so slippery. I see her first as a hovering thing at the edge of the porch. Then, I rub the startle out of my eyes and hear her say, —Emma, lovely to see you, my how you've grown. Help me bring in the vases, will you?

A familiar voice that takes me a second to place: our great-aunt Andrea, here from a few towns over.

—Vases? I ask.

She waves me down to her car, which is parked at the side of the long road up to the house. Her back seat is stuffed with boxes; she opens the back door, removes the nearest two, hands one to me, and shuts the car door with her hip. We lift the boxes up onto the porch, where Mom stands propping the screen door open with her foot, hands held over her chest, eyes wavering with sorrow.

—Andrea, she says. —Thank you, thank you. I appreciate you so much.

So much emphasis on the *so* that it's a miracle the word didn't kick up into the air and fly out the door. Andrea goes limp-eyed, falls into Mom's open arms.

Next to her beauty, her pretending, I'm grim, ugly, unkempt, haggard, blank. Were I on trial for murder, I'd be harangued, torn apart. I've got only three hours of sleep swimming in my system and my eyes can barely hold themselves open, my brain can barely tell me what day it is, my heart can barely hold what it's missing.

When Mom and Andrea pull apart, we begin opening the cardboard boxes, each with a snugly fit lid and stuffing made of tissue paper.

—You won't remember this, Andrea says to me, —but I've been making these for a long, long time. I made them for your grandparents—I'm sure those are around somewhere. I've been working on these ones all week. She pulls paper stuffing out, exposes the vases' tops. —Since the crash. What a horrid thing, to have taken them both.

Mom skates by it, but it flags in my ear. I almost leave it, almost, but the temptation is too great, a branch right before my eye, at the end of which is an apple I reach out to pluck.

I say, —Dad didn't die in the crash.

Mom's shoulders take up a new tension, visible beneath the garment's black.

—What? Andrea says. —I thought . . .

—No, I say.

Andrea turns to Mom for confirmation.

Tears brim in Mom's eyes and she jolts her head side to side, like she's trying to shake a ghost out of it. She says, —No, it's true, I . . . I had to . . .

Andrea's eyes are cloudy with shock and confusion.

—He was going to kill me.

Mom collapses. Andrea again rushes to her while I unveil the vases and admire the delicate painting. One, I realize, has been painted in commemoration of Ingrid, adorned with musical notes, dresses, and trees. The other in honor of Dad.

—He hadn't been the same, Mom continues, voice quaking, —since he came back from the war. So, so different.

She looks out across the room like his spirit hovers there and taunts her. She's good, so good.

—Oh dear, Andrea says. —How tragic.

Mom lowers her voice, just loud enough for me to hear, quiet enough for it not to carry. —I sometimes tell myself, she says, —that I deserved it. She wipes her face with the palm of her hand, gathers tears and snot. —That if only I'd been a better wife, a better mother . . .

—Oh no, Andrea says, —you can't go doing that. No, you are not to blame.

She holds the back of Mom's head in her hand like an infant's.

Over her shoulder, Mom catches my eye: she has transformed and something dark glints there in her irises, some warning. A flash of dread goes through me. I turn back to the vases, trace painted-Dad's long hair with a pinky finger.

—Will you join me, Mom says to her, —to pick up the urns? I don't know if I can bear it myself.

—Of course, Andrea says, cradling her cheek with a palm. —I'll drive, if you want.

—That would be wonderful.

I'm back to the vases, spinning them gently on their tissue-papered mats, watching them spin.

—Emma, Mom says as she and Andrea are stepping out the door. —Fill those beautiful things with flowers, won't you?

A flame is held beneath my stomach. —But nothing has bloomed, I say.

—The crocuses shot up early, don't you remember? She slips into a longer coat, also black, in her perfect grief. —Go trim some and fill those vases. They'll look just lovely for our remembrance

today we hear orrie is coming back home

we'll see him at the sad event

our side of town has missed him so

and rumor has it he's bringing a friend along

the way up to the house Pio leans in to me. Though he hardly remembers my father and barely knew my sister, he is here for me. His head is against my arm in the truck, his ear at my shoulder like he is trying to hear my thoughts. The feeling is a nice break from the wrenching inside. Sil smiles at us from the driver's seat.

Over the past few days I have been bedbound and ailing, with strange fevers working their way in and out of my body, and odd nosebleeds. Pio reports that I have woken him up by gasping in my sleep, unable to get air, but he's shaken me awake and it's stopped. (I don't remember it happening.) Would my body, I wonder, have closed my throat and starved itself of air, had he not woken me? But I don't need to ask, don't need to know, because he was there. It feels a bit like our souls have been floating around for a while in pursuit of each other. Across all those dew-drops of time.

I don't have any fancy clothes so I borrowed some of Pio's before we left. Pulled them on in the dark of his room, sweaty and nauseated and dizzy. Climbed into the car and rode here. Pio's been taking driving lessons from Sil and it was almost him that drove us here but he was too shaken at the state of me. He wanted to comfort me on the drive instead.

I arrive later than I should as a member of the family. There are already loads of cars lined up on both sides of the long road. We park at the back and I nearly keel over when I try to get out, but Pio steadies me and we hike up the hill, my hand on his shoulder, his arm around my back, hand at my opposite hip.

People are wandering the orchards and the nearby flowerbeds all dressed in black. Except for a few kids who totter around in brighter colors. The earth is normally dead at this time of year but the strange freeze has faded and some purple flowers have shot up early. They stand out bold against the brown. And as we near the house, I feel like I am stretching back into my bones. I peel away from Pio like I never needed him to hold me up in the first place. A strange lifting, an undoing, as we near the house and enter it. Enough to make my head ask itself, Did you really ever hurt?

Pio and Sil are marveling at the strength I have regained, but inside, I am cowering. Remembering the voice, how it told me to COME HERE and how, now that I am home, I am no longer in pain. For the first time in a long time, I am afraid: I feel it as a hair-lift in the skin, a shiver in the bone. A bewildering, miraculous thing, my ailment having fallen away.

It's been a long time since the house has been populated like this.

I can't remember a time it has been so bustling—it gives me an itching kind of anxiety.

A pair of arms assails me and I realize from the bright touch of citrus in my nose that it's Emma. She squashes me so hard that her hair is crushed to the side of my face.

—How've you been? she says. —You haven't called.

When she pulls away, I see it on her, clear as a cobweb in light: the absolute crushing loneliness she carries. I feel for a moment like the world's worst brother, shadow-shaded and absent—feel it as a sharp stab in my gut. Emma, Emma, I want to say, this whole world is yours.

I am near telling her about the illness but I'll save it for another moment. Feels good to have it off my skin for the moment, to radiate with something else.

—I'm going insane, she says. —Mom is . . .

My heart kicks at the word *Mom*. Emma looks around, makes sure she's out of earshot.

—Well, you'll see, she says. —Is there another bed at Sil's by chance?

I sense her trying very hard to say it like a joke. I smile and look around the room. —I don't think so, but maybe we can squeeze in tight. Two to a bunk.

The front room of the house is lovely, adorned with those same purple flowers in a couple of vases, which I realize are decorated in honor of Dad and Ingrid. A little sob tries to escape but I catch it and gulp it back down.

—You look so spiffy, Emma says. —Where'd this suit come from? I haven't seen you in this before.

—Oh yeah, it's Pio's. I look down at my shoes (Pio's shoes). But something in the way I say his name must ring with feeling because I look up and Emma's got her eyebrow raised.

She just says, —Oh. Smiles, a pleasant face like nothing is the matter. Doesn't push. She'll get it in time, she knows.

We turn and see Uncle Enzo's pickup approaching the house, that desert color shiny with overcast light. He parks and lowers the tailgate. In the back are a bunch of buckets, which he starts unloading two at a time. I remember a very old thing—in the buckets there is seawater, and soon he'll plop in bunches of hyssop. In the past, when we lost our grandparents, this was Dad's job. The driving to the ocean and the gathering. But today it's Dad's soul we'll scrub out of the house. After the day's events, we'll wash the place from top to bottom in the minty-herbed saltwater. A refresh, a starting-over. Wash our walls, our objects, our floors. Mom learned it from her mother and she learned it from hers and she from hers. And up and up the tree.

We walk out to meet him and help with the buckets. Sil and Pio are over at the side of the house and Emma waves to them.

—Hi, kid, Uncle Enzo says, pulling me into his side.

He tells us to carry the buckets over toward the shed where we'll keep them for now and throw the hyssop in soon. He leaves our side and goes into the house. Like little machines, we unload each of the buckets. I'm really only strong enough to lift one at a time but I challenge myself to grab two and feel the muscles mad in my shoulders. Enzo has cleared out the shed, moved bottles and canisters into the coat closet to make room for all the buckets. We make two neat lines of them down the middle, stand back and admire our handiwork: two orderly rows of gray-lidded things.

I walk back toward the front of the house, intending to let Uncle Enzo know we've finished unloading the buckets. But when I look into the house, I see Mom there behind him, notice their heads moving in sync, notice her hand slipping back to cup the nape of his neck. They're the only two in the house at the moment and it's gone all stuffy with a STAY OUT feel.

—Oh yeah. So now you know, Emma says from my left. —Don't know how you didn't see it earlier. It was so obvious.

I remember watching them walk up out of the fields that day

and sensing that strange body-tight sense. How it didn't stick, how I forgot it, I don't know. It may be true that I am lost in my head a lot, but I didn't think it was possible for my brain to lock me so firmly within itself that I missed things that were right under my nose. What else have I not seen, heard, noticed because I have been lost inside myself?

I blink away the bits of old life that swim in my eyes and Emma is no longer there. She has disappeared inside the house. Pio and Sil are at my side instead.

—What's the matter, boy? You feel sick again?

I shake my head and try not to think about what I've just seen. It's loop-de-looping before my eyes, that hand snaking back there, fingers twirling the nape-hairs.

Sil gives Pio a head-jerk like he should leave. He does so, wordlessly (my chest catches at this), goes to wander through the mostly empty flowerbeds.

—Yeah, Sil says, —that's a big part of why we haven't seen you in so long.

—What do you mean?

—Because I always knew about them.

My brain flips itself over. —Always? What do you mean, always? How long has this been going on?

He swallows and wrings his hands out like he's trying to rid himself of the facts he holds in them. I can see his eyes shifting, can see him deciding whether or not to tell me.

—About seven years.

—So since before . . .

—Since before your dad left.

The fact reverberates through me in slow motion like an echo booming in a canyon.

—I knew, he continues, —and I was going to tell your father about it. He didn't deserve what he was getting.

—So then why . . .

—She freaked. Said she was gonna ruin me if I ever told anyone.

—Ruin you how?

—I don't know. But some threats are scary enough on their own. She's one of those people that . . . well, I don't know what she would've come up with.

Looking up at the sky, looking for sense there, he clears his throat.

—Sorry, he says. —I know she's your mother and all.

I look around for Pio. He's down by the tree line, tossing rocks up in the branches, and my heart sinks thinking of earlier times. Of Ingrid and me. But then a loosening—I can breathe again.

Sil was still trying to explain. —She made it clear my only choice was to . . . be gone. But I never felt like it was right of me to take you and Pio away from each other. So when Enzo called and asked if we'd be good taking you in for a bit, I thought something felt very right about that. And I said yes.

Pio is still throwing rocks. At one point, he darts away from the trees with his hands up, scared one will rain back down on him. Sil is looking over there too.

—You're really good for him, he says. —You seem to have woken something in him. I know you don't know it because you haven't seen him in so long, but . . . he's different these days. Now that you're around. He's taken such a liking to you.

—But aren't you scared of the curse?

It falls from my mouth without my willing it. Been on my mind lately, with all the illness and voices. I've been wondering where the commands are coming from. Thinking back to the late-night bedtime stories, Dad's voice delivering them. The quake, the terror of them. Can't help the feeling that it's happening to me too now—coursing through me. It's followed me down all these generations through all these years and it's striking me down again and again.

But Sil laughs. —Stories don't scare me. There's something in you that's brought him out. I'd say that's worth whatever may come with it.

He rubs my hair with his hand the way Dad always used to, and a big swell of love fills me. I throw an arm around him before I know what I've done. He laughs and laughs, but he circles me with an arm too and we stand there in the overcast day. He's even got a dadlike smell, different from my dad's but equally like home.

Then Pio is there too. When I pull away from his dad, he is looking at me with such fondness I think it may cause him to explode. He seems in the firmness of his eyes to make some decision and he reaches out and grabs my hand. I wonder how Sil sees it, wonder what *us* looks like.

—Before everything starts, Pio says, —can you show me where the bathroom is? I have to go so bad and I've been waiting but I can't wait anymore.

I laugh and turn to guide him into the bright-lit

house is beautiful at this time of year all that lovely
architecture stood out against the gray of the sky
so kind of them to open their home to us in this time
of sweltering sorrow

we have lain out our grief-offerings
salads stews loaves and rolls pies and cakes soups and drinks
all that cuisine carried over from casserole country
out on the thick slab of their dining table
to feast on together once the rites are done

, I am done, I am done, I am done. Sometimes I feel like nothing more than a bleeding heart—there is no thing I feel halfway. Orrie has come in with Pio, their hands clasped (!!). He has seen Mom and Enzo together, and she has offered him nothing more than pleasantries. I want to clap my hands before her eyes, at either side of her head so the sound shoots into her ears, and say, YOU CAN'T LIVE IN MAKE-BELIEVE FOREVER YOU HAVE

HURT YOUR SON WITH YOUR YEARS-LONG LIE-DELUGE EVERYTHING IS NOT FINE. But she would blink away my words with that blank measured smile and turn back to her work and carry on. Slide back into the lie of her everyday life.

Her style is tempting. I'd take up the same sort of ritual if I knew how, I'd slip into some other skin, where nothing hurts and I do not rage. But I can't find it and wouldn't know how to get myself into it if I did. I contain too much, I won't fit into those bounds.

When it is time for the ritual to begin, I keep my eyes on her. The family plot isn't on our property, but it's just down the hill—we'll make a procession down to it. A big, long, orderly line, key players at front—Mom, then Orrie and me side by side, then Enzo, his breath huffing at my neck all the way down the hill—then other family, then neighbors, friends. But Mom's leading the way with the two urns cradled in her hands, to be interred one after the other. A gorgeous, trained tear-streak trails down her right cheek and drops onto her collarbone, melding into the fabric of her black dress. Hair twisted up behind her head in a tight, solemn bun.

And while I watch the rest of the afternoon happen, listen to her speak about how these deaths have rocked the fabric of the family but brought us closer together than she could have imagined, I reckon with a feeling, with a dreaming. In the past I have felt angry, I have felt violent, but I have never felt murderous. And today I am feeling something so close to it—it would be easy, wouldn't it, she wouldn't have to know. If I slid up behind her, quiet as night, sliced her throat open, poured her out into her husband's grave, atop his urn, a libation of sorts. For the first time, the thought gives me no pause but instead brings a calm, a comfort. I have raged, and shoved it down, and raged, and shoved it down, and all the rage has gathered into a clump of ruin. I could ruin her, I could ruin everything. She'd better hope I don't

try the chicken we want to say arlene cooked

it to perfection sandra's butter rolls too

soft and fluffy as anything sure you don't want

a scoop of dave's green beans flecked with little bits of fried shallot

or lily's mac and cheese with crispy bits

surely you want to shove

something down to keep the wellspring

of grief from rushing its way up and out

-side but we bring them in and spread them around the house so everyone can reach them. Pry the lids off now that the hyssop has been steeping for a while. Dip in our sponges and get to work. The family (the four of us) are doing the upstairs and the rest of the group is doing the downstairs. The thought being that everyone who wants to pitch in on the ground floor can do so and everyone else won't be waiting for the feast. But this is the part of the day I have been strangely excited for. The house will soak up the smell of the herbs the floorboards will sigh with new breath. I remember it clear as day. All the while, we're freeing the last pinnings of Dad's and Ingrid's souls. Letting them loose.

We have always believed the soul escapes the body in a tiny gust of air. So what that Ingrid didn't actually die here? Her soul found its way back to us, where it belonged. Till its next stop on the journey to dancing in the grass of some afterlife.

The things we do because people did them before us. How many times has the house been purged and restored, purged and restored? And still I fear the curse lingers in its build. One by one, we are being stricken away. But we all have to believe it as we scrub at the house to get the sick out: it is becoming bloodless, it is becoming bloodless.

I consider the possibility of coming back here. To a warmer place, a cleaner, purified place. While I scrub the banister, take care with each rail, I look down at Pio. His eyes are moon-bright, his smile hesitant: he is helping. As a child, he ran up and down these halls; the house contains a piece of him too. I just hope it hasn't left its mark on him.

A warm thought but a strange thing begins happening tonight. Every now and then, I shut my eyes and open them in an entirely different place. With no memory of the gap of moving my body between. I open my eyes and am by the window at the far end of the hall near my bedroom door. My sponge sits on the sill and its water leaks out, drips down the wall in three separate streams, like paint streaks. This has not happened before. I have never not trusted my immediate memory. But there's a slipperiness to the evening.

< you're back >

I hear it and turn to look toward the end of the hall, where I think the voice came from, but then I realize with a panic that it rang out from within me. I press my fingers to my temples and rub in small circles. I don't feel the pressure I felt at Pio's house, but I feel a strange presence in here, like another mind has joined mine, and I don't like it.

< you know what to do >

What am I to do? I don't understand. I hear from downstairs Mom gathering everyone together announcing the end of the cleansing ritual and ushering forth the plates and cutlery for the funereal feast but in an instant all comfort I felt at the house has evaporated and I'm itching to get back to Sil's. I try to get my legs to move me toward the stairs at the smell of the rolls being uncovered and the meat being sliced. Pio is at the bottom of the banister looking up at me with those big pools of eyes, extending his hand like he's beckoning me toward a dance.

I open my eyes and we're in the kitchen. People all around hold plates loaded up with food, trying to foster lighter spirits, but still everything is weighted down by death. Pio's eyes dotted with concern—he senses my unease. I smile, which takes twice as much muscle as usual, and push him toward the food. I go for lots of rolls and not much else. I'm in a bready mood; I want the soft melting of a roll's inside. I'm walking around the house trying to find a space to sit, waiting, bracing for the next time I lose myself. Because I feel a rush of anything-could-happen. And I just want to

know this is a hard time for you all
know this cannot be easy all this remembering
know you're tired of all the day-to-day
know the ending won't come for a while yet

it sounds nice, actually, to bring on the end of her. Not only something I *could* do but something I *want* to do, something that fills me, here at the end of the dining bench, feet crisscrossed beneath my legs, lifting individual nibs of green bean to my mouth, with a wash of bliss.

I could slip the black ribbon off her bun and wring her neck with it. I could splash her across the tiles, spell her name, my name, all of our names, in her blood across the wall. Blood binds all families and her legacy swims in mine.

I want to see hers spill, want to flood the house with it, to watch it rush out the crack beneath the front door, a river of dark.

Want her sinews to fall cold, her eyes to go hollow. After all the damage she has precipitated, the blood she has spilled, it's only fair—an eye for an eye, as they say. She led two of us to death, so she'll have me coming for both eyes. I can pop them out with my thumbs.

There's a bit of me that shakes itself awake at this, begins to churn. Where do the thoughts come from? The urge for murder, that isn't me. Harm, yes, verbal assault, yes, but not bloodletting. I'm looking around at the people at the table, as if one of them has planted the thoughts in me, and wondering if they recognize me anymore or if I have bloomed into something else.

I look over at Orrie and he seems similarly pale. I wonder if the same thing is happening to him, if some poison is spreading slowly in his head. Too slow to stop, too subtle to notice,

too late to stop the chaos it has been
brought down like rain
from some cruel god

oh god oh god I open my eyes and the kitchen is emptied except for me. I don't know where anyone is. But I feel a weight in my hand and see I'm holding a knife. The giant chef's one from the block, sharp and shining. My stomach drops. I let the thing go and it clatters down into the sink, a very loud sound, metal on metal. I look down at my hand, wonder how it could have committed to the act of grabbing this thing. Wonder where my brain was or the rest of my body. Swimming here, swimming.

The house is silent. I step out into the living room to see where everyone is. My shoes are on—I have tracked some faint mudsteps throughout the house. Before I reach the door, Emma bursts through it.

—Are you okay?

I shove down the feeling, don't want it flashing in my face. —Yeah. What do you mean?

—You ran up here all suddenly, she says. —I came to make sure everything is okay.

A shudder in my stomach. —Ran up here from where?

A dark look comes over her. She swallows, scratches the side of her neck. —We all went back down the hill. She hesitates a moment. —So you're feeling weird too?

I look out the window and in the distance I see them all down there, the lights of their procession. I imagine Mom again in her leading position, her face wrecked by grief, her body strong.

—Yeah, I say. —I don't know how to describe it but yeah.

—Me too. And I don't either.

We hold ourselves in that space for a while. There's an energy between us that we sustain. Something like: in this moment, we are both here and we understand our bodies as they are right now; nothing is being pulled from us. We look at each other and see each other. And on this slippery day that may be all I can ask for.

—You ready to go back out? she says.

I set a hand on her shoulder and she turns to lead me out of the house. We walk down toward one of the graves, our breaths puffing in front of us like little souls. Though ours, I know, are still

here is where the dead lie
here is where the memories will remain
what dark times have come before
what beauty we hope will come after

-ward it feels like a false memory, that strange sectioning-off in my brain, but when I see her again it comes back, that blood desire, in a strong enough burst to dizzy me, to flare up behind my eyes and dance around for a

while to recover of course it'll take time
as everything worth doing does

the world feel tilted or is it just me? I look around and can hardly tell where I am, can hardly feel the cold in my hands. The world has gone dark and my vision goes in and

out here the world is so quiet we feel such
privilege to be out here in the earth so much
of our crop comes from our potatoes our carrots our herbs
what a special thing to be a part of what a special thing

s are falling apart, it feels like, this instinct is taking over, I feel it in my hands and arms, spreading like molten lead through my body, it's all I can do to crawl up to my room and hide so I don't find a way to

hurt will recede in time as all
pain does time that beautiful healer these people will find
it when it flutters down over them like leaves

me in the shed in the cold. There's a fluttering in my fingers—they are reaching for something, I don't know what. They wrap around it, pull it toward me. Something wiggles in front of my eyes, tells them to LOOK. So I entertain the thought, open them wide, and they settle on a

drawer opening and closing letting the feeling
out keeping it contained
things go a bit like this like a ball at the end
of a pendulum grief will keep
them here leave them rocking

back and forth on the floor, I have locked the door and dragged a chair in front of it, so even if I wrangle myself onto my hands and knees, make my way over to it, I won't have the strength to get the door open. Every cell in my body is burning with this blind rage—my fingers itch to wrap around a throat—my teeth quiver with the urge to tear it open, they sink into my arm for at least something to occupy them, how long till everything is right

again and again the world spins around
the sun rises and sinks and the moon too
and again and again this feeling will wake with them there

in the drawer are several things and one of them I have taken into my hand; it is a box cutter. Big scary sharp retractable thing with the slider on the side. Mom always says, Don't play around with box cutters, if you need to cut open a box, just use scissors. Only the tip of the blade is extended and it's got a glint of red on it. Red, dark red, the copper-tangy red of life.

I extend it an inch and the whole blade is that same color and it even runs down onto the metal handle a bit. It's dark out here but the corner lamp is on and the light shines down on that red.

Why am I finding this, I wonder, why have I been led here? It quakes in my hand. I have the tingle-sharp feeling in my whole body that I have just been let in on something I was not supposed to see. I think of Dad in the bath, glass shattered on the floor, a few loose bloodied shards on the floor, his neck scored open. The blood on the blade doesn't seem years old, crusted to dust—it still seems fairly new. We have no livestock on the farm, so what could the blood have been from? And why was it returned here?

I wonder to myself for the first time if maybe she could've. She could've. Can't even think it. A gasp sucks itself into my mouth, a strange half-sob thing. What is going on in this

place memory is so strong none of us have
been this far up the hill in years maybe but the second we return
to the property it's like we never left so warmly
welcomed it's like we will never again leave

-s me in an instant. I look up from the former place and find myself strewn across my bedroom carpet, the door barricaded and locked, teeth marks all up and down my arms. The thing that gripped me now feels locked away like a years-old memory. Set it in its safe place, kept there.

I walk down to the living room and most of the attendees have left; only the family hangs around. Pio and Sil are near the front door, and when Orrie steps into the house, he drifts toward them. My stomach curls in on itself, watching them lumped up together, more of a unit than anything I have ever belonged to. I used to have my friends, used to have my siblings, but where have they gone, what have they left me with? The bottomless black well of myself, every thought and feeling ink-stained with hurt.

Orrie comes over to me. A sheet of pallor passes over his face, he seems one second from passing out. —We're gonna head back, he says.

—What do I do? I say. —I can't stay here, something about this place isn't right.

I can barely get the words out. Sil and Pio huddle near the front door, waiting for Orrie to join them.

—I don't know, he says.

Then, after a moment that appears to hurt him, he leaves. It's the final nail falling out of me, the one that has been holding me together. Mom and Enzo escort the three of them out and I stand there in the middle of the room, a pile of planks. Mom asks Orrie something and he's barely able to answer, barely able to look at her. Still pallid and pliant, guided out the door by the gentle tug of Pio's hand. A tug like that could knock me over and I wouldn't have the strength to get up. Mom would step over me, sweep me up with the day's trash. Some life I have lived, some life I am living.

The gentle turning-over of the engine outside, the tires tracking down the hill, fading away. Enzo stands there and looks out at everything, the gardens and the driveway and the slim trail down to the graves, and Mom comes back inside.

—Orrie sure seemed strange, she says.

She's running her hands along the table, the walls, feeling the place, its newfound purity.

—Did you tell him something? she says. —Something to get him that spooked?

She's looking at me now, her way of threatening: she never has to say a word because the daggers in her eyes are sharp enough to slice.

—No, I say.

—That's good. I'd hope you wouldn't spread your unfounded theories.

Maybe it's because I don't care anymore, maybe it's because I feel like every inch of skin has already been peeled away, so I'm no longer afraid of consequences. What further damage can be done? What further hurt can my heart hold?

—But they're not unfounded, I say.

Her hand pauses in its sweeping motion across one of Aunt Andrea's vases. —Pardon me? she says. But in the kind of way that means SHUT YOUR DAMN MOUTH.

—They're not unfounded.

I think of Nic, of Claire, the last two people to love me, and the promises they made when they left for the city, not to leave me behind. The polite, two-sentence email Nic sent when he learned of my father's return; the phone ringing, ringing, after each of my losses; the operator's voice. I have nothing left to feel, nothing left she can take. Nothing at all.

—They're not unfounded.

I haven't moved in ten minutes. I stand in the center of the room like I've been put on display here. A statue whose mouth is moving, won't stop moving, spewing its dark.

—I've known about you and Enzo for a long time. That wasn't ever an unfounded theory.

—*Uncle* Enzo.

—Oh, sorry. I've known about you fucking our *Uncle* Enzo for a long time.

—Language.

—It's only the truth.

Something falls over in the sink.

—You fucked our uncle and you killed our dad. You poisoned him with something and then you slit his throat. So what if he fucking attacked you, you were gonna kill him anyway. You are *evil.*

She is facing away from me now. Glad I can't see her face because by now her gaze must carry enough venom to knock me down dead.

—No daughter of mine speaks to me that way.

—No mother does what you have done.

She picks up the vase and flings it at the far wall. Little fragments of Dad's face fly around the room, still skidding across the floor after the explosive shatter-noise has fallen away.

She turns to me, approaches.

—By tomorrow, you are *out*. Understand?

I nod.

—This is no longer your house. No longer your family.

—When was it ever.

I can't help myself.

My cheek stings red and pinching. I didn't even see her hand move.

—*Get out,* she shouts.

And for a second, with her standing there, a blissful thought returns. She is inches away from me, teeth in my face bared like a bad dog, and I think about how easy it would be to reach out, squeeze, cut her words off.

Watch her beautiful throat narrow, feel its cords in my hand.

The windpipe, the arteries, the muscle. All the texture I want to feel.

Maybe we're not so different after all, she and I. Maybe we're one and the same.

As I begin reaching for her, fingers outstretched, cramped and eager to latch, she jerks herself away, looks me up and down. Fear is in her eyes, moon-bright—it's the first real time I've seen it there. She turns and heads toward the stairs, doesn't look back. Doesn't look at me.

crackle

19

all the way across town we go

and as we pass mile lines I keep sharp attention on my body. If the strange sickness is tied to the house, as I think it is, it's only a matter of time before things set in again. When we soar beneath the freeway overpass I notice a twinge in my right eye, a strange sort of flicker. By the gas station on the corner my stomach is swirling. I hear

< where are you going orrie >

and sweat breaks out at my hair line. And there's an ache too, a little misery inching its way down my face into my neck, my shoulders. Pio maybe can sense it because he sets a hand on the knee that's closest to him and traces little shapes on it. Or maybe he is just being kind. It's a nice feeling but it doesn't negate the rending in the rest of me.

I'M GOING AWAY FROM YOU, I want to tell the voice. You, whoever, whatever you are. But it doesn't like that, because it sends a wrench into my side and I buckle over, collapse into Pio's shoulder. I am trying to mask the feeling because I want to be at Sil's house—I don't want the other force to win. I want to live my life the way I want to live it. We pull into the driveway and I hang behind the others as they proceed into the house. My stomach turns over a couple times and I heave behind the truck. Nothing comes up but air: it's like my body is trying to hack my soul up and out of it.

Emma also mentioned feeling strange and I wonder what she meant—I should have asked. Wonder if she was having dizzy dissociative spells too or if it felt different for her. But when my stomach has somewhat settled, I head into the house and take a seat next to the others. Sil's at the head of the table with a full glass of red wine in front of him. He's swirling it around, looking at the glass like its trails of fluid are going to let him in on a secret. I look at Pio there in his little gray suit and my heart seizes—I could drown in that gray fabric. Among all the other feelings in me there is this great lifting. I think of Pio crying like a child when Ingrid and Dad were interred, think of the way I hadn't shed a tear. Something about him is more connected to the body, to the earth, and something about me is more detached, drifty. It was only when I saw him crying that I started crying. And then it was hard to stop. But at first, it was him.

But drifty as I am, I can't seem to get myself out of this strange hurting. When we're heading off to bed, changed into T-shirts and getting ready for grief-slick sleep, he says, —You seem off. Is it happening again?

I nod because I don't know if my body will allow me to speak. It takes all my effort to climb up to the top bunk and I lie there pale and panting.

—Let me know if it gets worse, he says. —Just shake me awake or throw a pillow down at me or shout at me or something.

Again I nod. He's standing at the edge of the bunk bed looking at me. Before he lowers himself to his own bunk, he leans his face right in close to mine, and after a second sets his lips where mine are. Just for a second. But if I weren't already lying down, I would have fallen over then and there. Fallen down and out into another dimension. I smile and he smiles and we allow ourselves this moment just to look at each other and smile. Then he sinks down into his bed and rolls over onto his side, which I have learned is his sleeping position.

Sil comes in and gives us both pecks on the head. Tells me we are okay and he is glad for us, his words bright with a bit of wine-breath. Then he leaves us in the quiet, clicks off the light, retires to his own room.

And things are okay for a while. There's a bit of nothing going on inside me and I think I'm going to fall asleep. Replaying again and again the last few moments, reaching out for the feeling, wishing to hold onto it, to live it for hours. But right at the edge of the black, I jolt upright in bed and feel a wetness on my face. Nosebleed, I'm sure, so I work my way over to the ladder to lower myself to the ground, but it's hard to hold myself up and I end up stumbling toward the chair, shirt over my face to keep the blood off Pio's stuff. One of my favorite shirts, too, one that was comically large in childhood but now fits me just right. Maybe I can get the stain out, but I'm doubtful.

—Orrie? Pio says, his voice soft and scared.

—I'm okay, I say and stumble across to the bathroom. The night light in the hall is on when I pull open the bedroom door and it illuminates my new dark.

—Jesus, that's a lot of blood, Pio says. He's standing there in his T-shirt and underwear, his eyes near-shut in the bright light, and he's gathering tissues to hold up to my nose, showing me where to pinch like a parent would. I want so badly to pull him in close to me, but now's not the time. Again, I'm hit by a wave of panic and a thrash in my stomach that pulls me to the ground, pulls my head over the toilet. Sweating buckets and buckets—my back is soaked. Pio lowers his hand to it but doesn't know how sweaty it is so I feel him recoil when his skin makes contact.

—What the hell is going on, he says.

< where have you gone >

I hear and I say, —I don't know, in response to both. There's a little bit of red in what I manage to spit up in the toilet. I think back to what I ate so I don't immediately flip out. But I can't think of anything red and there's another wisp of panic that rises.

—What do we do?

—I don't know, I say and then hurl again.

He strokes my back anyway, lowers himself to my level, sets his head against my shoulder.

—But I know I felt better at home. I think I need to go home. Can you drive me?

—I don't know. I mean, I've been practicing, but maybe we should wake Dad up.

I think back to Sil opening the bottle of wine when we got home. The first glass he drank and then the second. Voice my concern to Pio.

—Oh yeah. Maybe not the best driver option.

With my forehead against the porcelain there's a coolness in my skull. Feels like a relinquishing. I start to stand, feel the coolness in my feet. But my stomach pulls me down again. More blood in the bowl, swirling around in my spit-up.

—I think I should drive, Pio says. His voice quavers like he's going to cry so I take his hand.

—It's okay, I say without any sort of confidence.

—I'll get the car started and leave a note for Dad so he knows where we are.

He slips from the room and I'm alone there in the suddenly cavernous bright-white. I don't want the whatever in my head to win but I don't think I have the strength for it to be a choice. I have to give in—I have to go back.

Pio does what he said and then leads me again to the car, bearing most of my weight to keep me upright. It's like a replay of the earlier walk when we were headed to the funeral, except this time is much worse. I can barely see what's in front of me, can barely hear my own thoughts. I slide into a jacket though I'm burning up and shivering and we trek out to the car. He slides me into the passenger seat and runs around to the driver's seat. He's put a bucket in here in case I have to vomit again and I want to grab his hand and squeeze it so tight. I try to grip the bucket between my knees but I don't have the strength to hold it there, so it clatters to the floor. Rolls around between my feet and clangs against the door.

Pio shifts into reverse. I'M SORRY NEW FAMILY, I say to the house, I DON'T HAVE MUCH OF A CHOICE BUT I'LL COME BACK WHEN I GET THINGS FIGURED OUT.

He jerks out of the driveway, slams the gas. Hits the pavement at an odd angle and we go jostling.

—Sorry.

Once he makes it onto the road, I keep my temple held against the glass so the coolness rushes in. It's a cold cold night and my skin feels so hot that I worry it's going to melt the glass down. But it won't, I know, and for the rest of the ride I sit there with my head leaning. Breathing slow through each wave of nausea that flows over me and ebbs out.

We're in familiar territory, crossing roads I biked in childhood, passing my favorite grocery store, coming up our big long hill. I'm waiting for the discomfort to subside. But it doesn't yet.

He pulls up at the perimeter of the house, puts the car in park. All the downstairs lights in the house are off except for the living room night light—it appears everyone has gone upstairs for the evening. Pio's headlights bounce off the blue wall.

My head swells as I say, —I think you should just leave me here for the night.

—Are you sure? he says. —Are you gonna be able to get in?

I laugh a bit under my breath. The tension in my head has let up a bit. —Yeah, it's my house. I'll break in if I have to. You can wait for me to get inside if you want and then go.

—I want to stay, he says with a tenderness that warms me.

—I don't think you should, I say. —We don't have any guest beds right now because of . . .

The events of the past couple weeks. Dark spilling out of them all. I shove a lid on the whole thing.

—Oh, right.

—And besides, I need to talk to Emma and figure out what's going on here. Won't be very fun for you, I don't think.

—I guess not.

He looks out at the shed, which is partially illuminated by the light that refracts off the wall.

—Well, he says. —I'll call in the morning, or you call in the morning, or whatever you want.

—Okay.

And before I climb from the car he pulls my face close to his and sets his cheek against mine. Doesn't kiss me, doesn't touch me for long, just holds me there for a moment.

—All right, he says, resigned. —See you tomorrow.

His lights trace my path as I step up onto the porch and pull open the screen door. The front room creaks into view and I hear his tires crunch as he backs up. A light clicks on upstairs.

—Orrie? I hear Mom say from the railing. —What are you doing

here we are waiting in anticipation for the spring
season to arrive for the earth to be

tilled for their crops to rise we trust
in them to help sustain us

but I hear a racket downstairs and feel a warmth spread through me: he has come back for me. For a second, I get a whiff of some distant dream: Orrie and me and Pio, living with Sil, in that little house I barely remember. But I remember it's the kind of little that doesn't feel cramped but instead feels like home. The kind of place you can still stretch out in, the kind of place that warms and cools quickly, that feels familiar when you return to it. I have a little dream bubbling in me of going back there, making a home of it.

But I hear Mom's voice and I'm yanked from the dream, brought back to this place. She doesn't want to see me, I know, but I step out into the hall and lean over the railing.

—Orrie, come up here, I say.

He looks at me and I can tell he is scared. Some residual unwellness hangs over him still, there's a blankness in his face, a weakness hovering in his limbs. I turn toward Mom and a wash of anger hits me unexpectedly, enough to take me out for a moment. That feeling that makes my fingers twitch. When I turn toward the front door again, Orrie is gone: he has stepped back outside. The screen door swings behind him, kicks at the frame. For a moment he hovers out

there will be no aggie presiding over the season
as we have been looking
forward to since we heard of his return
none of his tender hand at work in their fields

all around me. The spacey thing is happening again. I looked up at Emma and blinked and found myself here. Some screen pulled down over my eyes. I'm being brought to my knees; my hands are sinking into the soil. This bit has been overturned recently: it's still fresh and loose, hasn't hardened to a crust the way the rest of the earth has.

I'm digging for something, then my finger makes contact with something firm and cold. My hand wraps around it. I unearth it like a vegetable by its root and see it's the box cutter again. I must have buried it here, though I have no idea why I would have done that. Maybe to keep it in a place I knew. To keep it from being hidden again. The handle in the moonlight is so dark that I can't tell what's blood and what's earth. I drop it back into the

soil on that farm is gorgeous and clean those folks know
what they're doing something about that place makes
it so easy for life to rise up and out

-stretched again, and I lower them. Mom has retreated to her bedroom, but still my hands reached out for the place she occupied. An energy gathered in my fingernails—I wanted to press them into her skin, leave marks there. Then it faded away like the last remnant of a dream.

Orrie is next to me now. His presence startles me.

—I keep . . . fading, he says.

He starts down the stairs, and I follow.

—What do you mean? I ask.

—Like I'm here and then I'm not. I keep . . . doing things I don't remember.

—I keep getting these feelings, I say. —That hit me really intensely and then disappear. Like it's . . . not coming from *me*.

Or perhaps, I think and can't quite face, it *is* coming from me and I don't want to believe it, don't want to know myself as capable of such hate.

We reach the ground floor and head for the kitchen.

—Maybe I shouldn't have come back, he says. —Maybe it was a mistake.

—No, I say, grabbing his arm. —I'm glad you did. I thought I was going crazy.

—But I was getting sick, he says. —Over at Pio's. Like I . . . *had* to come back.

—What do you think is going on? What do you think it is?

He looks at me with tenderness and fear, grabs a glass from the cabinet.

—The curse, he says.

—What does it want?

He makes a face like something unpleasant has spread through his stomach. I remember the voice he mentioned hearing, wonder if it has trickled through him again.

He looks at me, swallows.

—It said, YOU KNOW EXACTLY WHAT WE WANT.

20

because it's true it's all true we lied to you we're sorry we won't do it again

—What the fuck did you do to me? Aggie said when they were in the bathroom.

Cleo watched his limbs go slack and druggy, his blinks slow, his eyes get sluggish beneath their lids. She stepped closer, got right up next to him, looked down at his pale limp body as he struggled at the surface. His eyes in their slow-motion panic. A gleam came into them, a murderous thing, and she imagined it as what he saw in her eyes too at that moment.

He reached for her, slow-limbed but sure-sighted, and she released a guttural scream. The ruinous thing in her came unstoppered; she couldn't stop screaming. She reached down, grabbed a shard of the glass, and ripped it across like she'd seen in films. The shard caught in his muscle-cords so she tried again, slashed with all her might, but it wasn't working—the shard wasn't sharp enough. So she reached into her back pocket where she'd put the box cutter just in case. She'd have to hide it later, find a place for it that nobody would stumble upon.

THIS IS WHERE WE COME IN—

She extended the blade and a bliss lit her up like fire. His skin peeled apart like ripe fruit. How many slices could she manage, again and again and again? How did each slice feel better and better, fill her with a bigger rush? She sliced till his neck was red-rivered and the water was darkening and her hands and knees were soaked. Then she stepped away from the tub but slipped on a splash of water, or maybe he pulled her down, he with his ironclad vengeful grip, and she fell in, soaked herself

NEW VERSION OF THE STORY BELIEVE WHAT YOU WANT TRUTH IS A RESULT OF THE LIGHT

shines down on her in a different way once again. Last week I clung to maybe a purer version of who she was. Before I saw her and Uncle Enzo together in the kitchen kissing and slow-dancing like the rest of the world had fallen away. And now this vision, which has come from outside, but I trust it deep in the gut as though I was there to see it happen.

She's come out of her room, Uncle Enzo behind her. They've come down the stairs and the two of them look at me like I'm coming unstitched seam by seam right in front of them.

—Orrie, she says, —what's going on?

I look over at Emma and she's got a darkness in her eye that makes me want to physically recoil. A churn occurs in my stomach. I should never have come back here. Can't help but feel like every pawn has been set in its perfect place and now it's just a matter of waiting. What will the house do.

So I open my mouth to say EMMA I'M GOING OUTSIDE. But before I can get any words out, I feel my hand reaching into my back pocket

< cover their eyes they don't need to see this part >

Cleo sees the fangs, the bloodletting fangs, the snake eyes beading

< sing yourself a song in your head little one >

but Emma's look is the same in this light, something similar has come over the both of them

< something bright and melodious la la la la >

—kids, come on, look at me, please, look at me, it's me

< something that would've made you turn the radio dial up on your way to school in the morning >

—it's me your mother don't you remember your mother

< something to put a little pep in your step sorry to say >

—no no no no

< you're going to need it >

How long does it take me to open my eyes again? It's quiet as death in here. I'm afraid to see what has been done.

I open my right eye slowly, slowly, and see red so I slam it shut again. Nope not ready. My heart will not find a normal pace—it rockets away like it's going to fly out of me.

—Orrie, I hear Emma say.

But I give my head the slightest shake.

Again she says, —Orrie.

And her voice is a pleading thing, tremulous and desperate; it begins to soften me. All I can do is listen; all I can do is placate. So I let my eyes drift open a bit.

Red still. Lots of it. All the kitchen tiles stained with it. Mom's dark head of hair cast across and through it, a soft net over Uncle Enzo's face. His eyes stare up at the ceiling and don't blink they don't blink. There's a slit in his neck and a dark waterfall has run down him. The box cutter in the middle of a blood-puddle.

I look at Emma. Stand at one side of the room and she stands at the other, in the back corner by the pantry. Our mother and uncle between us and the lake of red.

Emma's hands and the knees of her pants are bloodied. My vision gives out for a moment and I think when I look at her that my soul is giving out. Blinking bright and dark like a light bulb winking out on a wall. How could she have done this how could

< so sorry children but it had to be done >

Emma shakes her head, lifts a hand to point it at a low part of me. So I look down at myself, raise my hands flat. See my palms—oh. An incomprehensible fact. What is the nature of fact, how does it sweep away the rest of the world. All that is here anymore is fact. Everything else has fallen away. All there is is this room and my bloodied sister and my dead family and my flatlined heart and the slick, stained floor and my own palms bloodied too.

ORRIE LOOKS AT THE
NEW EDGES OF HIMSELF
AND WONDERS
IF THIS IS WHAT IT MEANS
TO BE A PERSON

&

EMMA STARES INTO THE
WIDE-OPEN WONDERS
OF HER LIFE AND OPENS
HERSELF UP TO POSSIBILITY

1

one chance to fix but it all falls away quick and flitty like the heartbeats of birds

< ok here's how this is going to go >

< we are the runners of things now >

< we are your fates we take your bounds bend and ply them like putty >

< welcome to us we have been waiting >

In the days after the deaths the house gives way to water. Days, weeks, months, something along those lines, what even is time anymore, who's to say. But regardless, it's a giant storm the likes of which we have never seen here. Giant rainclouds brought on unseemly winds, water pouring onto us. It should feel false or dreamlike in its abnormality but every drop is skin-real.

From upstairs the thrumming on the roof is loud enough to make it feel like the whole house is going to cave in. An onslaught of water. Flooding field rows barely visible through the water-sheet.

Emma is here somewhere but I can't find her. I call her name up and down the halls and throw all the doors open but there's no sign of her. No food she's eating, no glasses she's drinking from, no crumpled bed she's sleeping in. Yet I feel her presence like a warmth in the body, the kind of sensation that feels like fact. Can't hear her but I can barely sense anything through the constant water-rush anyway. I sit at the top of stairs and hold my head in my hands like I'm waiting for my brain to tick-tock like a heart.

Eventually the flood rises on all sides of the house until it bursts through the back-door glass, rushes in and covers the bottom floor, mingling with death-blood. Rainwater with a tinge of red-brown. It lifts our couches and tables and pillows and rugs. It bursts through the front windows.

Then the roof gives and the storm is coming in that way, washing down the stairs, making waterfalls through the railing. I haul myself up the banister, fight for higher ground so the water doesn't carry me away. Emma is still nowhere in sight, her absence a cavern in me. I feel her all around but can't find her.

And somehow the storm only gets worse. It whips me left and right. It's a world-ending kind of water and I try hard as I can to hold onto that railing but eventually the water is too much and my hands are too tired and I let go.

I'm whirled down the stairs and end up in the kitchen where Emma is waiting (Emma! my heart squeezes itself in the middle) and she says something but the water is too loud for me to hear. She comes closer, says HELP ME, she needs me to tie a rope around her. Around the both of us. So I can secure her to the stair railing, so we don't get swept away.

But the rain-sound changes: a clattering, now, like the heaviest hail imaginable pelting the exposed wood. Box cutters, hundreds and hundreds, falling from the sky with the rain. My mouth hangs open as they plunge into the floodwater, toss with the current. I extend the rope-end out to Emma, but her fingertips are all gone, sliced off at the knuckle. From the wounds sprout carrot-tops like in the field. But I look down and find my hands have become box cutter blades glinting in the dim light. HURRY, she says.

I CAN'T, I shout back. And eventually the rising blade-water pulls us under. And I try to help but all I can do is cut and cut and cut. The water is so deep the light can no longer permeate it. But I'm still aware of the damage I do. The skin I shred to bits, all the people I try to hold and only harm. The world, slicing me open. Pulled back out of

< we're almost ready to lay claim to what we deserve >

**< *almost almost* the word sings
like honey on our tongues >**

the house is empty again, just like me and Emma and the pile of bodies we brought to the ground. The blood we let out of them like melted rubber on the floor. The rain just a trickle now. She sits across from me with her feet kicked out in front of her, slumped over in resignation. Her eyes are cast down and nothing I say raises them. In another time, in another world, she might have become a statue.

We're sitting there and I feel a building head-rush of something about to happen. Rain just a trickle, a *tap-tap* on the sills, a gush through the gutters on the roof perimeter.

Then I look down and up and my brain has done that skipping-ahead thing again. I've lost trust in the institution of my own mind. We sit in six inches of water. Emma has fallen face-first into it and will not get up. Out in the living room again, the stair-fall of rushing floodwater.

I run to Emma and try to get her out of the water and get her conscious, but her body is slack and unresponsive. She is dead. And besides, again, my fingers are blades; I slice her shoulder open when I try to pull her upright and collapse down into my own weight, the weight of

< we almost have what we need
in order to prosper >

< the world will feel so good
on our feet once again >

< the world we were robbed of
by the guilt that gathered as we worked our way
down the bloodline >

lost I have lost so much and I am only going to lose more aren't I. Floodwater rises, air charged with chill, with wetness, souls spiral around the room, the last death-breaths of Dad and Ingrid and Mom and Uncle Enzo spin through the splashes. Could try to chase after them, catch the slippery souls between my hands, but they'll only find another way to escape and besides, they don't belong on this plane. Upstairs, water sloshes over warped wood and maybe I will give in, maybe I will just let it take me where it wants

< almost time >

< oh good morning little one >

eyes are closed. The first thing I notice is the stench of me. Then the full-body sweat-sheen. I open my eyes in a room of blinding light, head thrumming with sound, with fear, with overstimulation. It's what the movies make hangovers seem like. I'm on the couch with four blankets thrown across me, toes sticking out the bottom; I can hardly feel them.

Emma comes in from the other room and a soaring light fills me. We have drowned in that lightless flood again and again and I am glad she is not yet drowned on this day. She looks at me and blinks a couple times.

—Orrie?

I cock my head.

—Orrie?

—Yeah?

She crumples with relief and runs to my side. Sits next to me, sets a hand on my forehead, feels my skin.

—God, you're so warm. Probably all these blankets.

I think of my furnace/freezer body at Sil and Pio's house (and my stomach drops out at the thought of Pio, where is he). I must still be looking at Emma with confusion, because she smiles a bit. Before realizing the smile might be a bit improper and shoving it down again.

—You've been out for a while, she says. —And you've been in and out of some weird places. I honestly wasn't sure if you'd ever come back. Your head went somewhere.

—There was a flood.

—Yeah, you talked a lot about the flood. Kept screaming out for me.

—Lots of floods.

It all felt so real. I can't wrap my head around the fact of it being not a fact. Lots I can't wrap my head around these days, my head is particularly unpliable. I keep turning toward the windows, toward the stairway, to watch for water, to avoid being swept away.

—How long have I been out?

—Four days I think. Give or take. Yeah. Yesterday was three. Today is four.

Four days. I swing my legs over the edge of the couch and stand. Nearly fall to the floor, unstable on unused limbs. But after a second I get the hang of it again and stumble into the kitchen. They are not there. There's caution tape around where they were, but they are gone.

—Where are they, I say.

—Ambulance came and took them away.

—When.

—Few days ago.

The tile and the grout are stained—I'm not sure if anyone tried to clean the area. Maybe I will try, find a bottle of something sharp-scented and chemical, let it soak for a while.

—How are we still here.

Her face buckles in on itself. —I really don't know.

< you're welcome for that >

sat here with Orrie, watched him swelter in his strange dreams, held him down when he flailed and screamed, fed him water and bites to eat between grief spells. The world felt like it was going to crumble. Those twenty-four hours played on constant loop behind my eyes, the blood spilled. And I don't know who spilled it, I don't know who spilled it—the blinders fell down over me when the dirty work was done. Orrie and I sat there and blinked our eyes and hardly understood what we were seeing. I thought of the feeling that had been flaring up in me for days, that white-hot blinding rage, and wanted to shrivel up.

The truth about the dark parts of myself is that I thought if I turned away from them, paid them no mind, they would remain recessed. But those big flares of emotions make me feel like maybe I can't trust the darkness to stay quiet.

< you can't >

This is how she tells it. We sat in the quiet of the kitchen for hours or maybe days. We heard the phone ring (or at least Emma did) but neither of us could rise to answer it. As she tells it, I had disappeared from my body. But as the sun rose and the room warmed, the calls kept coming, and eventually a car came and our door was knocked on—slowly at first, then beat on with insistence and eventually opened. And Sil found us all here, then bent over to vomit and turned around to shout at Pio, GO BACK TO THE CAR DON'T COME INSIDE. And Emma called out for him but he didn't answer, and when Pio came in later and screamed her name he couldn't see her couldn't find her but the trampling and light became more trampling and more light red and blue swirling things high-strung boots stomping through blood and vomit and no matter how many people Emma called out to and waved her hands at none of them saw her all of them stepped around her like she was a shadow across the floor instead of a grieving vacant girl unglued and emptied by the grief. Me too. They all stepped around me, no one laid eyes on me, I just lay there like a dummy. Emma wouldn't have believed I was breathing if she hadn't set her fingers beneath my nose and felt my life there. The bodies were lifted away and photos were taken and the world fell quiet. The house kept us sheltered and when the rest of the world was gone we were still there.

And we are still here. Emma speaks with eyes glazed over, thick with unconsciousness, as if they were still closed. I'm unsure if either of us has left our fevered state or if some of its muck still lingers in our brains. I wander upstairs and come back down a moment later, pull a pair of socks over my feet.

—How is this happening, I say.

I say it but I think we both know. The way she looks at me, eyes wearied, shoulders resigned, confirms it. A floorboard creaks upstairs—just a draft, a shift in weight.

She can tell there's another question on my tongue that I'm trying to swallow. My eyes stationed at the entrance to the kitchen. If she looked closely she could see my pulse pounding at my throat.

—What is it, she says. —Spit it out.

—Who did it.

I bet she'd love to fling the guilt at me, love to lay the weapon in my reach, love to believe herself incapable of committing the act. But we were both bloodied, both beaten, when we woke. So she shakes her head slow and solemn and says, —I don't know.

< sometimes
it's hard to tell >

And the worst part, the part I couldn't tell Orrie: I finally heard a voice of my own. In the interstice between waking from the horrific killings and watching Orrie sink into his panic-sleep. Three words that nearly sent me into a panic of my own, reverberating somehow from deep within myself:

< one week left >

2

two days left down a hollow path empty light gestures toward ending

< you want a crumb of the others don't you >

< worried for them as you are for you own kin >

—I just dropped him off, Pio said in the car. —He was so sick it seemed like he was gonna die. So he asked me to drive him here.

Sil had just pulled up to the house and found the life-spill and made the calls. Hurled on the floor, added to the acrid air, emptied himself out. Came back to the car and sank into the seat and tried to keep himself from retching any more.

—I dropped him off and he went inside and didn't come back out.

He was doing a strange sobbing thing that Sil hadn't heard before. The kind of sound that made the word *keening* rise up in his head. The kind of sound he'd noticed coming from him when he felt Angio's pulse peter out in the hospital room. He wasn't in his body or he would have reached out to comfort him.

Pio threw the door open. Needed to find belief with his own eyes.

—Don't go in there, Sil said. —DON'T.

But Pio threw the front door open wide and screamed ORRIE EMMA ORRIE into the house. Heard his own screams careen off the far walls, up the staircase. From the front door he could see red on the kitchen floor and he turned to the wall, crushed his eyes shut, tried to squash the sight out. Then the suited people showed up with their lights flashing and sirens blaring and pulled Pio from the house, did their work.

Abduction was suspected, but who did it nobody could guess. Sil and Pio were cleared from consideration as the blood wasn't fresh and Sil's sister was in town and corroborated their story (his aunt was somebody Pio had greatly looked forward to Orrie meeting, but with a flip of his gut, he realized: not this trip).

Nothing of Orrie's or Emma's had been taken. It seemed as if they'd simply stepped out of their lives. The house had not been burgled; every piece of furniture and jewelry was in its place.

A box cutter was found beneath the lip of the kitchen cabinet but it had no prints on it. Blade bloody, handle whistle-clean.

Sil and Pio held all this inside themselves and let it swim there.

< you see the curse robbed us of life too >

< trapped us in its walls held us there >

< and we decided we wanted another shot >

We decide to test the bounds of the property.

I describe to Emma the way things went for me. The further I got, the worse my ailments were. The boiling-freezing in my blood and the pressure in my head and the retching. It's her turn to see if anything will happen to her. She has not left the property in weeks.

When I balk at this she says, —No driving. Mom's orders.

So I wave it away and we go for a walk. Step out onto the porch and sit there for a minute, feel the sun on our skins. It's a chilly morning but the light is warming and pleasant.

—I don't notice anything yet, she says.

—Me neither. Just wait.

So we venture down to the oracle tree at the front of the house. Sit at either side of its base. I am not brave enough to ask anything of it but she is staring at it like she's demanding its innermost truths. Then I notice her eyes have narrowed and she's crawled closer to it, set a finger against the bark.

—Not good, she says.

—What?

—Looks like some sort of fungus or rot. Gotta keep an eye on it.

I walk to the other side and see what she's seeing. The black-spotted patterns infiltrating the bottom of the bark. Thicker and darker at the bottom but narrowing and fading as they work their way up. Strange spirals of not-good.

I look down at my hands and feel the rot there too, remember the blood. Consider whether the deed was my doing. Or maybe was done through my body, during that strange blank period before I opened my eyes and saw. I tremble with what I do not know.

Here at the oracle tree, too, I feel okay. But the sickness normally doesn't happen till I get off the property. At the funeral everything was fine, but maybe the house knew I was coming right back after the interments; maybe it had no reason to act upon me. All just theories I crumple up in my hands till they make a mash. All I've got to work with.

So we trudge forward till things start fuzzing. Blur at the edges the way they did in Sil's car (I try to push away thoughts of Sil and Pio so my legs do not give out).

—Are you feeling that, I say. —In your head.

—Yeah. It's like a tightness.

—Yeah, that.

—Like when I get a cold and get those horrible migraines.

We're crunching down past the graves and I'm remembering Emma laid up in bed, her hands held to her head because she thought it was going to explode if she didn't lie perfectly still. Hasn't had one of those really bad colds in a while but I remember them like it was last week. One of the few times Emma was truly quiet.

—So this is what it's like, I say.

I remember Ingrid tending to her (I want to cry out), floating up and down the stairs with tea and hot rags and medicine in her hands. The way she itched to help.

—Oh, it's getting worse, Emma says from my left. Her knees begin to buckle beneath her but she steadies herself and carries on.

We're at the bottom of the hill now. Once we cross the street, we'll be at the bus stop where we used to hitch rides to school when Dad first left. Swing a right and head down a while and we'd be at the gas station where we used to stop on the way home for after-school snacks. With hidden pocket money, bellies soon full of sugar and secrets. On the left is the fire station.

—Left or right? I say. The eternal question.

—Neither, she says. —I think this is the end of it for me.

She collapses onto a big rock near the base of a power line and holds her stomach with her right hand. Leans over it and spits up across the gravel. Nothing substantial, just enough to get the feeling out.

—I don't know how you seem so steady right now, she says.

Maybe because I've seen the sickness at such an extreme I thought I was seeing the light of the afterlife. But I don't want to one-up so I help her climb to her feet, guide her back toward the house.

In truth, a bit of me is leaping up and down. Until now, I was the only person to feel the strange symptoms. To see Emma experiencing it too confirms its reality, confirms that I am not merely losing my mind but that something real is happening here, happening inside both of us.

I grip her hand. —You'll feel better soon, I say.

—You don't know that for sure, she says.

But I do and it's like clockwork. The intimate knowledge of the way it melts off you. We hobble up the hill and cross the perimeter of the porch and a lightness enters her that I can feel instantly. In her spirit and in her body, a levity in the way she moves into the kitchen. She's looking at her hands like the answers are written there somewhere. She looks up.

—Why is this happening? she asks the ceiling.

< we love you child can't you see >

< we wish you could hear us all the time
wish we always had the energy to reach you >

< but our words and actions drain us
and if we want to get what we want
(which we do)
we have to be frugal >

<and we need you
to stay here >

< yes that too >

< don't you want
to help us orrie >

< don't you want us to be able
to breathe again >

Orrie is in the bathroom with his shirt off a couple hours later, looking through to something on the other side. Brows creased, concerned. He's rubbing his chest with his right hand, hard. A few acne spots there, blips of red against olive. I can see his ribs poking through his skin.

—I can see through to my soul, he says, —and I can see a black stain on it. It won't rub away. Can you see it too?

The air stings with rubbing alcohol. Cotton balls line the rim of the counter. My heart aches: all I see is a boy chafing his skin, which reddens in his fingers' wake. His shoulders are slumped, his eyes heavy, sleepless and afraid. But I just smile, hug him. He freezes up at first, then leans back into me.

—No, I say, —I don't see anything.

I've been thinking something and I figure he's been thinking it too: we are all that's left. We sit in the living room, wait for some sound to poke through our quiet. Metal-clanks in the kitchen, the clatter of pots and pans, the hiss of boiling water. Or the noise of earth-tending outside, the whir of machinery, the scrape of boot-bottoms against stair edges, the clearing of a throat, the sniff of a nose running in the cold. Any of it. Seated downstairs, waiting for him to rise from his fever dreams, I was alone. As medical professionals and law enforcement entered our house, stomped around me, I sat shrouded, alone. I'm so glad to have him back, awake and blinking, I could squeeze him so tight he'd never escape.

Till we figure out how to get ourselves free of it, our feet unstuck.

I still haven't told him about the voice I heard when we woke, warning us of one week left. Five days ago: if the voice was real, and if it was right, and something was coming in a week, it means we have two days left. But I push it away: so much around me I have been forced to believe in, and the voice is something I can still refuse.

—Orrie, you don't have to . . ., I start but don't know how to finish. The weight of his guilt sinks down onto me too.

—I don't what?

—It wasn't us.

—But what if it was?

—But we don't know.

He's crying now. Oh, the poor sweet thing. I pull him into my arms and hold him there, feel him shudder against me.

—How can you live with it?

Nothing I come up with is sufficient, no answer feels more than half-true or more than an excuse, so I just hold him there, hands set against his cold back, and wait for him to calm.

< sure you have some things to live with
but at least you can live with them
and not hold them in frigid dead hands
did you ever think about that >

From here it is a matter of what we do, Emma and I. That night I am lying in bed teeter-tottering on the edge of sleep, holding onto this fact for a while (I have moved back up into my bedroom, which has taken on a stale smell). For dinner we microwaved some leftover funeral potatoes and shoveled them down. By dinner I mean a meal we happen to have eaten at nighttime, because when was the last time either of us really cared about what we were eating or if we were eating or what day it was.

When I look up and notice a woman in the corner. No one I have seen before—a woman half in shadow, dark hair obscuring her eyes. A terror-yelp lets itself out of me and I throw the covers back and rush to the hallway. Where Emma is already waiting—of course she's already waiting.

—What's going on? she says.

She's clutching a blanket around her shoulders. (It's quite cold in here but the thermostat has stopped responding to our touch and it's stuck on a low setting—is there power, I wonder? But we got the microwave to work, so there must be.)

—Your room, I say.

She leads me in there and I curl up in her bed.

—I saw something.

—What?

—Someone.

—Who?

—I don't know, some woman in an old gown. I think she was holding something.

—Where?

The image comes to me again and again in flashes; whenever I shut my eyes, it's there.

—I couldn't tell what she was holding. I didn't really get a good look at it.

She sets a hand on my forearm and rubs it gently. The way Mom used to when we were children, to put us to sleep. It sends an instant, involuntary calm through my body.

—I think you just need some sleep, she says.

—Don't talk to me that way, I say, not mad so much as fatigued.

—What way?

—I know what I saw.

The words are clunky in my mouth and ring hollow in the air and I feel like a crazy person in a movie. But I was fully awake, looking, breathing, thinking. It wasn't a lie or a trick of the light: there was a figure there and then she disappeared. In between the two blue wall-corners, there was a woman waiting. And holding something. But I couldn't tell what she was holding. And after a few minutes of Emma's calm-summoning, I'm removed from the intense desire to know. I watch it float away like a balloon untied from a wrist.

< i think i deserve the first turn in the body
since i've been in here the longest
and gathered you all >

**< no i think i deserve it
as the newest and youngest >**

**< oh shush woman there is no way
you are giving it the first spin >**

**< the truth is we're all getting a turn
and most of us have been in here for years upon years
so what does it matter >**

< well mildred aren't you such a diplomat >

< no i just know the value of patience >

**< well you can take that patience
and shove it >**

In the morning, while Orrie is still asleep, I visit the yard again, crouch down to the base of the oracle tree. The mold or fungus has gotten even darker since the last time I looked, and when I prod it with a finger, I find the wood is soft and squelchy. I rip my hand back, repulsed, and that repulsion is the strongest thing I have felt in days.

I think back to when I used to feel anger strong enough to want to rip the tree from the ground myself, and it feels like a years-old memory. Now I feel wispy, content to float through the breezeless air of my life. If I don't move a muscle, don't blink an eye, nothing else will happen to me; I will just exist.

I feel forces acting upon my life, like gods breathing through me. Pressure from all around, waiting for the inside to give. Fine, I want to say, hands thrown up—act away. Do what you want with me, to me, through me. I no longer have the capacity to care.

It's sort of a waiting game, I think, till the tree rot spreads to my body, guts me, turns me to waste.

Orrie comes outside and sits in one of the chairs out on the porch. Doesn't do anything, just sits there and looks out at the world, and something vicious courses through me. Something I can't bear to feel, because it's going to tear me apart when we lose each other, like we have lost everyone else. It's coming, isn't it? I know it almost as surely as I know my own heartbeat.

I look up at him and my heart twinges for him: poor boy, caught in the crossfire of his curse. A tall tale in childhood, something he cupped in his palms and whispered about in the dark. All his life he has been waiting for it to rain down on him. And here it is, stinging his skin like wind-whipped sand.

But his curse is not my curse. I am not beholden to it; it does not move through me. So I run to the garden shed. I have never seen a fungus like this, something that has driven a tree to ruin so quickly, so insidiously—I feel an obligation to fight back. I throw the door open, rummage through the shed, find it curiously empty. Normally there are bottles of fluid, canisters of chemicals—field and garden stuff—but the shed is empty, from when we filled it with hyssop water for the funeral. I think deep, try to remember where Enzo moved everything.

A glint of memory comes to me: watching him carry things up the porch steps into the house, then coming back down again, refilling his arms. I leap up the porch, into the house. Dart into the kitchen, check beneath the sink but find only kitchen cleaners and soaps. The upstairs bathrooms are empty too, and the hall closet.

Finally I stand at the perimeter of the living room, where Orrie now sits.

—Orrie, I say. —Do you remember where Enzo put all the bottles from the garden shed?

I don't think he'll answer, figure he's deep in another half-dream, but he says, —Coat closet.

And I realize I walked right past it on my way into the kitchen, paid it no mind. I pull the door open, root around on the floor, pull out a purple-capped jug of fungicide. The pestilence that spreads across the tree—black, rotted, like a portal into the dark parts of the world—looks nothing like the varieties pictured on the bottle, but I've got to try something. Better to fight back than to let the tree die alone, defenseless.

It's a concentrate, so I mix a capful of the stuff into a pitcher of water. Carry it outside, dump it bit by bit onto the tree, down into the roots.

I take a step back and spend a second thinking about things. Try to bring the hyperreality closer to where I stand. Parents dead, Enzo dead, sister dead. Only Orrie and I left, alone, all the way up here. Sil and Pio not seeing us when they came to visit. The authorities not finding us when they came to collect the bodies. The whole world has that nightmarish grayness, that sense of falsity, to it, like I'll sit up in a rush any minute now and hear Dad snoring down the hall, smell sausage in a frying pan downstairs. Like this whole week with Orrie has been nothing more than a dream. But every time I fall asleep, I wake still in it.

The fungicide has sunk into the dirt, into the black cavern at the base of the tree. I can only hope it's enough. But I have a dark feeling it's all too late.

3

three words never to be heard from the leathered dead mouths threaded through shuttered shut ever again

< ladies ladies quiet down
you're disturbing the boy >

< and he's plenty disturbed enough isn't he >

< ha >

< i like to think he enjoys
my presence more than most i'm slightly less severe
than the rest of you >

< you're a quack is what you are the great great aunt quack
whom he hardly remembers i'd bet >

< but i'm sure he's having a riotous time with me now >

< hold onto that hope lady it's probably all you'll get >

Emma and I begin to realize that maybe the house isn't actually the house. Find ourselves in some version of the truth with rougher edges. I went to get a bite to eat earlier and found that the kitchen floor had been cleaned up and the fridge cleared out. Grackle-spackle-crackle. Flutters of life outside the house. My stomach grumbled something fierce and now I sit in the living room and think. The outside shimmers through the windows like it'll ripple if I touch it. I worry I'm going to walk out the front door and find myself in space or in the future two hundred years from now. While I'm in the house, there are choruses in my head all the time, talking about I don't know what. Some louder and some quieter but always this calm flood of sound. Occasionally, one voice pokes through and says something meaningful, like

< orrie there you are my good child >

that rouses me to attention. I hear some sort of rumble outside

< my dear it appears we have a visitor >

and I run to the window. See Pio out there alone: he's hijacked the car in the late afternoon. Been so long I wondered if he was a hallucination, if I'd ever see him again. The sound of his shoes on the deck steps. He reaches the door and tries the handle but the bolt is locked. His eyes are heavy like he's been in a long sleep. Or been awake for so so long.

I shout, —LET HIM IN.

< are you sure >

—YES.

Never been more sure of anything, never felt anything this deep in the body. I try to grip the doorknob and tug it open but it doesn't budge. But Pio tries the handle again and it gives. I'm so happy to see him, so knee-deep in relief, I could cry. But he looks right through me, looks around the emptied room.

—PIO I'M RIGHT HERE.

But his eyes never land on me. It's like I'm a current the air vent has sent through the room. And I can't touch him with my hands; they go right through. Objects pelted at him sink right through him. It's like we're on two separate planes of existence and somehow the house is letting me peek through to his. I don't realize I'm crying till I try to call out again and the sound catches in a sob.

He calls out for us up and down the ground floor. I step into the kitchen and again its tile and grout are ruined, deeply blood-stained—no scrubbing could clean them. I blink, try to rub the red out of my eyes, but it's there again on the floor. It was gone earlier and it's back now. How? I saw it so plainly.

Pio ascends the stairs and does the same up there. I hear his shoes soft-tapping on the hardwood up and down the hall. I want to pull his hands to my face, make him feel my heat, my chest rising and falling with life. For him to know I am here and breathing. But there's no way for my plane to meet his. He makes his way back down to the bottom floor and takes one final, solemn look around the house like it's set to be demolished tomorrow. Then he walks out.

I run out behind him, try to knock him down, to climb into his car, to stop him from leaving. But the car just goes through me like wind through a screen door. In my head I hear,

< it's for the best >

and I'm lit up with rage. Who's to decide what is best for me? Who's overlaying thoughts onto me and cluttering my skull with voices?

All useless questions. I throw them at the wind and watch them get lifted away.

< not useless at all dear it's us don't you recognize us >

Us, they say: this chorus of women's voices young and old. Some wearied and time-worn, others sprightly and brand-new. I don't recognize them.

Emma's in the kitchen, seated at the table, staring at the wall. Not doing or saying anything. Didn't notice Pio was here, didn't notice me shouting at him. No tea or water or anything, just her small body slumped there over the wood. Her turn to dissociate. There are so many worlds for us to lose ourselves in: the ones forced upon us and the ones we invent for ourselves, carve out in our minds. I am fighting my way out of each one—I want no place in any of them. I want a world with my sister and Pio and Sil and the rest of my family back. I want Ingrid and Mom and Uncle Enzo there. I want it to be a full world we can all breathe in. Bloodless and gentle and love-full and gleaming.

< sweet boy >

said with the sorrow of the knowing.

< let's work some of our magic now >

< it's always fun to feel powerful isn't it >

< by the time cleo makes her way to us we'll be near unstoppable >

When I wake, on the edge of some black dream, I hear a single word:

< tomorrow >

It booms through the room, though I know it's coming from inside my head. Not Orrie's voice—a woman's. A brief, quick thing that nevertheless hangs in my ears as I toss my legs over the edge of the bed. There's a twist deep in my gut at the memory of the first voice I heard, the one that warned me about the week. Only one day remains.

Then I notice a loud hammering sound. Again and again, coming from downstairs, shaking the foundation of the house.

The world is different today. The light coming in the window has a red hue. Red streaming down the windows almost, if I squint hard enough. Like the world is taunting us, saying, LOOK WHAT YOU DID. There's a flash, for a moment, of that red-feeling I had, that I-could-kill rush. Not only I-could-kill but I-*want*-to-kill, and the shame that swept through me afterward revisits me now too.

As I descend the stairs, I locate the sound as coming from the kitchen. I pop my head in and see Orrie on the floor, chisel and hammer in hand. Eighty percent of the tile has been stripped away, and the concrete is exposed. Boxes of tile are spread out behind him, and orange buckets with thick, gluey mixes inside and a heavy smell. All sorts of tools, trowels, paddles. I feel, again, disoriented, like I stepped out of one dream and into another. With the hammer, he sends the chisel through the floor, through the last tile—it sends a sharp spike through our ears. He turns to me, grinning.

He must not have heard the voice. He would wear it on the skin if he had, the dark aura of it. But I don't believe in it anyway. It was a remnant of a dream, a trick my mind played on me. Nothing else, nothing more. I begin to breathe slower.

—Morning, he says. —I remembered seeing these out in the shed.

Some dark thing crosses his face then, perhaps at the memory of what else he'd seen there, what it led to.

—What are you doing? I ask.

—Getting this ruined tile out of the floor, he says, —and laying new.

—Do you know what you're doing?

—Yeah. He smiles, glows at a distant memory. —Remember when Uncle Enzo and I redid the bathroom floors last year? And the laundry room?

I do have some vague memory of it—the same bang and shatter as the old tile came up, the same smell of adhesive.

—These tiles are bigger, he says, —so I'll have to do a bit more cutting than I'd hoped, but I can get this done no problem. I'm glad you slept in. I was worried I'd wake you.

Looking closely at the exposed concrete, I notice thin pencil-marked tile placements all along the floor behind him. He's filled two of the buckets with old tile and mortar.

I hear it again. Tinny in my head, not the actual voice but my memory of it. < *tomorrow* >. I scratch my arm and look at the blood-light outside again, look down and notice I've been scratching myself for quite some time. Red welts up and down my forearms, like Mom is visiting me here, rising up in me.

At which point a thought hits me that I don't want to sit with for even a moment. I push it to the very back corner of my brain, hold it there till it runs out of air. Orrie notices me struggling with something, goes concerned.

—We should eat something, I say. I haven't thought to eat in a while and the weight of remembering hits my body with a loud grumble. —Wonder what's in the fridge.

He shifts, swallows. —Probably a lot of rotten stuff. Produce all gone bad by now.

His tone is light but there's a dark layer beneath, like he's trying to keep me out of the fridge.

—What?

He gulps again. —When I was in there earlier, he starts. Swallows. —There wasn't any food.

My stomach groans. —What do you mean?

—It's . . . cleared out. I don't know. I was gonna eat earlier but there was nothing in it.

I slide on my pair of shoes that's by the front door and walk into the kitchen, set ginger steps on the exposed concrete. I pull the door open. It's fully stocked, as ever. I turn back toward Orrie and he's shaking his head with a dark glow in his eyes.

—I'm serious, Emma, he says, —it was empty earlier.

—I believe you, I say.

But it leaves my mouth with a curious, nonbelieving lilt. I peer in at the food, try not to think about the voice, but every time I get away from it, it rips back to the front of my mind, the warning there that my dream-ears lasered in on.

—Omelets? I say.

One of the first meals I learned from Dad before he was drafted. I remember standing here in the kitchen with him and watching him try to teach me the assured wrist-flick for a flip. How many eggs did I break, sling along the backsplash—how many yolks ran down the stripes there? I dig through the drawers, find half an onion, some shredded cheese, some wilted spinach, grab a couple limp tomatoes from the counter.

—Sounds good, he says.

But he's still looking at the fridge like it's going to leap out and gnaw on him. A kind of fear I haven't seen in his face since he was a young child, afraid of a nighttime hall noise or a tree shift outside or a bit of curse lore. Scary movies did him in too, that kid. And now he's plopped down in the middle of his own and he doesn't know what to do—neither of us knows what to do.

I have processed everything on some level but it still feels false, like a twist that happens at the end of a movie before you walk out of a theater into the bright day and resume your life. I'm waiting for that resuming to happen. But there's only the thwacking of the flooring, the sound of the saw slicing through tile, the paddle mixer on the drill whipping up the mortar, the scrape of the trowel, the tap of the mallet to level the tiles, the making and spreading of grout, the wet swish of the sponge. Then Orrie's excited voice at sundown, telling me to come look. The bright-white tiles; the smooth, clean grout. Still, I wait to open my eyes and find everything gone back to how it was. Any minute now.

< march seventh the ides of the ides >

< double beware >

< rough estimate really you never know in this business >

< but by then we should have the life force to live again >

< when are we deciding which body we'll be inhabiting >

< my personal vote is for orrie something about that boy he can see the world so beautifully >

< but wouldn't you want it to be emma wouldn't you want to live as a woman again >

< i know i want to feel the power of a woman >

< eh my soul is woman that's all i need to know >

< and what are we going to do with the other >

< we don't have to talk about it >

In the middle of the night I roll over and open my eyes and the woman is back with two others. My body is sore and my brain is foggy from working on the flooring all day, but in a moment I'm up, my spine rigid, my eyes wide. The women are shrouded in the dark of the room but I know in my marrow that it's them.

—What do you want, I say to them.

< we're testing your body taking it for a test drive >

They're speaking in front of my eyes but their voices ring out inside my head. No travelling sound waves but I get it all regardless. The strangest thing.

I ask, —Testing it why?

< why not aren't we allowed to have a bit of fun >

—I don't even know who you are.

By now I'm quaking like several tiny bombs have gone off in my limbs and they've destabilized my whole structure. Trying to take in all the barely perceptible flecks of light that crop up along the far wall.

The women are closer without moving. It's a not-motion.

—Who are you.

< who aren't we >

One of them snickers, a high, silly sound.

< sorry we're being coy >

< but the less you worry about us the better >

—How am I supposed to not worry when you're in my head?

< so sorry darling >

< everything will happen as it should >

which is not in any way a comfort. It sends itchy chills up my arms and I pull the blankets up higher over me. Maybe if I cover my eyes, I won't see them. But I don't like not being able to see the enemy, it only makes me think about them more, so I pull them back down again but when I look at the corner of the room, they're no longer there. The whole thing had the here-and-gone sense of a dream. But it was so real. If I look closely enough at the backs of my eyelids, I can still see them printed there.

4

four letters that spell out the woman the life-giver the last to join the spirit-clan caught in amontillado

< in the mood to be sad then listen to this >

The boy sits in his room and he's almost crying. He hasn't let himself cry in years but the thoughts are bringing him near that edge, bringing things toward spilling over. It has been five years of shoving-down and finally he's allowed himself to let the slightest thing out. A vulnerability, light and giving, like air in his hands—though he was terrified, and it wasn't as easy as it had seemed. He was gnawing his lip the entire time, tearing it to shreds.

He finds a sweatshirt on the top bunk, that's what starts the whole thing. He finds it and pulls it down and holds it to his nose. And it smells like him—it smells so strongly of him that the boy has held it to his face there for a minute or two and allowed a figment of imagination to slip in. He's back, he didn't disappear, he's still out there. Hope is a thing built to disappoint, but if it also brings him this relief, so be it.

< we never said it was going to be easy for everyone >

< oh don't be going all soft now we're so close >

< i'm not going soft i'm just empathizing >

< bit late for that isn't it
and besides where's the empathy for us
trapped in the walls for all this time
aren't your soul-bones tired >

< been tired for so long i don't even know
what it'll feel like otherwise >

< exactly >

< i got my first taste when amphithea first figured out
what we were capable of
and since then it's been a sweet taste i've been craving >

< can't forget it can you >

< well we would've had the thing done by now
if the little one weren't sulking in the corner >

< c'mon little girl it's okay
your brother and sister will be fine
in most senses of the word >

< god look at her over there

crying her little soul-tears
god help her >

—It's happening, I tell Orrie when he comes down in the morning.

The sky is bloodier than it was yesterday, like an always sunset, clouds floating in it red-tinted at their edges. I point out toward the oracle tree, and he gasps when he sees how the rot has accelerated, the brown-black spotting spreading up the trunk, the bottom nearly given to it entirely. The high-up branches have begun to lose their integrity, bent toward the earth like they've gone invertebrate.

—Like it's being devoured from the inside out, he says. —I wonder how long till the whole thing gives. Let's go look at it.

—Can't, I say.

—Why?

But he figures it out for himself when he gets to the front door and it doesn't budge. No matter how firmly he twists the handle, no matter how many times he checks the locks, how much of his weight he throws into the pull, the door doesn't move an inch.

—Oh, and also Pio came by again, I say. —To check. This time he couldn't get in the front door and he was confused.

His eyes take on a faraway sheen, like he's popped out of his body and cropped up at Sil's house.

—It might be a good thing, I say. —He seems suspicious. Maybe it means he'll keep coming, keep checking.

He's tracing his fingers on his pant legs now, writing things. —Or that he'll get roped into everything too.

—But isn't he already? I say.

He can't really argue with this, he just keeps tracing his patterns. Letters, maybe, things he wishes he could say, if it weren't too late. And the whole time there's an itching beneath my skin, a temptation to scratch at my arms, to scrape out the truth. I've got to give it away sometime, I figure, this thing I've been holding in, or it'll dig its own way out.

—I knew this was coming, I say.

—What? he asks.

—Today. It's the end, I think.

—What do you mean?

—I heard a voice.

He catches at this. His soul, in some faraway place, is yoked back to his body; his face reddens, his shoulders tense.

—When?

I don't want to say, I want to keep it inside myself, don't want to hurt him. But hurt him I must.

—When Mom and Enzo died, I say.

—And you didn't tell me?

It booms from him—I know he doesn't mean for it to, but it does nevertheless.

—I didn't believe it, I say. —Thought it was a dream or something.

—Emma, he says. —This whole time.

—And I heard another one yesterday.

—And you didn't tell me *again*?

Another rise in volume, in pitch—another dart thrown.

—But they were warning me about today, I say.

—What did they say?

He's in the living room now, in the chair across from me, seated at its edge, like at a moment's notice he might have to spring up and defend himself against something.

I tell him what they said and try to describe how the words moved through me. He nods along fervently as I go, reinforces that everything was the same for him. As he nods, my eyes begin to water, and I wipe away whatever spills over.

< was it mildred who discovered the earth might also offer us energy and power >

< knew she'd someday be good for something >

< oh hush >

< i'm speaking in jest >

< you never speak in jest to me i remember you
running around the house with that wooden spoon
in your hand
looking to lay into me with it
you've always had it out for me >

< please i did no such thing >

< that crazed look in your eye
like the devil'd gotten into you
i remember it like it was yesterday >

< ladies ladies please we've got one mission here
haven't we let's not tear each other up in the process >

< i will tear into whomever i please
thank you very much >

I sink into a brief couch-nap (sorry, Emma, I know you wanted to figure out how to tend to the tree together) and when I wake Emma's struggling with the front door.

—What the hell, she says, kicking at it with her foot. She throws her weight against it, testing if it'll give in the other direction. But her body does an awkward crunching against the meaty door and she lets out a cry. —Goddammit.

Then we hear a giant shifting sound and look out into the yard to see that the oracle tree has come unmoored. A giant, tangled net of roots and soil clumps, its heavier upper half giving way to gravity.

—NO, she cries.

I am too stunned to speak.

The trunk topples away from the house, strikes the ground with a heavy, earth-trembling thud. Branches rattle and thwap against each other. Now that the tree is inverted, we can see the horror at its base. The rot has taken over its root system and the soil—the whole mess is crawling with that death-black. Tender networks of rotted roots cut off from oxygen; lifeless clumps of black dirt.

—I've never seen anything like this, Emma says.

Looking out the eastern windows, we see the blackening has begun to spread out into the fields. It's just beginning to push past the fences. Dread fills me to the brim.

< sorry children we have to sustain ourselves somehow >

I think of whomever is living in our rafters and sharp anger joins the fear-blades in my blood. Putting voices in my head, sucking the life out of the land. Leeches, the lot of them. Covering my eyes, making me do their dirty work, and for what. In an instant I'm the closest to fury I've been in weeks.

—AND FOR WHAT, I shout at the walls.

Emma leaps in fear. I sense a nudge at my shoulder and turn back toward the hall.

—Emma, I say. —Do you see that.

—See what.

I walk down the hallway and Emma follows me. One gentle step at a time, as if she won't be able to turn back.

On the triangle of wall beneath the stair steps there is a door. A door that has never been there before, that exists where we knew only a smooth field of cream-colored paint.

< come on down >

The handle gives, soft in my hand like a knife in butter, and the door creaks open.

Stairwell, down, down. To what, I don't know. I've never been under the house, never known of any lower chambers. But it's got to happen. I feel it deep in me.

—Our answers are down there, I say.

I'm resolved to follow the yellow brick road, but it's only when Emma grips my shoulders and spins me around that I note the fear pooled in her eyes.

—Answers or a trap, she says.

—Don't know, I say. —But we can't do anything up here. We can't even get outside. So there's really only one way to find out, isn't there.

She thinks about it for a long while, during which I don't know what to do with myself. I look up and down and toward the red-skied windows and the rotted soil. Finally, she steps in after me and we begin to descend.

< good children
always been good children >

5

five four three two one welcome to the end feel it all again

As soon as we step into the stairwell, the door shuts behind us and the daylight disappears. But there's a glow from somewhere beneath us that beckons us down the steps. Emma sets a hand to the door, feels for the handle, but no door is there any longer. Only a wall painted the same cream on the inside as the outside.

—God, she says, —we can't get out.

Her breath starts coming shallower and faster like river-rushes striking rocks. I pull her toward me till it starts slowing down again.

—We have to do this, I say, filled with a sudden conviction, a lack of fright.

Palms and pits sweatless, eyes set straight ahead. The chamber carries a musty smell that intensifies as we descend further. The kind of aged and barren smell that suggests this dark chamber has been here all along but hasn't been opened for years and years. I can feel the tremble in Emma's creaking steps, like she might tumble down the stairs, collapse onto the floor at the bottom.

Till about two-thirds of the way down, when the sound of shaky footsteps fades away. I turn to check on Emma and she is not there. My stomach threatens to spill over.

—EMMA, I shout. —EMMA. WHAT HAVE YOU DONE WITH HER.

< come on orrie you've almost arrived >

Arrived where and to what? My limbs are rickety, my throat hoarse; my sister is gone. I feel the departure: there is pressure on my heart at her absence. I stumble to the bottom of the stairs and find myself in a large, concrete room. There is nobody here but me, yet the room feels full, strangely populous.

< we've been stuck here >

I feel-hear it from every wall. It seems to bounce from one to the next

< we've been waiting for you to set us free >

< i could scream i could cry so delighted am i that you're finally here >

< calm down you're scaring the boy >

< *i'm* scaring the boy >

cacophonous voices, different textures, different timbres.

—Who are you.

< who do you think we are dear >

I try to identify the source of the flickering lights but can find nothing. There's a heartbeat pulse to them like candle flames wavering in wind. But no candles. The light seems to flash from inside the walls themselves.

—I think you're the curse.

< not quite but something close >

< though if it would comfort you to think of us as the curse
then think it all you want >

—What are you gonna do to me?

< we're not gonna do anything *to* you
merely *through* you
haven't you always wanted more friends >

—Not like this.

< well i'm afraid you don't have much of a choice >

< well it could be him or her >

—What could be him or her.

< mildred shush >

—Him or her . . . me or Emma?

< yes darling >

—What are you doing with her and don’t call me that.

< the problem dear
sorry i know you just said
is that we need a bit more energy than we have >

—What do you mean, energy.

< we want to live again dear one
the curse stole our lives from us
just like it stole your fathers and sisters and mothers
before you >

All the dead lined up in a little line.
—So does that mean you’re.

< we have lived in this house all this time
and as long as the house stands we’ll be here >

< till mildred realized we *can* live again
we just need a vessel >

—A vessel. And that’s what I am.

< precisely >

< well you or the girl >

—And what happens to the other one.

< well >

< as i said we need more energy >

< we thought your mother would be enough >

< but unfortunately your little sister isn't cooperating >

I picture her in there, wherever the souls are cramped and alone.

—Ingrid, I call out.

And then I hear her voice, mellifluous and inch-tiny.

< orrie >

< i'm trying to stop them >

< but they're too strong >

It's a voice I held close across eleven of my years. A hole funnels through my heart.

—Ingrid, I say. My eyes fill and my chest goes petal-tender.

< i don't know how to get out >

—Don't worry, I'll figure it out. I don't know how either but I'll do it.

< ok little one that's enough for now >

< dear orrie we don't know
who we want to live through yet
you or your sister >

—And how do you find that out.

< well we test you of course >

< don't you love tests >

—Test me how.

< just with questions and memories >

—Where do we start.

< answer me this >

< orrie are you a good person >

My stomach quivers. I push away several memories that spring to the backs of my eyes. Heart leaping with conviction, with unfettered belief.

—I think so, yes.

< are you sure about that >

—I have to be, I croak. —How can I live otherwise.

< are you positive >

< i think we might need to refresh your memory >

I open my eyes and I'm in another place. Another room. It's Mom's room—I'm outside of myself, looking at myself sprawled out across the bed. It's late in the day and the windows are dark. I think for a moment that this must be—but no, I don't want to think about it.

If I listen closely, I can hear chatter happening in another room, maybe the bathroom down the hall. Then, a scream: Mom's voice, at that pitch I'd never heard, and I watch other-me stare at the notebook in my hands but I don't even seem to be focusing on it, my eyes have that glazed quality of an old window. The pen in my hand is frozen on the page. It doesn't move, doesn't add a single mark.

< you can hear them >

the voice says

< why aren't you doing anything >

—I don't know, I say.

So I start shouting at myself. —ORRIE. ORRIE.

But the kid on the bed doesn't move. He's still got those fogged-glass, downcast eyes.

Why didn't I move? Why didn't I get up to run into the bathroom? Was it out of malice? Did I know somehow what was happening in that bathroom?

—It wasn't me, I say. —It was you. You made me stay there frozen.

< was it us or is that something you are trying to believe to make yourself feel better >

—No, I wouldn't do that, I would go help. I would do something.

< are you sure >

I blink and I'm in another place. On a highway, a lonely stretch of winter road. The sun is low in the sky. It's mid-afternoon, but already the light is preparing to leave us. I recognize the highway that leads down into town. Two lanes of traffic moving in either direction with occasional intersections. Few stoplights. It never gets this cold in A____; we all think it's a strange occurrence, the road covered in slush, hiding black ice beneath. I'm standing beside the road in the cold, watching the scene. My breath forms plumes of fog. My jaw judders and I clutch my arms around myself.

I spot a truck in the distance that looks so familiar I can place it in an instant, can place myself in it all through my childhood, riding on the bench with Dad. Heater blaring, radio cranked to something I wanted to turn off—but it was better than riding the bus to school. Used to get rides to school from Dad back when he was here. Used to sit in the middle between him and Emma. And he'd always say something at the door, what was it.

—No, I say with a knot of dread in my stomach, because I know what's coming. Because what else could be coming at this moment but—

The truck comes closer, the little girl perched in the passenger seat looking out the window with bright eyes. The awkward man driving, clutching the wheel like he's never seen one before. He's going fast. I can feel it in the ground's rumble, hear it in the engine's rev—faster than you should go in these temperatures, never know what kind of threats are lurking. And when the curve comes up, he misses it. I try to look away, but the room won't let me, not entirely. He overcorrects and veers off the roadway toward the ditch, bounces in it once, comes up on the other side, and launches toward a row of solid pines. Closer to me than ever for a second—I think the vehicle is going to splat into me, split all my bones apart—but it only skims me, shoots past my right shoulder and wraps itself around a tree.

< why aren't you helping you're just standing there >

< you're right there what are you doing >

—BUT I'M NOT, I shout at the voices.

I'm only there now because they're putting me there. In reality, I was happy at home, unaware of what was happening down here on the road. I was sitting at the table with Emma, talking about something, splitting a snack—normal afternoon stuff. But in the vision I'm seized by a desire to help. I try to sprint toward the vehicle, but the distance stretches into eternity. Every step I take leaves me further away than I was before.

—Let me over there, I shout.

But nothing happens; time only continues stretching. I watch someone else show up on the scene and pull Ingrid from the truck. I see her body shattered and reddened but I keep running I keep running I keep running.

—Why would you show me this? I yell. —This is fucked up.

In truth, I don't enjoy cursing, but it's the only word that feels right for once.

< still think you're a good person dear one >

< you haven't done a thing >

And they're right, that much is true. The thought brings me to my knees in the hard snow-ice. Maybe I really was there, I don't know anymore, can't tell the real from the fictive. Maybe I sat and did nothing.

< ready for the next one dearie >

We sink back into the gloomy half-light of the not-basement.

—I thought I said stop with the nicknames.

The snow is still freezing on my kneecaps, starting to soak my pants. The kind of cold that seeps in deep and starts to sting.

< but you're our dear little one
youngest in the line >

My fingers are losing feeling.

—And you're about to kick me out of my body. Don't think that sounds like royal treatment.

< oh no we're not going to kick you out
we're just going to snuggle up next to you
like at a sleepover aren't those fun >

—Where is Emma.

< she's in a trial of her own
but she's fine don't you worry about her >

—Can I see her?

< not until the trials are complete >

—When will they be complete?

< when you've decided >

—Decided what.

< next up >

I'm at school now. My pants are again dry; my skin feels like it never touched the snow. Haven't been here in what feels like so long—only two weeks in reality, but those two weeks have been so full of grief they've stretched out into years. This is earlier in the year, when the leaves have just started changing color, far before Dad came home or any of that. The sky is a glacial color in early afternoon as the sun is about to start going down. The wind is starting to nip at my cheeks and nose, turn them red.

—Why are we here?

< watch and find out >

—I'm impatient.

< just hang on feel it all again >

Feel it all again. Okay. The sun on my skin is warming the parts the wind has touched. The grass fields casting up their just-mowed smell. My too-thick jacket, the moisture gathering in my armpits. The wind doesn't go through it and the air is still warm when the wind-gusts aren't there.

< good remember these feelings >

I see my friend Jacob leave the school building. One of the silly but quiet kids, the kind of silly that emerges as the layers of quiet recede—it's a privilege to get through to it. The teacher of my last period tends to let us out a few minutes early, so I'm always at the front of the school quicker than the others. But Jacob comes out and nods at me, crosses the grass to get to the student parking lot. Blake, one of the athletes, appears behind him, stops Jacob, and they start talking.

My stomach goes sour—I know why I'm seeing this now. Again, I can't close my eyes, can't look away.

They appear to be just talking, could be any two people in a conversation. Until Blake's fist launches out whip-fast and Jacob's head careens back; a big arc of blood flies through the air. He falls on his back and Blake keeps going, kicks and punches him, and from twenty feet away I hear the impact in Jacob's body. All those sounds of pain being absorbed into him.

< stuck in the mud orrie why aren't you running getting help breaking it up

In truth, I find myself captivated by the mechanics. I've never seen a fight this close up. By now people are energized, drawn to the fight, crowding around. Not much of a fight, considering Jacob lies there pulped up and Blake just keeps going.

I watch what I do next and try so hard to move my body elsewhere but I'm stuck in my actions. I become part of the crowd, become a bystander, forget I know anything about either of these people. Forget about Jacob as a shy character with not a mean bone in his body. Forget about him going for it and asking Thea to homecoming even though he knew she was going to laugh in his face. Forget about Blake as one of those ramped-up football players using every moment of every day as an opportunity to illustrate dominance. Every muscle, every limb, quivering with potential energy.

Just watch. Listen. Feel it all again. The squelches of feet and fists impacting soft organs, the crunch of cartilage and limp exhales.

Certainly isn't a walk-it-off situation. I watch a pair of coaches come up—takes them a while to get through the crowd that has gathered—and they pull Blake off the poor kid and kneel at Jacob's side. Maybe they think he is dead at first, flattened against the ground. I watch Jacob lifted onto a stretcher, hear him make death-groans, blood clogging his throat as they wheel him to an ambulance.

I felt sick the rest of the day. Why hadn't I done anything? Why hadn't I called for help, why had I been glued to the scene? What dark part of me relished what I saw, was fascinated, curious, fulfilled?

When I found out the cause of the fight (Jacob had said something in passing about Blake that he thought would never reach his ears but you know how word travels in air vents and through floorboards, and you know how high-schoolers stoke fires, encourage the winds) I took a vow of hall-silence with myself. Knew I wouldn't be able to stand up for myself in that situation. Knew Blake would beat me to flattened, bloody ruin too.

< are you good orrie >

< why are you turning from your darkness >

—I don't know.

< let it in >

< let us in >

I feel a kicking at my ribs. Something trying to get in. It leaves a sludgey feeling in me. I shove it out with a big push.

< see we still can't get in we need one more >

< one more >

< stop resisting us child we'll get in sooner or later >

—I don't want you.

< it doesn't matter what you want
don't you get it
the end comes for us all anyway >

—And you haven't accepted yours.

< we were robbed
and we're willing to fight for what we want
willing to fight for what is right
but are you >

It stops me cold.

< so far it seems like
not quite >

Back in the basement room again. Still cold; a shiver radiates outward from my core.

< more orrie more >

< then we'll know for sure >

—Know what.

< then you can't hide from your truth anymore >

And I can't hide. I'm launched up a floor, find myself in the corner of the living room. I am watching myself again, this time standing next to Pio and Sil. The night of the funeral. From here I can see the way I look at Pio, like I've found my resting place.

Emma stands back by the stairs and looks at me. Looks at us the three of us standing there, huddled all together.

< what kind of brother would do this >

Emma and I approach each other and speak. I watch the light leave her eyes gradually, as if on a dimmer switch; I watch myself turn and rejoin the others. Eventually, the three of us peel away from the house, slip through the front door, and only Emma and ghost-me stand in the living room. Her hands hang at her sides and her shoulders sink. She watches the front door, hoping it opens again, hoping we'll come back for her.

< how could you leave your sister behind >

The light bleeds out, and when I blink, we're up in Emma's room. She's on her computer, typing an email to somebody. She looks at her phone, scrolls through her call log—all the unreturned calls. Glances at the clock, then back to the computer.

Leaning closer, I see that she's writing an email to Claire. One of her best friends that I haven't seen or heard from in a while—nor, it appears, has she. There's a long email drafted on the screen. I watch her select the whole thing except the first paragraph and delete it.

< abandoned from all sides >

My heart lurches. I didn't know. But I also didn't ask. Why didn't I ask? Where was I looking to have not seen her hurt?

Then I plummet downstairs and find myself standing in the kitchen. Emma is there too. Mom. Uncle Enzo. All of us bunched together in one room.

—No no no, I say to no one.

< don't look away orrie >

The world is blurry, tilted. I can't tell if I'm going to be sick or pass out.

< confront who you are >

—Come on, Mom says, shoulder to shoulder with Uncle Enzo. —Look at me, please, look at me, it's me.

Her hands are held out in front of her like she can ward us off with magic. Emma and I are at either side of them with blades in our hands. Emma's got the chef's knife from its magnet strip above the sink. And I've got—

—It's me, your mother, she says. —Don't you remember your mother?

< how do you want it to end orrie
what would make you feel best >

I watch myself step closer in the dream-scene. Still the old tiles on the floor, before they were stained, before I did the work of smashing and replacing them. Pure, unsullied, simple.

< maybe you'd like to shoulder all the guilt
and you'd feel better if it were you >

I step back.

< or maybe not >

Emma's mouth twists. Dim in the kitchen bulb's amber glow. She steps closer.

< maybe you'd like to cast it all on your sister
absolve yourself >

I step closer too. We're tight in on the two of them; they're running out of ways to smash themselves together, to make themselves smaller.

< or maybe guilt is a thing
best when it's shared >

—No no no no.

Those words from Mom I never wanted to hear again.

< what do you say child >

—I just want the truth, I shout into the room. —I just want the truth.

< all right >

< if you're sure >

I watch myself step forward, hear my foot-taps against the light tile. I raise my arm. Blade there. No light in my eyes—I've been taken over by some *thing*. They're voids, from my dream-vantage point, as depthless as drained pools.

< you asked for it >

Mom lets out a shriek as I rip her neck open. The room is full of screams—she's screaming with what throat she has left, Uncle Enzo screaming too (and me too, from here). I reach out to silence Enzo. Emma, I notice, has her eyes shut, her arms placid at her sides, like nothing is happening.

I watch myself turn toward her. Death-fear in her now-open eyes, she knocks at my wrist and the box cutter falls to the floor, skids a bit. She crouches to take Mom's head in her hands like she can shake her back to life. Blood pools and it touches her knees, her hands.

Then the end. The moment when I blinked myself away and took it all in.

I feel it all again.

< what do you think dear >

What do I think.

I believed it was all the house. On some level I still do. But I look down at my hands and see blood on them still, blood that won't wash away. The tarnishing marks on my soul.

< orrie >

Because I did this. I did. My body.

< orrie child >

< what do you think >

My hands. My dark-curtained soul.

Emma and I face each other, standing over the dead. We walk toward each other, footsteps sticky with blood, and raise our weapons at the same time, extend them toward each other's necks. We hold our poses for what feels like minutes. Wait for some divine command. Eyes locked, hearts athump.

And at the same instant in time we rip our blades across each other's necks, tear through skin, vein, muscle, artery. We collapse. Truth or forecast, I don't know. Watching Emma clutch her neck, roll in her own blood-puddle, I am overcome with anger at the injustice. But watching myself splutter and flail, I feel the peace of retribution. The evil has been eliminated—the evil that radiates from my core, affecting everyone I encounter.

It all goes dark like a curtain call.

Back in the not-basement now, the lights dimmer than before.

—It should be Emma, I say.

< what should be emma >

—Who lives.

< ahhhhhh >

< dashing >

< we can work with that >

A newfound chill in the air. A cavernous sound behind me.

< up the stairs you go >

I turn to look and there's a harsh glow at the top of the steps. My eyes have adjusted to the dark and I have to squint to see that the door has appeared again and it's open. I take the stairs two at a time. Call out for Emma the whole time, need to see her.

< in the kitchen >

Of course: the place where everything began is where everything must end. The end of the line. The family brought to ruin.

Emma is there.

—I'm sorry, I say and pull her in, hold her tight. If it were possible to put a lifetime's worth of weight and guilt into one *sorry*. Every up-and-down mood, every mini-moment, slammed together into one. On an elemental level I do feel better having said it, not quite in the soul but in my bones.

—What's going on? She sounds miles away, like her brain has locked her on some other planet. —Why are we here?

< i think you know >

—This is the end. Of everything.

—What do you mean.

—We have to do it.

—Do what.

—It's the only way to dispel the curse.

< weapons too >

—Go to the shed, I tell Emma. —Get a box cutter.

—The police took it for evidence.

—There are more out in the tool box.

—I don't want you to die.

How many times have I seen Emma afraid like this? Unvarnished. Fear written into her shining eyes, her tremulous lip.

—Just go get it, I say. —They're in the far shed in the middle of the fields.

She'll have a few minutes of walking to get to them.

Her eyes go blank, the fear melting away. I know the house is guiding her rather than she guiding herself—it lets her twist the knob, open the door. She's outside now, venturing toward the shed to rummage through the tool box.

And now I get to test a theory I've been formulating.

Not positive, but I'm pretty sure the house can only act on one of us at a time. It can show us things, alter our perceptions, at the same time, but it can only make one of us *do* things. So while it's guiding her out to the shed, I race toward the hall closet.

When we cleared out the garden shed to make room for the buckets for the funeral service, we brought all this stuff inside. Jugs and bottles of chemicals, plant stuff, car fluids, antifreezes, oils and the like. As I run toward the closet, I pray it hasn't all been put back. I remember Emma rooting around in it the other day, remember her looking for something. While I was in some fog. I hope it wasn't what I'll need now.

I pull the door open and sink to my knees, rifle through all the bottles and canisters. At the back behind a bottle of antifreeze—there it is. I breathe out, relieved. Red can of gasoline. That's all I need, all I wanted to look for.

Something the voices said keeps playing in my mind: < *as long as the house stands we'll be here* >

So there may be a way to set them free.

I'm thinking of the voices as little gas-bursts of souls, trapped in the wood of the walls. Last breaths caught in here all this time.

Got to set Ingrid free.

I run upstairs, let the gas leak out onto the floor a little at a time. Gaze into my bedroom, hug its door one last time with my left arm. A door I never closed but a door I cherish anyway for its tack-holes on the back and its bevels.

Don't think about it.

Emma's room. Ingrid's.

For a moment, I imagine what Ingrid's room would have looked like through the years. Had she never died, had she continued to grow and change. All the books she would have filled it with, the music she would have learned to play. But I don't have much time. I shove it all away. Can't get too sentimental. Things are just things; they can be replaced.

A big dash of fluid in front of Mom's room.

A trail down the stairs, a little waterfall; I try to keep it from sticking to my shoes.

A ring all around the downstairs. Through the kitchen, around the table and the island (pull something from the kitchen drawer, turn on the oven and all the gas burners), back into the living room, around the couch and chairs and TV, across the wood leading to the staircase. Stop at the front door.

Emma is near. She stands at the edge of the lawn with two box cutters in hand. She has no idea, does she.

I've stepped out the front door now; I'm looking back at her.

—ORRIE, she says. Her voice is strained and hoarse—she's trying to push through the control. —I CAN'T STOP IT.

She's crossing to the house now, soft footfalls in the dirt. Black-rotted dirt: the soil of the whole property has gone black now and the rest of the trees are beginning to curl in on themselves. She's got one of the blades extended in her trembling hand.

I've pulled out the box from the drawer and I'm trying to strike the match.

—ORRIE RUN. RUN. I CAN'T STOP.

She's making a death-moan now, her throat juddering in her neck. She keeps stepping forward, hard as she tries to resist.

I keep striking—fast, slow, I can't figure it out. The precise rhythm I need. I think of Mom lighting birthday candles, camp-fires in the yard.

—ORRIE RUN!

She's ten feet from the steps now. Finally, the match catches.

I hold it out in front of me and she notices it too—it captivates us both. She stops in her tracks and we just look at it for a moment. I consider blowing it out, letting her catch up to me, letting her end things. It's what I deserve after all I have done.

Something changes in Emma's expression. She struggles against it but her hand begins to lift the blade toward her own throat. Presses the cutter against her skin. A giant gasp leaves her; there's a bloom of red at the spot the blade touches.

The match, burning down, scorches my finger and I let it go. We watch it fall toward the front rug, toward the gasoline with its hungry glimmer, before the bright

6

He sees the smoke from miles out on his daily drive past the house, which he disguises as driving practice. He's already got the license but something about the daily ritual pleases his father, so he keeps it up. Makes him seem busy: he's on the road for an hour or two after school and before homework, math problems, books for English class. It all adds up to something that resembles a life.

The town has mostly written off the murders and disappearances—investigation is still happening but it's half-hearted, lethargic, like the entire police force has been given a sedative. Once the initial sharp grief cleared, Pio noticed a bad taste in his mouth and wanted to slap everyone awake. He's trying to resist taking the whole thing into his own hands. TWO PEOPLE ARE OUT THERE SOMEWHERE, he wants to shout. FIND THEM.

Every time he returns to the property, he notices slight differences. He's always been praised for his eye for detail—in English class, on the off chance he raises his hand, and further back, in childhood, solving hidden-picture puzzles in kid's magazines, running laps around the track. And these past few days, after the long drive out, he's poked around the property and noticed a steadily accumulating rot in the trees and flowers, in the farm's soil, like the whole earth has curdled in the absence of the family. He's tried the front door, stalked the halls, called out for his friend, his dear friend. Funny how someone who's been absent for six years can come back with such force—funny how you can think about a person when they're there, when they're not, you can find their name sewn into your brain-layers. A song that plays again and again and never wears out.

But today the difference at the property isn't slight. Black clouds billow up from the tree line, merge with the cloud cover. He inches down on the gas, accelerates. Dread simmers in his stomach.

He has felt strange these past few weeks. *Help me feel real again,* he has said to the property, the trees and gravel and plots for crops. The land hasn't answered. There's some mystery lingering here, something in the soil that he has not discovered yet.

When he gets closer, he sees that the tree in the front yard has toppled. A chill goes through him. The blackness, the rot, has spread, the tree has given way. And the smoke, all the smoke. Billowing up and out, dark and thick. The bright flames are the last thing to come into view around the curve of the hill. The front door an open maw.

He slams the car into reverse, ready to floor it back down to the fire station, but then he sees the forms on the porch, bent over each other like folded sheets of a letter. If he rushes to the fire station, the forms might be beyond saving; if he rushes to help, the house might collapse in on all of them together.

It's no choice, really, especially when he notices the sweatshirt the boy is wearing, its resemblance to one that's been missing from his own closet. So he puts the car in park and sprints up to them. He buckles to his knees, sets his hands to their chests to feel for breath, life. Sets his fingers to their neck to feel for pulses. They are alive, their blood is beating. Sooty and roughed up, starved-looking, gaunt in their faces, but alive.

The improbability of it all makes the moment feel hollow, but later he will look back on it and joy will flood his system. For now, he scoops them up beneath the armpits and drags them down the porch stairs, hauls with all his might to get them out of the smoke. Does it as quickly as he can to minimize breathing it himself, hacks hoarsely into his elbow.

—Hang on, he tells both of them.

Wishes so terribly that he had a cell phone.

Then he leaps into his car and kicks the dirt up, speeds on down to the fire station.

7

The first time I open my eyes, I'm bound in a bed. Bright fluorescent light and clean sterile white hospital walls. Time looping in my body. Over and over.

The feeling of blood moving through my fingers. Never had the sense of it before but each cell is making itself known to me. I curl and uncurl my fingers. Crush air in my hands, feel it whoosh out. If I look closely enough, I can see the air molecules moving like a fountain furling.

Humming, beeping, air flowing all around me. Machines keeping an eye on me. The hallway door an inch open. I haven't seen anybody pass but I can hear the distant sounds of another life.

I can barely turn my head and when I do, there's a sharp crackle of pain at the back. An under-skin sort of soreness down to muscle and bone. Six feet away from me is Emma, in a bed the same as mine, watching me.

—How do you feel? she asks.

I try to speak and a rough, scratchy sound comes out.

—They think you'll be mostly healed in a few days, she says. —Couple weeks for some of the bigger stuff. But nothing is ruined or anything. You'll be good as new.

I look down at myself. The body may not be ruined but the soul is. Black-smudged, irreparable.

I think of Ingrid. All the others too but mostly her. Free from the house now, or so I hope. I'll need to go back to see for sure. But for now, I think, yes—I've let her out.

I remember when Dad was here. Wonder if he was in the same room as me, wonder if he looked out into the same hall, saw the same sterility.

—We need a story, Emma continues quietly. Her eyes keep darting toward the door and she scratches her leg through the hospital gown. She's in much better shape than I am, able to move freely in the bed, able to speak. —And we need our stories to be exactly the same or else they won't believe us. So for now, just say you don't remember anything. Until we can figure it out.

I try to nod but my head doesn't like it, so I try to mutter assent but my throat doesn't like that either, so I just sit there and hope she understands.

—Oh, and they're not letting Pio or Sil in to see us. 'Cause they're not technically family.

I exhale through my nose.

—Rude, I know.

I picture them here. Sil's comforting voice and Pio's soft hand. Fall back asleep.

8

We claim amnesia. Tired, jostled, smoke-addled brains. Smuggled across state lines, held captive in our own hometown, who knows, who's to say—not us. When news spreads to us that the house has burned down, I have genuinely forgotten this fact and the world crumbles anew. Orrie thinks I'm acting and gives me a subtle thumbs-up, but the news collapses me genuinely.

—Let us know if anything comes back to you, I hear before we're left alone again.

Orrie is healing, after what appears to have been a bad fall, and his voice is coming back after the smoke inhalation and burns. When dark comes, and we're truly alone, we begin to plan.

9

Pio and Sil make it in to us eventually. A day or two days or a week later—time slips. Pio takes both my hands in his as if to get any closer to me or handle me without the greatest gingerness might crush my bones. But his eyes say what my brain is saying, which is a series of small explosions, bursts of color and light.

—Your aunt Andrea has agreed to take you in, Sil says. —But I also thought . . . and wanted to offer if . . . you both might want to come live with us. At least for a little while, until some things are ironed out. And your aunt would be okay with that.

Pio's looking away but he's got a puppy-soft longing in his eyes. And I look at Emma with probably the same look.

—And there's obviously lots of stuff to be worked out with the farm and all that, Sil says. —So I thought it might make more sense for you to stay with us, where it's closer.

Emma's nose twitches as she smiles.

—I would love that, she says. —And I think Orrie would too.

I croak out, —Yeah.

And apparently the resulting feelings are too strong because I conk out. Wake with a big puddle of drool on my pillow, slimy and stuck to my cheek. How many hours has it been? It's dark now, the moon a bright thing in the window alongside the TV's glow. I wipe my cheek clean and scoot away from the drool-pile. Emma is lying there with her eyes closed but I can tell she's not asleep. She's not in one of her sleeping positions; she's too dead-still.

I ask her about the trials by disembodied voice. They're on my mind. I want to confirm them as real things in our histories, to bring us together in that regard. She doesn't have to talk about it if she doesn't want to, I say. I know mine had some things in it I wouldn't like aired. But how was it for her.

Her eyes, open now, take on a faraway look. Aimed at the TV but looking beyond the TV as if she can see through its twinkling grid. The news is on and the story is about us, though the volume is muted.

—What trials? she says.

I nod and let the moment pass. Her brain, I reason, has covered the whole thing for her. The way the house used to pull shade across our eyes. It was all too real and too painful, and so it has been banished to some far corner. Maybe later she will remember and she will find herself back in this moment. She'll say ah, yes, those trials are what he was talking about.

Or maybe the house had a way of wiping something from her. It could cover our eyes, so maybe it could cover our memories too. I roll around, scratch at my arms, because I can't stop thinking about all of it. I'm alive here in this hospital bed and for a little while I'm going to be allowed to live with Sil and I'm going to see Pio every day, I'm going to wake up and know he is in the bunk beneath me, I'm going to get to watch him eat cereal in the mornings. But do I deserve it, do I deserve any of it is the question.

It's like the end of a movie where the bad guy gets to go free—I'm going to be loose in the world. I'd like to say it was all the house making me do everything, but I don't know what to believe anymore. I stared at each of those deaths in the face. I felt implicated in them.

But Emma doesn't need the burden of all this. So I let her fall asleep as the TV flickers.

10

Orrie mentions things I have no memory of: trials, a strange basement, voices. He's sustained more injury than I have—head trauma, bone fractures, esophageal damage—and I'm unsure how much of what he says is ailment, hallucination. I don't know how to let him down gently, so I nod: Yes, I remember; yes, I was there. Yes, I am here for you now, in these strange deluded night spells. One foot stuck in the muck of the past, the rest of the body cleared.

11

I keep waiting to see the women again. The three of them nestled into the corner shadows. But they do not appear. Sometimes, in here, I notice sounds and think the voices must be returning. A whoosh in the vents as the air kicks on or the shuffle of a shoe out in the hallway or a slight croaky cough from Emma next to me. Or some light-show will happen in my periphery and I'll think the (glimmer)s have returned. But they haven't and they don't. For now at least.

12

Apparently, some stuff from the house was found intact under all the rubble. Our first assignment, post-hospital, is to stop by and check out what remains. Walking out of the building, I feel briefly unmoored: my feet are carrying me toward a car which, in my mind, will lead us to the home I've known for nineteen years. But that home no longer exists. It's been brought to the ground, every plank and tile and beam. So home means something different now. Home is the boy who follows me out the hospital door and hovers at my side, lost in some corner of his mind. I pull him into me, smell his weird, smoky hair. Everything will smell like smoke for a while, they tell me, if it smells at all. Better get used to it.

Orrie wears it well.

13

I feel Emma watching me sometimes. Watching for anything strange, holding eye contact a second too long. She must not believe the dark thing in me has been banished. Maybe not the one in herself either. She's waiting, waiting, for one of them to rise up again.

14

—It'll be a tight fit, Sil says as we walk into the house.

It's smaller than I remember—I haven't been here in years, and last time I was much tinier. Something about its atmosphere, though, is like sinking into a still-life. I can feel the frame dissolving around me, can feel the lines of my life blurring. I'd be happy, crushingly happy, to dissolve here.

—But if Pio sleeps on the couch, Sil continues, —you can both share the bunk bed, until we get something else figured out—

—Oh, no, I cut in, —I'll take the couch. Please. Don't move a thing for me.

—It's no problem, Pio says.

I cut in again. —Seriously, I say, —keep your bed, everything, as it is. I'm more than happy with the couch. It's not long, anyway. Till we'll be with our aunt.

—It's actually pretty comfortable, Sil says, as a compromise. —It's a pull-out, a good one.

I smile. —Perfect.

But Orrie's got a strange distant face—he stands at the border of the living room and kitchen, and rocks, one foot in, one foot out. I approach him while Pio and Sil are talking about the furniture configurations. —What's up? I ask.

He cocks his head, plays innocent. I raise a brow.

—Something's up, I say. —You're easy to read.

—That's what Pio said too, he says, dismayed.

—Well, what is it?

He glances down the hall. —Let's go to the back, he says.

I follow him, cast passing glances at the photos on the wall.

When we cross into Pio's room, he pulls me in tight. Confused, I wrap my arms around him, hold him till he pulls away. His eyes are wet and he wipes them with his thumbs.

—I feel, he says, —like I haven't been there for you.

—What do you mean?

—The whole time I was here, after . . . and you were at home, and I wasn't . . . and Claire . . .

My stomach drops. —What about Claire?

He sits down in the office chair, leans back in it. —When I was in my trials, before the house burned down, I . . . saw something. I saw that Claire wasn't answering you. Ignoring your calls, not responding to your emails.

It's like a kick to the throat. —How did you see that.

—I don't know. He's shaking his head, rhythmic, trancelike.

Pio comes to the door. The way he looks at Orrie, concern knitting his eyebrows, sends a rush of warmth through me.

—You okay? he says, looking at Orrie, then me.

—Yeah, Orrie says. —Just confused.

—It'll all come back, Pio says, tone artificially light. But Orrie buys it, or chooses to look past the artifice, and smiles a bit, stands to rejoin the others in the living room.

15

We get masked up and go back to the house to look at all the old belongings that have been pulled out. We wander through the rubble-dusted stuff that somehow survived the fire, look up and down the piles. Some things are laid out on tables, most of it just left along the ground.

Emma tackles questions and things with a very adult air of suppressed emotion and I'm so proud of her ability to steel herself shut. The only thing I want to save, the only thing I find worth saving, is Ingrid's charm bracelet. I drape it across my wrist to keep a bit of her here with me. The rest can be donated or sold or thrown out, I don't care.

While we're here, I listen for soul-sounds in the hollowed-out rooms, in the splintered wood, maybe traveling through the tiles. Nothing from anywhere—not a single peep. The house feels emptier than ever, so empty it raises a lump in my throat. I swallow it down and take a few deep breaths through my mask. Twirl my new bracelet, look at all the little charms there. My favorite one is a book—she told me once which book she thought it was, because of the red cover, but I can't remember it now.

16

In the mornings, I have coffee in the living room with Sil. He tries to slip by my bed-couch quietly when he puts the water on to boil. I roll over and pretend I've been up all along, join him with an empty mug in hand, wait for the drip machine. The boys are still sleeping while he and I catch up. I am surprised by how much of him I remember: several things I attributed to Dad were actually imparted to me by Sil. It makes me wonder what I ever knew of my father, how much of his lore was just what sounded lovely.

—Or remember when I showed you how to make omelets? Sil says.

I color over the occurrence in my head, in which Dad crouched behind me, watched me stir and sprinkle and season.

—You splattered the wall so many times. Got all frustrated and stormed off.

But he's nearly laughing while recalling it.

—Not your brightest student, was I, I say.

—Oh, definitely bright, he says. —But such a temper. Definitely not my most *patient* student.

—Some things never change, I say.

—And, he continues, —speaking of students, you graduated from high school, right? A year or two ago, if I remember.

—Yeah, I say.

He sips from his cup. Maybe he senses some soreness there when the light goes out in my eyes. He asks how I feel about it.

—I really wanted to go to college, I say. —But I felt bad leaving everyone behind. Especially with Dad gone.

—You could still go, he says. —This year, next year. In ten years. It's not over, it's never over.

He says it so casually, it stuns me. I haven't even considered going back—I've been thinking only of Orrie, how he needs me now more than ever, when we're the only ones left. But when he and Pio shuffle sleepily into the kitchen and join us, rubbing their eyes, I look at Sil, watching them with such fondness. And there's a little crack, a little splinter, in my resistance.

Another morning. I'm sitting in the recliner, and my fingers drift down to the frayed fabric at the cushion's edge. A familiar feeling, this fabric, and another memory to recolor: I always thought it was our living-room recliner that I tore apart.

—Was that you? Sil asks, watching my fingers work, twist and tear.

I hold in a laugh, just nod.

He laughs, though. —Neither of my kids would confess to it, back in the day. I should've known.

—Well, it could've been Orrie, I say. When I invoke him, he pokes his head around the corner of the kitchen, raises an eyebrow.

—I don't think so, Sil says, looking wistfully in the direction of the kitchen when we hear cereal clink into porcelain bowls. —He was never in the house. Always out on the trampoline, or playing pretend in the woods.

We smile, sip our coffee. He skirts around the topic of *what happened in that house,* as always. Deathly curious, I'm sure, but unwilling to let the question loose. Orrie and I haven't yet decided when we want to reveal our version of the truth.

—I really don't remember anything, I say. —It's so strange. But I don't feel . . . weighed down by it. It's almost like I was in a weeks-long dream.

I look out the window and watch a pair of rabbits chase each other in the grass.

—But maybe that'll change, I say. —Who knows.

He nods, offers eggs. I accept and he ducks into the kitchen.

—Or you could make us all omelets, he calls out.

I laugh. —I'm better at them now.

—I'd hope so!

17

Pio and I are going out to the rock again. Time number two to make up for the fright of time number one. The air is chilly but nothing a good coat can't handle. At the lookout point he finally bridges the lip-distance and I don't hurl anything up this time. A giant kick in my stomach, at which point I fear some voice or vomit will emerge, but I realize it's just normal nerves. Times like these, people get nervous. So I push it away and focus on the happy.

18

Maybe my favorite thing about the house is getting to watch Orrie and Pio together, when they finally wake, bleary-eyed, near noon. How they roam around in the quiet, always in each other's orbit. How instinctual their togetherness is: the way, when Orrie is slightly down or off or unleveled, Pio will walk into the room and pick it up like a scent. How he'll comfort, with words, with proximity. I can't help but wonder how things will be at Aunt Andrea's, how often they'll be able to see each other.

Walking by the bathroom later, I see Orrie peering in the mirror again, shirt pulled up over his shoulder.

—What's going on? I ask. I'm just beginning to dream about college again, about distant coasts and textbooks and friends, people my age, and the sight of him yanks me back into my body.

—That soul-mark is still there, he says. —But it's fading now. Kind of gray.

—It'll be gone before you know it, I say.

19

Pio's eyes go distant sometimes. I think some part of him doesn't believe the amnesia Emma and I have manufactured: it's too pretty and too clean. But sometimes stories are like that, I want to tell him. In truth, his buttery-sad eyes are nearly enough to make me spill the whole truth out to him. The truth as I see it, which—whether it's real, who knows.

Up there on the rock, I wanted to kiss his eyes shut so they wouldn't look at me and pry me open. But once you tell something, there's no reeling it in again, so I tried hard to keep the real thing from coming up.

20

The farm, the whole property, goes up on the market. The town is trying to keep the sale local and familiar—they want the farm and its goods to carry on, for its crops and blooms to continue nourishing them. There are multiple interested parties, I'm told.

The thought of losing the house sends sharp hurt through me. We spent our whole lives there. But we've already lost the house, I tell myself, all our memories have been suffused with the smell of smoke. We lost it to free ourselves, maybe—if that's what Orrie has to believe, it's what I have to believe. And Orrie and I aren't prepared to manage the place on our own; we'd have to bring in help to keep it all going anyway. It's probably for the best, but it brings a grimace out of me.

We visit the place one last time. The rot, somehow, has cleared up—the soil that was black, the trees that withered, all restored. The trees stand tall; the soil, which I bend to touch, is soft and brown.

The oracle tree, which rotted and fell over, is still toppled, but the fungal growth has receded—only a hole in the side of the tree remains.

—When I came here, Pio says, —it was the strangest thing—it looked like the soil was . . . *dead*. It looked so unhealthy.

Orrie and I look at each other. My stomach turns over. —So you saw it too, I say.

—Wait, you remember it too? says Pio. —I thought you didn't remember anything.

My cheeks burn, and I hope the redness isn't noticeable. —Just the one thing, I say. —Being here brought it back.

—Huh, he says, then wanders up to the porch. The fire didn't quite reach the steps, but they've got a new groan beneath his weight. He stands at the top, turns back to us.

—I found you both here, he says. —Collapsed right here. I dragged you down the steps and out of the way of the smoke.

—What good timing, I say, —you showing up.

—I'm just glad. His voice goes gravelly here. —That you're both safe. I was so scared.

We walk down from the porch, and Pio startles.

—Wait, he says. —There's something you haven't seen. Let's get back in the car.

We glance around, one last time, at the whole place, the flowers and sheds and fences and neat rows of crops we tended for our entire lives, and the house, the blackened house, and we climb in after him.

—It'll always be here, I suppose, Orrie says, eyes cast at his hands folded in his lap.

Just what I was thinking—a slight smile warms me.

Pio pulls out of his spot near the garden shed, rolls down the hill. He puts the car in park near the gravesite, and it dawns on me. I keep my eyes on my knees, the clouds, the shifting trees, afraid I'll cry if I look at him, at either of them.

He'd packed some things up in a grocery bag before we left, and he grabs it from the trunk. We walk over to the two new headstones, see the flowers laid out by mourners. All that time we were trapped in the house, the world carried on around us: people mourned, people processed. And we were stuck.

Pio pulls the bag open and withdraws two branches, two bowls; two Mason jars, the large one filled with white liquid, the small with amber. —Milk and honey, he says. —To pour out. And olive branches.

How he remembered our libation practices from the funeral, I don't know, but Orrie's knees nearly buckle. We empty half of each jar into the bowls, mix them, then pour them slowly onto the graves where new sod has been laid. The liquid settles down into grass and soil.

As I pour atop Mom's grave, I think of her last words to me: *This is no longer your house, no longer your family.* As I pour atop Enzo's, I think of his: *I don't feel like you've given me a fair chance. I've always felt like you hated me. But what have I done?*

I shudder with shame. Trapped in the house, my emotions festered. Now that I'm out, roaming the hospital and Sil's house and the greater property here, I feel freer, lighter—the fury has a place to go, it can float off me like ash. All the ruin that bred itself in that house, unleashed at long last.

I'm sorry, I think, head bowed, as I stand before each headstone. Sorry I allowed my emotions to rule me, sorry I couldn't see them clouding me, sorry I blamed others for my own darknesses. I am not healed, I am not better, but I am bettering: inch by inch, day by day.

Orrie wipes his eyes with his thumbs and lays his olive branch on Enzo's grave, so I lay mine on Mom's. Finally, in the afterlife, a kind of peace.

The wind picks up above us, rustles his hair, casts it into his eyes. Pio pulls it back, kisses his forehead. Orrie pulls me closer and we stand there, the three of us, and watch, silent, as the last of the libations are absorbed into the earth.

Acknowledgments

First, I must thank Christine Neulieb, who plucked this manuscript from the slush and sharpened it beyond belief. Thanks for nerding out over words with me, for reading and editing with such care and thought, and for preserving the project's intrinsic playfulness (and for letting some of my real weirdnesses remain!). I feel so lucky to have been able to work with you, and I'm so grateful for all the ways you've made this a better book. Thanks as well to Feliza Casano and Aubry Norman for their marketing and behind-the-scenes work—the Lanternfish team is truly special.

Enormous thanks to Matt Bell, my thesis chair, whose enthusiasm fueled the germination of this manuscript (in, uh, my last semester of grad school) and whose craft wisdom guided me in its tightening and polishing. Thanks for asking all the right questions, even the ones I hoped you wouldn't but, because of your eagle eyes, you did anyway. Thanks for loving these characters and for encouraging me to be bolder, to write weirder, to risk more riskily. This project is all the stronger because of what I learned from you, in our meetings, the novel workshop, and in courses long before.

Thanks to Tara Ison, whose careful attention to character development and relationships I kept at my side as I planned, drafted, and revised this project. Thanks to Jenny Irish, whose full-throated encouragement to follow every artistic impulse and whose wonderfully varied reading recommendations pushed this book toward its truest self. Thanks to Mitchell S. Jackson, whose attention to the sentence, to every syllable inside it, taught me to better listen to the prose.

Thanks to everyone in Matt's novel-writing workshop who nurtured this project in its earliest days and encouraged it to bloom open: Jules; Christie, Christina, Colin, Winslow; Amber, Arya, Asna, Frankie, Haylee, Maya. What an honor—and a treat—it was to experience all of your works in progress.

Thanks to Sarah Ruden, Mary Lefkowitz, and Emily Wilson, whose recent robust translations of the *Oresteia* (and *Oresteia*-adjacent works) provided the initial spark for this novel.

Thanks to Creekside Arts, who graciously hosted me in 2022 while I took the pile of raw words that was my rough draft and sorted it into something more presentable. John and Janet, your cabin, with its awning windows that let the scent and sound of rain in, its wood stove (that I never used, but that was beautiful nonetheless), and its motion-sensor alarm—also affectionately known as Zoey—was an unparalleled space for reimagining this work. Sorry, again, for inexplicably shattering two of your wine glasses. Tanya and Calder, Olli, Joey and Rich—I loved getting to know you. Maizy—behind-the-ear scratches for you. Ashaki, Rhombie, Andie, and Jon—what a privilege to create alongside you. Co-op cookies forever. Japhy's Soup & Noodles—I will miss you endlessly. Gone too soon. (And, speaking of fallen eateries, Crazi's Hot Chicken, in AZ—I think of you every day.)

Thanks to Colin—I think having your overwhelming Aries energy in the apartment allowed me to tap in and absolutely demolish the first draft of this novel. And thanks for the brewskis (and soft pretzel) when production wrapped. Thanks to soft pretzels in general, for existing. Thanks to my creative writing students, whose craft discussions and wonderful work have kept me energized.

And, finally, to my family and friends. So much of the writing life, more than is often understood, is about what happens off the page, between chapters. Thank you for nurturing me, nourishing me, entertaining me, teaching me. I love you all.

About the Author

Hayden Casey (he/him) is a writer and musician who lives and teaches in Phoenix, AZ. He holds an MFA in Fiction from Arizona State University. He has previously published a short story collection, *Show Me Where the Hurt Is*, with Split/Lip Press. His short fiction has appeared in *Witness, West Branch, Bat City Review,* and elsewhere, and his long-form work has been longlisted for the Dzanc Books Prize for Fiction and the Palette Chapbook prize for poetry. Find him at haydencasey.co.